LIZA KASNER S

IRIS GLAZNER LEIGH

LIZA'S SECRETS

A CAPE COD THRILLER

Enjoy your adventures on Cape Cod with Liza

Best

Iris G. Leigh

Black Rose Writing | Texas

The author grants the final approval for this literary material.

First printing

This is a work of fiction. Names, characters, businesses, places, events, and incidents are either the products of the author's imagination or used in a fictitious manner. Any resemblance to actual persons, living or dead, or actual events is purely coincidental.

ISBN: 978-1-68513-394-8
LIBRARY OF CONGRESS CONTROL NUMBER: 2023949100
PUBLISHED BY BLACK ROSE WRITING
www.blackrosewriting.com

Printed in the United States of America
Suggested Retail Price (SRP) $21.95

Liza's Secrets is printed in Book Antiqua

*As a planet-friendly publisher, Black Rose Writing does its best to eliminate unnecessary waste to reduce paper usage and energy costs, while never compromising the reading experience. As a result, the final word count vs. page count may not meet common expectations.

I dedicate *Liza's Secrets* to my grandchildren, Alex and Margaret. As you journey through life, you will meet lots of people who will say no. Be resourceful, flexible, and kind. Never stop trying. *Yes*, is right around the corner.

PRAISE FOR
LIZA'S
SECRETS

"In *Liza's Secrets*, everyone has a secret, and some are about to explode. As Leigh guides the reader toward the inevitable confrontation, her compassion for her characters and her insight into their broken lives keep the pages turning by themselves."

–Jacquelyn Mitchard, #1 *New York Times* bestselling author of *The Deep End of the Ocean* and *The Good Son*

"Liza Kasner has a problem. She is jobless, friendless and short on money. Her psychopathic husband is hunting her down. *Liza's Secrets*, the delightful debut suspense novel by Iris G. Leigh, is about one woman's survival. In this twisty, atmospheric novel, Leigh lovingly captures the off-season vibe of the Cape after the tourists and summer people have left, and gray skies and damp cold have replaced the sunshine and ocean breeze. Writing with good humor and insight, she perfectly describes a place peopled by intriguing characters, both local and off-Cape *washashores*."

–Paul Kemprecos, *New York Times* bestselling author

"When you sense danger and it's coming from someone close, you become desperate. In Iris G. Leigh's debut novel, *Liza's Secrets*, a novel of suspense, you'll discover what it feels like to completely change your identity, leave all behind, and make your way to safety. It's a thrilling story of lost love, new love, and a page turning adventure onto the back roads of off-season Cape Cod."

–Barbara Eppich Struna, author of *The Old Cape* series

"*Liza's Secrets* is an enjoyable romance belonging in anyone's vacation luggage for reading on the beach. The main character, Liza, is on the run from her brutal husband and winds up in the town of Chatham on Cape Cod in the winter. During the off-season, she is able to find a house-sitting arrangement, two part-time jobs, and a number of friends who live there year-round. Jeff, the owner of the hotel where she stays the first night, quickly becomes a love interest."

–Carolyn Geduld, author of *The Struggle*

"Franny is a victim of domestic abuse, and the abuse is escalating. She needs to get out now before her husband, Barry, kills her. With a new name and matching ID, her cat, and a different car, she leaves her old life behind. Or does she?"

–LeeAnne James, award-winning author of *Justice for Loretta* and *The Dusty Road to Homicide*

"If you are looking for a story that will be impossible for you to put down, look no further than *Liza's Secrets* by Iris Leigh. Leigh economically uses words to keep you enthralled in this piece. Leigh's characters are crystal clear, and truly pure. I loved every page."

–Trey Everett, author of *Beneath the Surface, For It Will Be Yours*

"A desperate Liza escapes her abusive husband, cutting herself off from all who are dear to her. But past pain prevents her from revealing her situation to those who might keep her safe. Just as she begins to feel comfortable, Licorice, her cat, goes missing, unleashing an unbelievable chain of events that kept me guessing until the end. What a fun read!"

–Marie W. Watts, author of *Tough Trail Home*

"*Liza's Secrets* is a poignant story of a woman trying to escape the cruelty of her cheating, physically and mentally abusive husband, who she knows is plotting her demise. The reader will follow Liza through her escape plan as she forges new friendships and a new life for herself, keeping the reader riveted until the very end, when the final outcome is accomplished."

–Lucille Guarino, author of *Elizabeth's Mountain*

"*Liza's Secrets* by Iris Leigh is a delightful yet suspenseful piece of escapist fiction. Leigh does a fantastic job of mixing cozy, atmospheric descriptions of the Cape with nail-biting suspense, and the overall effect is pure entertainment. Don't miss this one!"

–Laurel Osterkamp, author of *Beautiful Little Furies*

"Hate tasted of blood and rage. With these powerful opening words, author Iris G. Leigh introduces us to a story that is all too familiar. *Liza's Secrets* is the story of Franny Blackman, an abused wife who finally gets the courage to break free. Changing her name to Liza Kasner, she is reborn, and as she struggles to grow and reclaim herself, her life, and her soul, she learns the true meaning of friendship and love."

– Karen Brees, author of *Headwind, Esposito Caper,*
Crosswind

LIZA'S
SECRETS

Chapter 1

Franny/Liza

Hate tasted of blood and rage. Franny bit her lip, gripped the steering wheel with a leather-palmed glove, and rubbed her jaw to ease the pain from clenched teeth. A glance in the mirror revealed no sign of Barry's car. Although her hypervigilance was based on years of terror, she was certain she left with no one noticing. Keeping her speed steady, Franny was careful to avoid an accident. The newly minted blonde reflected in the mirror looked shattered and scared. Hot tears fell, and Franny swiped at them with the back of her hand. It was difficult to erase her whole life. She said her new name aloud, "Liza Kasner." Franny Blackman did not exist anymore.

The early morning trucks kicked grimy slush onto the windshield, and she peered through the melting mounds, squinting, and afraid to stop. "If we keep a steady pace, we'll be safe," she whispered to Licorice, the sleeping cat in a carrier on the back seat. It was more than irresponsible to leave without a plan, but she had to escape while Barry was out of town. "Don't worry, Licorice. We're going to a place where Barry will never find us." The silence from the back seat was welcome. Licorice was out cold from the kitty tranquilizers, and she envied her.

Liza took stock of her situation. She had $63,000 in bank checks, and $2,000 in cash, and was heading north on the Interstate. The note on the kitchen table was a lie. Liza wrote she was going to Florida to see her cousins. Barry was on a business trip in Hartford. She hoped this would buy her enough time to find a place to settle before he realized she was not visiting relatives. A rivulet of cold sweat running down her armpits added to her discomfort. Would her cousin Lucy in Florida cover for her? Not likely. The woman did nothing for free.

The bridge over the Hudson River signified the gateway to New England. When she spotted the sign, Liza maneuvered the car into the traffic. Driving a new-to-her car, complete with a transponder, ensured Barry could not trace her route.

Last summer, they vacationed in Chatham on Cape Cod. The quaint town and proximity to the ocean were perfect. Liza loved walking along the endless, sandy beaches and admiring the antique houses with gardens of bright flowers. If she found cheap off-season housing, she could conserve her money, weigh her options, and stay in paradise forever. Doubts took over. Would Barry look for her there? Liza shook her head. No. He hated everything about the place and would never think of searching for her in Chatham. Could she blend into a small resort town in the winter? Why not? Anyway, she had no choice.

Although Liza was dying for coffee, she convinced herself to go a little further. The snow had stopped, and the roads were clearing. By the time she reached Providence, Rhode Island, Liza was optimistic. She had cash, a car with working brakes, and identification for Liza Kasner. Franny was gone and Liza could figure things out on her own.

After another hour, her initial rush of adrenaline was waning. It was time to stop for coffee and a bathroom break. She would have to be quick, so as not to leave a sleeping kitty alone in the cold. So far, Licorice had remained in a drugged stupor. The large convenience building welcomed her. Returning, she was relieved her luck held and Licorice was still asleep. Liza's stomach growled, and she realized she was starving. Running away gave her an appetite, and Liza unwrapped the turkey sandwich from the picnic bag and devoured it. Brushing the crumbs off her parka, a tiny blob of mayo stuck to the nylon. She swiped and licked it off her finger, relishing her newfound freedom.

By the time she reached the Cape Cod Canal, the sky was clear, and her earlier trepidation gave way to excitement. Licorice began rousing. "We're here, Sweetie." Her kitty responded with a small whimper. "Get used to it, Baby. We're in this together." Driving along the canal, the stretch with large houses nestled in the hills was postcard-pretty. The sky was the color of blue topaz and the water sparkled. It was so picturesque that she considered getting out and taking pictures. However, her Subaru dashboard gave the temperature as ten degrees. There was no way she wanted to leave the warmth of her car. Liza had to keep going before night came. She had made it to the Cape and was safe. At least for today.

Chapter 2

Barry

By the second hour into the drive to the sales meeting, Barry could not stop yawning. He knew this was going to be a bust. Why did he even invite Donna? His personal trainer was nice to look at, but she was not well-endowed in the brains department. In addition, Hartford lacked excitement and had no appeal. The restaurants near the hotel were awful, and the bars were dreary. A proper city, like New York, would be thrilling, but the company always had their meetings in low-cost places. At least his wife, Franny, was not there to pester him. That was something.

Listening to Donna for hours was irritating. Although she laughed at his jokes and was pretty, he found himself drained from her incessant talking. What did he care about clothes and jewelry? Conversations about their future together and her feelings were annoying. When did everlasting love and moving in together become important? Barry could not understand where she had dreamed up these ideas. He never promised her there would be a forever in their relationship. He took it one day at a time and wanted it to stay like that. However, he was bright enough not to argue and wind up on the hideaway couch in their hotel room. Barry planned to stay in the king-sized bed and knew it would be better to make her happy. It was time to say something. "Babe, you're the best. We'll have a great time tonight. Just you and me."

His cell rang, and he glanced at the screen. He recognized the number and felt his breakfast rise in his throat. "Hey, Donna. Let's stop for gas. I bet you need the ladies' room."

Donna nodded. "Sure, that's a great idea. I've got to go."

Barry rolled his eyes, turned off the highway, and followed signs for the nearest gas station. "Okay, Doll. Take your time. I'll be waiting right here." While the tank was filling, he returned the call. His sweaty hands shook, and he rubbed them on his pants.

Sal picked up on the first ring. "Hi ya, Barry. Glad you called back so soon. I don't like to be kept waiting."

Barry felt the chill of terror run down his back. One of his old buddies introduced him to Sal when Barry could not get enough money together to make a payment. Sal was not a guy to screw. "I'm good. How are you?" Better to be friendly.

"Let's cut to the chase. You're in for over 185 thousand and I need it real soon."

"Sure. I'm working on some sweet deals with my old lady clients. I buy their run-down houses and hire a cheap builder who fixes them up. Once they're sold, everyone makes a bundle. It's foolproof." Flipping houses was never foolproof, but he was not about to confess this to Sal. On his latest venture, the damn builders found black mold everywhere, and it was going to take even more dough to clean it up.

"Listen, this isn't the bank of charity. The interest's adding up."

"Just a few more weeks. I promise. One's ready to flip. I guarantee a big payoff. I swear." Barry's stomach burned. He needed a little more time.

"I'm a friendly guy. I hear you loud and clear." Sal cackled. "I'm going to keep a close eye on you. If I don't see the money soon, well, you know..." He hung up.

Barry could only imagine the rest. Why did he get involved with these guys? He just needed a quick loan last month to cover expenses. The loan was too much to pay off in one payment, and he would never finish the old house on time. Barry made a fist and hit the car door. He seemed to do that a lot lately. The last time he was with his wife, she begged him for a new car. If it were not for Franny pleading for things all the time, he would not be in this mess. How had life turned out like this?

Donna approached the car and smiled. "All done. I even got us some coffee."

It amazed Barry that she did not notice how upset he was. At least he would not have to explain anything. He attempted a smile. "That's great, Honey. You always know how to make me happy."

After a few minutes on the highway, Donna continued to prattle, "Oh, Barry. I can't believe we're finally together. It'll be so much fun."

Barry brightened. Maybe this would not be so bad after all. He deserved a mini vacation, away from the stress. He was clever and would come up with a way to pay Sal. Everything was going to be okay.

They checked into the hotel and Donna changed into a bikini. "Hey, Sweets. Are you sure you can't skip the meeting today? Come swimming with me."

"I'm sorry, Babe. I've gotta make an appearance. You look hot."

"Later, Big Guy. I'm out of here. Come find me at the pool when you're done."

Barry barely made it on time to the afternoon session with the head salesperson, the alpha commander. They competed against each other in teams. The team who sold the most policies would win the opportunity to vacation in Aruba with other insurance sales agents and their wives. The men were mostly in their fifties and would sit around the pool in baggy trunks, drinking beer, slapping each other on the backs, and yakking about the Yankees. Their boring wives wore swimsuits that covered everything but cellulite. Barry wondered what the second prize was and daydreamed through the sales videos.

On the second day, his boss, Chuck, asked Barry to meet him in his suite. It smelled like spicy food and spearmint gum. The wooden desk, covered with papers, displayed a picture of Chuck's family that was propped against the back wall. The kids were all short and fat, like their father. Chuck's tall and willowy wife stood next to them. Too bad the kids looked like their dad. Chuck stood close and shook his hand. Barry did not need a menu to guess what his boss had for lunch, as the aroma of egg rolls and spareribs was overpowering.

Barry backed away and Chuck moved closer with a serious expression. "Hey, Barry. What's going on? You're not doing so well this quarter. If you don't get your accounts back up and make your quota, I may have to let you go. You've been with us for a long time. You know I don't want to get rid of you."

Barry smiled and said, "You know me, Chuckie, I always deliver. I love working for you." Good thing Chuck could not read his mind. Barry could not stop thinking about the man's ugly children.

Barry endured one more day of meetings and finished the last night in Hartford at the hotel bar with Donna. Too much liquor made it difficult for him to keep up with her antics. Falling asleep, Barry wondered if he needed to see his doctor. He chalked it up to constant stress and decided he deserved a real vacation, with a beach and drinks with tiny paper umbrellas.

Returning to New Jersey was exhausting, with a pointless conversation about seeing each other the following weekend. Barry had no way of keeping his promises after he was back home with Franny. However, Donna's chatter passed the time, at least until they got to Donna's apartment.

"Why can't you stay here? Just tonight?" she pouted.

"We'll be together soon. You're so special. My beautiful girl." Barry kissed her and closed the door quickly behind him. He needed a break from everyone and wanted to go home to some quiet. Too bad Franny would be there. Trying to delay confronting his wife, he stopped at his favorite bar and had a beer. It took the edge off. After another, his mood was lighter, and he headed home.

It was ten, and the house was dark. He assumed Franny went to bed early. He hoped he would not have to give her details about the conference. Before he left, Barry told her he was signing five new clients a week for annuities. Franny thought he was making a good income. He used to do much better. That should account for something.

Barry discovered the door was unlocked and wondered why Franny forgot to bolt it. He turned on the light and waited for the cat to leap out at him. He hated everything about that repulsive animal. Licorice was a dumb-ass name for a cat. He wanted a dog who barked at strangers and kept him company. Sure, a cat did not need to be walked, but scooping cat poop into a bucket was not his idea of paradise. This cat hated him, too. She was always underfoot when he tried to walk through the house. He called Franny's name and entered the kitchen. Except for the hum of the refrigerator, the house felt empty. No one was home. When he spotted Franny's note, written on pink paper, he grinned. After he read it, he was in a much better mood. She and the cat were both gone. His wife would drive a lot of miles with bad brakes all the way to Florida. He hoped she would find an icy road on the way, skid off, and self-destruct. He would collect the life insurance and be free. It would be better than hitting the lottery.

Barry went upstairs to the bedroom, took off his suit, and threw it on the floor. Then he followed with his shorts. When he threw his socks into the air, one caught on the ceiling fan. This was the most fun he had in days. No one to nag him about hanging up his clothes. Barry liked this bachelor life. He had not been this free in a long time and turned on late-night TV. After flipping through the channels, there was nothing he wanted to watch. Smiling, he turned to the empty side of the bed. Franny was gone. There was no one to boss him around or whine about the things he had not done. Then it sank in. He was lonely.

He needed to talk with someone right now. His son, Sam, was the one person in the world he cared about. Barry's money problems were, in part, because he did not want to be like his old man. He quit college when his father got into serious gambling debts. Barry shuddered at the memory of his dad. It was not unusual to see his mom cowering so as not to provoke him after a binge. The doctors diagnosed his dad with liver problems, and Barry had to get a job so the bank would not take the house. It was not until he met Franny, and her father set him up in the insurance business, that he felt secure.

Sam picked up on the first ring. "Hey, Dad, you're up late. What's up?"

"Not too much. Your mom's gone down to Florida to visit her cousins. I just wanted to hear how you're doing." Barry swore he heard laughter in the background. It delighted him that his son was so popular. The kid took after him.

"I'm in the middle of a study session for a test. Can I call you tomorrow night?"

After they disconnected, Barry was still restless. Although Franny was gone, he hoped she had stocked the refrigerator with food before she left. She probably had. He padded downstairs and brought up a big bowl of chocolate chip ice cream with hot fudge sauce. Franny would never approve of him eating something so messy on their pristine bedspread. Well, too bad.

Tomorrow, he would call Donna and invite her to dinner. She could make him a nice meal of steak with baked potatoes without a discussion of his cholesterol levels. Barry did not intend to start a pattern of her staying over. He would drive her home, have fun, watch the news, and come back. Yeah, that would be great.

Chapter 3

Hot tears fell as Liza followed the road to the main Cape Cod highway. Being up all night, the caffeine was not enough to keep her alert. She had to stop soon and find a place to sleep. Licorice began wailing in the back seat. "Hey Precious, it's okay." The cat quieted at her soothing tone. Liza knew she could not drive much further, as they needed a warm place to rest.

After getting off at the Hyannis exit, she passed upscale chain resorts and malls. Liza longed to check into a name-brand hotel with an indoor pool, room service, and a comfortable mattress. It made her even more furious at Barry. How could he do this to her? Liza glanced back at the restless cat. "I'd love to sneak you into a luxury room, Licorice. But at the first meow, we'd be out in the cold." She lamented at their dilemma and sniffed back tears.

Last summer the commercial two-lane highway along Nantucket Sound was lively. Today, Liza spotted boarded-up gift shops, stores with Cape Cod tee shirts in dingy windows, and vacant mini-golf courses. There were unoccupied lots in front of restaurants illuminated with dark, neon billboards. Small 1950s-style motels with signs announcing, *See you next year,* dotted the landscape. Liza missed the aroma of fried clams wafting from seafood restaurants. Now, the thoroughfare was almost empty.

In Yarmouth, she stopped in front of a motel with ten small cottages surrounding an office building. A lit vacancy sign announced Pilgrim's Landing was open, and the lights through the office window confirmed occupancy. She followed the plowed driveway to the front office and said a prayer. The building was white with red shutters and needed a coat of paint. The cottages nearby were red with green shutters. They were not too close together and there was a covered pool with a playground on the right. Two older trucks, one with a rusty fender, sat in front of the cottages furthest from the parking lot. Entering the office, Liza smelled hazelnut coffee. It reminded her of home, and for a fleeting minute, she considered getting in the car and heading back to New Jersey. The homesick moment passed, and she continued to the front desk. Early American pine furniture covered in orange and pea-green plaid crowded the small space. A tall, bearded man stood behind a countertop reading *The New York Times. The Times* and hazelnut coffee? This might be a good omen.

He appeared to be close to her age and dressed in clothes she thought more fitting for a fishing trip, a red plaid flannel shirt and faded jeans. The man had mid-length brown hair and blue eyes that looked straight into hers. "How can I help you?"

Liza could not stop herself from blurting everything at once. "I need a room for a few days. I have my well-behaved cat with me, and I can pay cash." So much for finesse, and she hoped he liked cats.

He looked her up and down. "Nice clothes."

"Thank you." Where was this conversation heading?

"I worked as a designer on Seventh Ave." That was the New York code for the fashion industry. "I bought this place last month and plan to fix it up by summer. My name's Jeff."

She followed his glance and noticed the new wood beams in the ceiling. It looked like the beginning of a renovation. This explained the incongruence of such unsightly decor from a fashion designer. After getting over her initial surprise, Liza realized she should not judge Cape Codders by their clothing. Men who dressed for a fishing trip might have fashion design backgrounds. She would fit right in. She was not who she looked like, either.

"I'm...Liza." She halted, not having practiced enough saying her name aloud. "I need a place to stay for a while. I'm moving to the Cape." Why didn't she blab about her entire life story?

"A couple of section eights live here. It can be noisy."

She did not know what he was talking about. Her confusion must have shown on her face.

"Section eight is low-income housing. Affordable family apartments are impossible to find here. In the winter, many families cram into motel rooms. The government picks up the tab for their *luxury* accommodations."

She understood what he was trying to explain. Families with children would be neighbors in these small cottages. "Those poor people. How do over two people fit?"

"People make do with what they can afford," he replied and looked at her with disdain.

Liza shut her mouth and smiled sweetly. She did not want him to think she was a snob.

He continued, but his tone was less friendly. "I'll need a hundred and fifty dollars a night for the room and an extra deposit, say fifty, for any pet damage. You can keep your cat here if you don't disturb anyone. I'll put you near the office, away from the families. It'll be more private."

She smiled warily. "Thanks. I'm sorry about my comment. I don't want any trouble. We just need a place to stay." Jeff nodded and handed her the keys to cottage 104. She kept quiet, not wanting to say anything else to offend him. He was her first human connection on the Cape, and she needed a friend.

Licorice and she moved into their early-American haven. It was so outdated; it was retro-cool. She could only imagine her cousin Lucy's caustic comments. "Dahling, you can't stay here. It's awful and so green."

The room had white walls with a wagon wheel light fixture hanging from the ceiling. An upholstered chair, covered in green-and-gold plaid polyester, sat next to a desk with the initials DW scratched on the top. A small television on top of it completed the amenities. Liza frowned at the three-drawer dresser that would never hold half her clothes. However, the gold shag rug looked recently vacuumed, with the pile matted in the same direction. Liza approved of the faint bleach smell from the olive green-tiled bathroom. The stacked generic wrappers of soap in the bathroom, and thin, but crisply laundered white towels, also reassured her. A small fridge with a microwave on top occupied a place in the corner under the window. This was not the Old Cape Inn but was affordable, safe, snug, and clean. "It's only for a few days," she announced to her now awake kitty. "At least we can eat in the room. How about bread, juice, milk, cereal, sliced deli turkey, cheese, and mayo? Oh yes, and more cat food for you."

Licorice ambled out the open door of the cat carrier and sniffed. She appeared a little hung over, but strolled tentatively toward the double bed. Curiosity won out, as she jumped onto the worn chenille bedspread and examined the room from her perch. She kneaded the bed coverings and closed her eyes. Liza turned the thermostat as high as it would go and was pleased to see how quickly the room warmed. Surveying the room for a spot to put the litter pan, she settled on the bathroom floor and tucked it behind the door. She made a mental note to buy cleaning supplies to wash the floor and guarantee the return of her fifty-dollar cleaning fee. "Okay, Honeybun. Have a good rest and try to be quiet. I'll be back soon with food." She turned on the TV to keep the cat company and locked the door behind her. Licorice and she had found a home, at least for now.

Chapter 4

After making sure everything was secure, Liza headed to the motel office. Jeff sat at the front desk, still reading the paper. He looked up. "Hello. Everything okay?"

Liza nodded. "It's perfect. Can you tell me where I can buy some food?"

"Sure. You'll find a small grocery store down the street, going towards Dennis. They probably have everything you'd need for breakfast and lunches. For dinner, try the Lobster Roll restaurant. It's right past the grocery store and isn't too expensive. Their chowder is great." He gave her a warm smile. Jeff was a New Yorker, and he sounded like her city friends who were foodies. She knew she shouldn't jump to conclusions, but he struck her as someone with good taste.

"Thanks a lot. I appreciate your help." Liza left the office and hurried to the car, trying to avoid being out in the cold. The winds were picking up, and the temperature was dropping because of the non-existent midday sun. In the late light, the Subaru's few dents and rust spots were hardly noticeable. When she tried to buy a new car, she found Barry had over-reached their credit limit. With help from an old high school friend, Rick, she swapped her Audi with questionable brakes for this car. The Subaru came with falsified papers, license plates, and a transponder. It was not a luxury car, but it ran and was warm.

The Subaru started right up, and Liza drove on near-empty roads. She admired the solitude of the Cape in winter, a refreshing change from the congested suburbs of New Jersey. Although the market was small, Liza discovered many upscale items on the shelves. Homemade fudge sauce and fresh-baked loaves of bread sat next to dried beans and rice. The store appeared to be geared toward a diverse clientele of wealthy retirees, tourists, and the local working class. Finding all the essentials on her shopping list, Liza added some treats to the basket. How could she resist the homemade jelly with a plaid ribbon on the jar, fudge in a small woven basket, and bright pink napkins? They looked so festive, and she convinced herself they would add cheer to her new adventure. Next to the register was a local newspaper, the *Lower Cape Review*. Liza had her heart set on moving to Chatham, where she stayed last summer. However, her online search was unproductive. Maybe the locals advertised in the small Cape paper?

After food shopping, the ride to the Lobster Roll restaurant was uneventful. Crossing the threshold, Liza admired the brightly lit cafe with red-and-white *Formica* tables. She grabbed a real estate brochure from a wire rack and glanced around the room. Most of the tables were empty, with menus leaning against the paper napkin holders. A woman behind the counter waved her arm and pointed to a booth near the front. Leafing through the menu, Liza noticed the smudges on the page describing six types of chowders. These must be popular choices.

The same server, walking with a slight limp, arrived at her table. Looking close to Liza's age, she was a short, stocky blonde. Instead of a uniform, she wore black jeans, a white turtleneck, and sneakers.

"Coffee?" she asked.

"Sure. I'm dying for caffeine. What's good today?" This was an opportunity to speak with another person, and Liza was excited.

"The chowder's always a good choice." She scrutinized Liza's designer clothes and asked, "You're not from around here. New York?"

That was too close for comfort, and Liza realized she needed to blend in better. "Chicago," she replied. She did not know how to sound like a Midwesterner and hoped the woman did not either.

Ten minutes later, the server returned with the most delicious fish chowder Liza had ever tasted. As she ate with gusto, Liza perused the real estate brochure.

After clearing the dishes, the woman asked, "Everything alright, Hon?"

Liza found endearing comments from strangers irritating, but the woman seemed genuine and friendly. "Yeah, I'm in the market for a rental." Maybe she knew someone with a place to rent.

"Oh, it's incredibly expensive on the Cape, with the summer folks who'll pay anything for a week in the sun. The rates around here triple in season."

Liza felt discouraged and the server must have read her face, as she added, "Don't worry, it's winter and you'll find something this time of year. By the way, did you like the chowder?"

"Yes. It's amazing. What's your secret?"

"Well…," she hesitated, as if guarding a numbered Swiss bank account. "In the fish chowder, we put real cream and in the clam chowder, we also add lobster stock. It makes it much richer."

Liza was glad there was not any lobster in the fish chowder. It was not her favorite seafood. However, the cream daunted her. She envisioned her arteries constricting and worried that

Sam would not find out if she had a heart attack. Would anyone care? She put this out of her thoughts, paid the bill, and walked towards the door.

"Good luck," her newfound friend called out.

"Thanks." The drive back was not long enough for the heater to warm the car, so she was shivering when she reached the cabin.

"Hi, Honey. I'm home." Liza greeted her kitty, as the warmth from the small cottage embraced her. Licorice opened one eye and went back to sleep on her bed. Careful not to disturb her curled-up friend, Liza spread the newspaper over the quilt to read the ads. Looking through the paper, she found a few Chatham rentals. One was available until June. That might work. It would give her time to decide if she enjoyed living on the Cape and wanted to stay through the summer. Although if she rented it, it would force her to pay the high cost of summer rentals. Liza did not want to wind up camping with a cat. However, she was desperate, and called the number.

"Hello," a woman with a low, cracked voice answered.

"Hi. My name is Liza, and I'm calling about the ad in the paper."

"Hello." Again, there was no further comment.

"Do you have an apartment for rent?"

A shrill voice in the background came closer to the phone. "Ma. Who is it?"

"I don't know."

"Give me the phone."

More crackling and an annoyed woman came on the line. "Who is this?"

Liza was ready to disconnect, but she remembered she had no other options. She re-explained who she was and where she saw the ad. "Is the rental still available?"

"Are you a nurse?"

"What?" She must have heard wrong.

"I said, are you a nurse?" The woman spoke louder, as if she had a hearing problem. This was not going well.

"No, I'm not."

"Oh. We're looking for someone to help my mother. She has some memory problems. Do you have any experience caring for people with Alzheimer's? My mom needs someone with her all the time. I have a job and can't stay home with her."

Liza hesitated. She could not think of a way to convince the woman to hire her with no experience. "No. I'm sorry."

The loud click on the other end was harsh. Liza looked through the rest of the ads and paused at the last one. It intrigued her, and looked promising, "Sublet my two-bedroom house and provide house and pet-sitting services. References required." Liza loved animals. This would mean the house came furnished, would be pet-friendly, and ready for occupancy. Her big hurdle was local references. How would she get them and from whom?

She called the number. A breathy voice answered. "Hello, this is Aurora. How may I help you?"

"Hi, I'm Liza Kasner. Is your home still available for rent?" She said a silent prayer.

Aurora replied, "What sign are you?"

She almost fell off the bed. What the hell? "Aquarius. How about you?"

"I'm a Taurus and want to make sure you'd be compatible with my cat, Zeus. He likes people born under your sign. I try to avoid Virgos, if you know what I mean."

Liza did not know what she meant, but forged ahead. "Can I come and see your place? I'm looking for a house in Chatham. I have a cat and would love to have two." Was Licorice going to be a deal-breaker? "My cat's a lovely tuxedo. Friendly," she added. This was not true, but she was desperate.

Aurora remained silent. For what seemed like an hour, Liza held her breath. "Okay, both of you can come tomorrow at twelve-thirty." She gave directions, and it did not sound hard to find.

Liza could not believe her luck. Was this woman for real or was she a crackpot? Maybe dangerous? She convinced herself not to dwell on it. It was time she got a break. She was exhausted and got ready for bed. Licorice spread out on the quilt, looked at her with one slit eye opened. Liza shifted her furry friend to the other side and moved onto the warmed spot. Sleep came easily, and she dreamed about oceans and summer beaches. When she woke, it was still dark, and she asked her cat, "Where the hell are we?" Her heart pounded as she sat, looked around, and remembered she was in a motel room. "Okay… safe." She fell back and drifted off again.

The next time she woke, the clock next to the bed showed it was ten. The sun was shining through a crack in the heavy bottle-green drapes. Licorice yawned and stretched, and Liza looked out the window and admired the blue-skyed day. After sleeping so much later than usual, she was famished. Liza shared a turkey sandwich with Licorice and turned on the television for the news. No mention of her on the *Ten Most Wanted List* of unsolved mysteries. She hoped it would be a long time before Barry started looking for her. She was glad she thought of writing a note to throw him off track.

"One day at a time. We made it." She hugged Licorice, feeling liberated. Not a bad way to start her day. What should she wear to meet Aurora? She dug through her suitcase for something crunchy and artsy. Liza chose blue jeans, boots, and a colorful sweater to make a good impression, and walked to the full-length mirror. She pushed her curly blonde hair behind her ears. Although she wished she were tall and lithe, reality told her otherwise. Liza fingered the fresh bruises on her arms that were fading. Soon they would be gone, along with other reminders of her life with Barry.

At noon she wrestled a yowling Licorice, transferred her into the cat carrier, and carried it to the car. It was too big for the front seat, so she gently placed it on the back. "Come on, Sweetie, it's just a brief ride." She wanted her kitty to make a good impression, too.

Licorice whimpered up Route 28 and Liza was afraid it was going to be a stressful day. She did not have a choice, as she could not stay at the motel forever. Summer rent prices were exponentially higher than winter, and her funds would eventually run out. She and Licorice could not take a chance at becoming homeless. Heading toward Chatham, Liza passed boarded-up storefronts from closed summer businesses. The village of Old Bass River looked quaint, and she drove through Harwichport, savoring the beauty of Cape Cod and her freedom. When she passed a painted black-and-white sign, *Entering Chatham*, her heart raced. "What are we getting into? Is this woman a nutcase, or can this arrangement possibly work?"

There was no answer from the back seat until she slowed down, and Licorice started bellowing. "Okay, Girl." She used her most soothing tone. "It's not too far." The kitty quieted, but soon started protesting. Passing an older strip mall, she took a right toward Harding's Beach. Close to a boat landing, Liza found the narrow road, with old-fashioned bungalows scattered along the drive. Number 37 Seashell Lane was on the curve. The house's green shutters matched Aurora's description. How adorable. She lifted the wriggling carrier from the car and walked toward the house. A tiny porch with a red screen door and a dark-blue concrete floor greeted her. The porch's well-worn wicker furniture looked inviting. Although there was a coating of snow on the floor, Liza imagined sitting in this cool refuge on a summer day, with a glass of lemonade and a book in her lap. She raised her hand to knock, but the glass-paneled door opened before she made contact. A tall, slight woman with long, wavy black hair stood in front of her, wearing a gauze multi-colored skirt and an embroidered blouse. Her accessories of a colorful scarf and long crystal earrings were exotic.

"Hi, you must be Liza." The striking woman studied her.

"Yes, thank you for having us over. I'm pleased to meet you." Liza answered in a perky voice. "Your home is sweet; I can't wait to tour the entire house." Aurora did not respond, but smiled with amusement. Liza realized she could view the entire place from the front door. It was a doll's house, tiny and complete. "Oh," she continued, "I love it. It's so warm and cozy."

Liza entered the main room furnished with a drop-leaf table and chairs, a floral hooked rug, a striped pink-and-blue couch, and a rocker covered in chintz. The fringed lampshades were perched on side tables covered with lace doilies. The cottage had a fireplace at one end and a small galley kitchen with white cabinets and blue walls at the other. Directly off the living room were two bedrooms, painted in bright colors. The closest one was azure blue and the other coral. Beaded curtains pulled back over the bedroom doorways added to the dramatic décor. The house reminded Liza of a fairy home in a bright-colored children's book.

Aurora examined Liza with pensive golden eyes. She took her hand and said, "You're in trouble."

Liza could not imagine how she read her so well. It was unnerving. She thought about telling a lie, then broke down and turned beet red. "I've got some problems...." She hesitated, not believing she was on the verge of telling this stranger her secrets.

"I know," Aurora replied, with a grave look on her face.

"I really can't talk about it."

"Yes, I understand. You'll be okay," she stated emphatically.

Liza wished she had Aurora's crystal ball because right now, she did not feel okay.

Aurora stared directly at the cat wailing in the carrier. Liza opened it and Licorice hopped out. "What a beautiful cat," she said.

Aurora walked toward the blue bedroom. Licorice and Liza followed. One of the largest gray-and-white striped tabby cats Liza had ever seen sat on a brightly quilted bedspread. The cat stared at the petite black-and-white cat. Aurora pointed to him and smiled. "This is Zeus."

Here was the moment of truth. Zeus closed his eyes and turned around. Licorice gave a brief hiss, exited the bedroom, jumped on the couch, and staked out her territory in the living room. Liza hoped this was a truce and they would get along better after they became roommates.

Aurora looked a little dismayed, but stared at her visitors for a long time. "I wanted a cat lover that didn't have a pet. However, I sense you need to be here and that you're in pain. My mom had a stroke and lives in California. She needs me to take care of her, and I can't bring Zeus. I'll be away until at least next September. I'm looking for a house sitter I can trust with my...my everything." Her voice faltered.

Liza looked up with teary gratitude. "You don't know how much we need a safe place to live. I promise to take wonderful care of Zeus and your home." She wondered how she would get around the problem of references.

Aurora said, "I guess references are out of the question, aren't they?"

Crap, she read her mind again. "Yes, however, I have enough money to put down a good-sized damage deposit. I swear I'll do everything I can to make Zeus happy."

Aurora did not answer right away. "I need to think about this and will call you tomorrow." She paused as if her next comment was an afterthought. "Do you have a job?"

"I'm in the interview process," Liza exaggerated.

"Tell me about it."

Liza shifted her weight and looked down. This called for a creative response. "I've already met my new boss. She's lovely."

Aurora gave a small chuckle, and Liza knew the woman knew the truth.

Chapter 5

Barry

Barry woke from a fitful sleep with an unsettled feeling. He had not heard from Franny in a week. That was not like her. Where was she? His wife had better not be cooking up something with one of her thieving relatives. If Franny were unhappy, she would whine to her cousin Lucy. That monster would set her up with a divorce attorney, who would try to take him to the cleaners. Of course, they could not get what they could not find. He chuckled and sat up.

"I'm just hungover from last night and need breakfast," he croaked. After wiping his crusty eyelids with his knuckles, he got out of bed, looked in the mirror, and grinned at his reflection. He looked great. He smiled, thinking about the party last night, where the booze and girls were amazing. Why was he thinking about Franny? Later, he would give her cousin a quick call. Barry pulled out a clean shirt and rifled through his drawers for a tee shirt and shorts.

"I bet Franny did the laundry and didn't bother to put my clothes away." He went downstairs and opened the dryer. It was empty. He checked the washer and yelled, "Franny, I'm gonna kill you!" The red towel in the machine with his clothes infuriated him. His underwear was crimson and matched his face. This was going to be a commando day.

Barry was late for work again. He scoffed at the other guys, making cold calls. He needed to get some serious money real soon, so he would not have to keep coming to this prison. Later in the morning, he tried Franny two more times, and the phone went to voice mail. He hoped Lucy could get in touch with his wife, so he called her. "Hi, Lucy, how're ya doing?"

She sounded sullen. "I'm fine, Barry. What do you want?"

He tried to be upbeat. Franny's cousin could be a real idiot, and he did not want to deal with her moods. "I'm just looking for Franny. Is she around?"

Lucy hesitated. "Why don't you call her yourself?"

Barry balled his fist. "You know how she is. She probably forgot to recharge her phone."

Lucy responded, "I don't know her itinerary. I'm not in charge of her, you know. She was here for a few days and went to Betty's for the rest of the week." Then she added, "Franny's probably traveling around the cousin circuit to make sure she doesn't wear out her welcome."

Her comment made perfect sense to Barry. Franny had worn out her welcome in her own house. However, there was something about Lucy's tone that made him suspicious. Was she lying? "Lucy, what's going on? I need to speak to my wife."

"I swear, Barry, she's just trying to visit all of us before she goes home."

Barry thought about it. Maybe Lucy was telling the truth. "Thanks. If you see her, tell her to call."

"Sure." Her tone had a sarcastic edge, but that was the way Lucy was.

Slightly mollified, Barry would give Franny another few days before calling again. At least she was not home bugging him. "It's not like I'm calling the governor of Florida to find her. She'll call soon." This decision made sense to him.

Chapter 6

After leaving Aurora's cottage, Liza drove around the outskirts of Chatham. She parked at Harding's Beach and took in the expanse of sand, ending in a view of a distant lighthouse. If it were not so cold, she would take a walk on the beach. Liza was pleased to see hearty New Englanders strolling through the sand. If she got the cottage, they might be her neighbors. This was the first time she believed everything might just work out. She and Licorice were not just on an adventure, they were starting over.

When she returned to their motel room, Liza opened the cat carrier. Licorice jumped on the bed and stared at her. "So, Licorice, what do you think about the cottage? Do you like it? What about having a new friend? Do you think he's cute?" The cat looked at her with contempt and refused to answer.

Liza perched on the edge of the bed and petted the soft black-and-white fur. She thought about her white lie to Aurora and panicked. She had to find a job. What could she do? Although she had a fake social security card, a professional job would leave a trail and make it too easy for Barry to find her. She had been an English instructor at a community college in New Jersey, but could not imagine herself getting a job like that here. Who would hire her with no resume and references? She regretted leaving on such short notice, but she had had no choice. When Liza discovered her husband was going on a business trip, she knew she had a brief window of time to escape. Barry's abusive outbursts were happening with increasing frequency. She told her boss she had a family emergency and did not know when she would return. Liza was not lying. She had a family emergency. Hers. If she stayed much longer, Barry would kill her.

It was late afternoon, and a knock on the door startled her. Liza grabbed a hairdryer, the only weapon she had handy. Had Barry found her? Peering through the small peephole, she laughed. It was only Jeff. She was not sure what she would have done to protect herself armed with a hairdryer. Liza inspected the room and kicked the clothes piled on the rug in front of the bed into the bathroom. After closing the bathroom door, she sighed, took a deep breath, and opened it.

He stepped inside and grinned. "How're you guys doing?"

"We're fine," she responded, wondering what he wanted. Was he checking for cat damage? She glanced around the room. The place looked fine to her.

"You said you were new to the Cape, so I was wondering if you'd like to come over for a glass of wine and appetizers."

What? She had not had an offer like that since high school. Her palms felt sweaty. Oh, grow up. It is only a glass of wine, not a marriage proposal.

He misinterpreted her hesitation. "Oh, you're busy. Is it a bad time?"

Sometimes she forgot other people had insecurities too. "No, I'd love to. Just let me feed my cat and I'll be over."

He responded with a big smile, and his blue eyes sparkled. "See you in a few minutes."

After Jeff left the cottage, she paced the room. Looking for something to wear more presentable for an evening out, Liza rifled through the clothing in her suitcase. She scattered them on the bed and complained to Licorice, "This is nuts. I don't even know him. Get a grip." The kitty surveyed the gigantic pile, snuggled on top of the assorted garments, and kneaded a red wool cardigan. "Good taste, a designer brand." Licorice took it in stride and rolled over.

After a few false starts, Liza selected jeans and a black cashmere sweater. The understated, comfortable, and warm outfit made her look at least ten pounds thinner. She poured a hefty amount of kibble into a bowl, picked up the clothes in the bathroom, and added them to the pile on the bed. Liza walked towards the door and glanced back at the kitty. "Have a good nap, Sweetheart. Don't wait up." Licorice opened one eye and went back to sleep.

Ambling across the parking lot, Liza had misgivings. For a moment, she thought about Barry and how hurt she was by his betrayal. Last week, she vowed never to have anything to do with men again. Here she was, about to have a drink with a single guy. Was he single? She did not need complications in her life, but she desperately wanted a friend.

Jeff answered the door wearing his usual work clothes. So much for him feeling insecure and trying to make a good impression on her. She wished she could come back in another life as a man and not worry about how she looked. After crossing the threshold, it surprised Liza to see such understated, but elegant, decor. The roaring fire in the fireplace and candles on the mantle exuded comfort. Placed on the trunk that served as a coffee table was a plate of Brie, crackers, and fruit. Jeff guided her to an overstuffed leather couch that looked inviting. This was a masculine room with delicate touches. His home was incongruous for a man wearing a red flannel plaid shirt. She wondered if this was typical for Cape Cod.

"Nice place you have," she commented.

"Oh, it's just the beginning. Most of my stuff's still in storage."

The old oval braided rug was in shades of green and orange, definitely early Americana. "Well, it has a nice feel and looks very comfortable." Liza's goal was to steer the conversation away from anything personal.

Of course, that was not the direction Jeff took. "So, tell me about yourself."

Liza giggled. Was he asking about Franny or Liza? This could be a long night.

He looked at her and appeared a little insulted. She realized it was an internal joke that he thought was at his expense. "Oh sorry. I was just thinking about my day and the interesting woman I met in Chatham. She was very unusual, and has an amazing house for rent."

"What happened?"

This was a much safer topic, so she provided an extensive account of the day ending with, "I kind of told her I had a job. She won't rent to me unless I can show a steady income."

Jeff gave her a pensive look and did not reply immediately. "Have you ever worked in a restaurant?"

She answered truthfully, "Why no, but I certainly have kitchen skills."

"Bonnie's my friend who owns the Lobster Roll. She's having a knee operation and will be out of commission for a few weeks. She's looking for a server to fill in until she can work again."

"You think she'd consider hiring a stranger? Can I use you as a reference?" Liza could not believe her luck. He was offering a suggestion for a job, a reference, and wine and cheese. She had hit the lottery.

"Sure. Just don't blame me when your feet are killing you at the end of the shift."

"I'll go in tomorrow and speak with Bonnie. Thanks so much. Don't worry. I'll take responsibility for my actions." This was not quite true, but explaining her recent past would take another week and require more trust than she had. The warmth of the fire and the wine relaxed her and, for the first time in months, she felt safe with another person. "This is really nice." She took a sip of wine.

"Stick around and you'll find people on the Cape to be welcoming after they get to know you."

"I've not made many new friends in a long time. It's been quite lonely."

"Well, now you know me." He poured some more wine and offered her the cheese plate. "So, I hear from your accent you're from the New York area. Am I right?"

She did not want to lie to this man. "Yes. I lived in the metropolitan area my whole life."

Jeff was a delightful host, and they shared their love for Broadway and the New York scene. "It's a big change living on the Cape. What made you come here?"

"I've always loved the ocean and vacationed here last summer." Talking about Barry and her escape was off-limits. "Tell me about life on Cape Cod."

"I love the small villages. Chatham's more expensive than other towns, but it's got character. I moved to Yarmouth because the motel was for sale, and I could almost afford it."

Liza looked around the room and smiled. "You're doing great things with this place."

"Unfortunately, I'm depleting my savings at an alarming rate to remodel the motel, but I hope to attract a new clientele this summer."

By eight they had exhausted the wine-and-cheese conversation and called an end to the evening. Thank God romantic moves never came up. He walked her back to the cottage, and they hugged good night.

Liza had eaten little and realized she was not hungry. This achievement impressed her. Spending time with an interesting man removed her desire to stress-eat.

Entering the cabin, she found Licorice asleep on the bed. Liza read that cats sleep over twenty hours a day, and from her feline's behavior, Licorice was setting the world record. It was too early for Liza to sleep, so she looked through her clothes. Cape Cod was not a haven for chic fashions, and Liza had very few items that did not announce she was an *outsider*.

Liza examined her wardrobe and decided to only keep clothes that looked like Cape Cod outfits. What did the locals wear? Liza needed to spend some time watching people. However, she was positive she could pare down half of her wardrobe. She would not require clothing for a Metropolitan suburban workplace anymore. One by one, she sorted the clothes on the bed with a discerning eye. On the right was a pile to keep. At the top were black and brown pants, three V-neck sweaters in muted colors, and a low-cut black sweater. She also added jeans, tees, two plain skirts, and three dresses. The last ones were just in case she won a Tony award for best acting on Cape Cod. She gave up trying to part with everything, as she had some fabulous clothes that were impossible to discard. By spring, Liza planned to buy more summer clothes, capris, lightweight shirts, and a new bathing suit. She only brought enough items to convince Barry she went on a warm-weather vacation. Liza's goal was to lose a few pounds by summer. She could only hope that would happen.

It was a teary-eyed moment when Liza fingered the black dress with the gold silk jacket she had worn to Sam's high school graduation party. She held the dress against her body and peered into the mirror. Overcome with a fleeting moment of panic about Sam, she comforted herself. "Listen, he'll be fine. When you sort this out, you'll figure out a way to contact him." Although they did not speak every week, Liza knew she needed to get a hold of her son and assure him she was safe. She wanted him to know everything was going to be all right.

Was that true? Nagging worries crept in, and she doubted her optimism.

Liza kept busy avoiding thoughts about Sam by folding the rejected clothing and putting items back in the suitcase. She would ask Jeff to direct her to a high-end consignment shop in the area that would turn her beautiful garments into cash. In a place like the Cape, there must be the wanna-be-wealthy and thrifty Yankees, who would appreciate the value of designer labels at bargain prices. Liza hoped there was a market for the ample-sized, well-dressed woman, and sighed with exhaustion. She put on her flannel nightgown and picked up a book. Although it was one of her favorite mystery writers, after ten pages, she could not keep her eyes open. Moving Licorice to the other side of the mattress, they curled up together and fell asleep.

Chapter 7

The next day greeted Liza with bright sun, blue skies, and fluffy white clouds. It was glorious, and she felt optimistic. Her 1960s-decorated room was becoming home. Even Licorice was a little livelier, purring loudly on the bed, and wiggling closer to the window to bask in the winter rays shining on the spread.

Liza made a bowl of instant oatmeal and drank a glass of juice. Later, she would head over to the Lobster Roll for coffee and a job interview. Although no one was expecting her for an interview, she adopted a positive attitude. Dressed in black slacks and a gray V-necked sweater, Liza was excited. Funny, these were her stay-at-home clothes in New Jersey. Now they were her going-to-impress-a-prospective-boss outfit. "Keep safe, Licorice," she called out and left. Liza shivered with dread, as she did not want to become an old lady who talked to cats. She needed a life.

When she turned into the Lobster Roll's parking lot, Liza's heart pounded, and her hands shook. What if she did not get a job? Or worse, what if she did and failed? She calmed herself with deep breathing. Liza had not felt such terror since she let go of Sam's hand on the first day of kindergarten.

When she sat at the counter, the hostess from the other night took her order with a friendly smile. Liza felt an instant connection to the woman, and she wondered if the server knew why she was there. Like Aurora, could everyone on the Cape read her mind? She laughed at the thought. She was going nuts.

The friendly blonde asked, "How're you today? What can I get ya?"

"Just coffee with skim milk and sweetener."

"So, how's the house-hunting going?"

"Excellent memory."

"We don't get many new people in the winter. I'm Bonnie, by the way."

Liza realized she must be Jeff's friend and gathered courage before answering. "Nice to meet you. I'm Liza Kasner." It thrilled her to remember her new name without messing up. "I think I found a perfect place in Chatham, but I'm waiting to hear from the owner, who I met with yesterday."

"That's great. I hope you get it." Bonnie walked away.

Liza continued before she was out of earshot, "I'd be house-sitting. I also spoke with Jeff at Pilgrim's Landing about finding a job. He said you were friends, and he thought you might have an opening for a fill-in server." She finished her sentence and exhaled slowly.

Bonnie hesitated, as if sizing her up. It made Liza more anxious, and she wanted to disappear. Did she overstep her boundaries? Was it too soon for this type of request?

After a few moments, she replied, "I'll be off my feet for a few weeks. Gloria, one of my regular servers, can cover some of my shifts, but we'll be short from early morning until lunchtime three days a week. It's less than twenty hours and we work for tips in the winter, if you get what I mean."

Oh yes, under the table. This was perfect. Liza smiled.

Bonnie continued, "So, what's your restaurant experience?"

"Well," Liza dragged out, "I worked in a restaurant a while back, but I think it's like riding a bike and will come back really easily." This was so lame, even she did not believe her own words.

Bonnie laughed. "No experience, huh? Okay, everyone needs help sometimes. Times are tough. I'll tell you what. If you're willing to help here for a week with no pay, just tips, I'll train you and we can see how you do."

A restaurant internship, how unique, thought Liza. "Sounds great. When can I start?"

"How about in a few days? You can wear those black pants. You'll need a few white shirts. Get some comfortable sneakers. We wear black ones. Make sure everything's washable. You'll be cleaning up all morning. Come by at seven a.m. Thursday and we can start you out slowly."

Liza drank her coffee and tipped generously. Thanking Bonnie profusely, she headed to her car. Now, if Aurora called, she would be all set. She had a good feeling about today and went online to check her horoscope.

Chapter 8

Barry

Looking around the smoke-filled bar, Barry searched for his latest pickup. When he went to the bathroom, the woman had disappeared. He finally spotted her sitting on a stool talking to a guy with a sleeve of tattoos down each arm. Good riddance to her. Barry peered into the bar's mirror and admired himself, with his blue silk shirt and gold chains. The bartender came over. "Hi, my name's Mike. What'll you have?"

Barry smiled. "I'm Barry. Glad to meet you. How about a beer, something on tap?"

Mike pointed to the empty stool next to Barry. "What happened to the lady?"

Barry nodded his head toward the girl with the long legs and low-cut spandex top. "She's over there." He pointed across the room. "Can't count on broads for even five minutes."

Mike laughed. "Well, there'll be another Suzie or Sarah or whoever showing up soon. Your luck will change. I'll be right back with that beer."

"Great." He felt a buzzing in his pocket and realized he had turned the sound off on his phone. He looked at Mike. "Damn. It's my phone and I've gotta take it. I can't believe someone's calling at this hour." Mike left, and Barry fumbled through his pocket until he found it. "Hello," he growled, waiting for the person to talk. Barry felt a chill of excitement go through him as he wondered, "Could it be the police? Was Franny in an accident?" He could only hope.

"Hi, Dad."

Barry pulled himself together. "Oh hi, Sam." He expected his son to call him earlier. It was nearly eleven-thirty. Didn't the kid have classes tomorrow? They had so much free time at college. Days off during the week and endless vacations. Why was he paying all that money for school? The kid hardly went there.

Sam laughed. "It's early for me. We usually go out after studying to blow off steam." He paused and added, "I'm sorry. Did I wake you?"

Barry glanced around the noisy place. "No." He moved towards the front door to cut down on the background sounds. He did not want Sam to know he was in a bar. "I'm awake and just watching TV."

"Sounds like quite a show," Sam replied.

Barry covered for the loud music. "Well, it's one of those reality shows." He wondered if this was convincing, but continued, "So, how are you?"

"I tried calling Mom and haven't been able to reach her."

"Oh. She's in Florida with her cousins. I haven't talked to her, but Lucy says she's fine. Is there anything you need?"

Sam hesitated and finally replied, "My roommate was just diagnosed with hepatitis. The school sent him home, but I wanted to talk to Mom about my latest shots and find out if there is anything I need to do and all. I could always call the health center, but I thought Mom would be easier to talk to."

This was Franny's area. She kept track of everything from hemorrhoids to sore throats. Where the hell was she? She should be the one answering these questions. "Look, Sam, it's too late to call Florida. I'll see what I can do to find Mom tomorrow. Make sure you take precautions and get to the infirmary in the morning." Shouldn't Sam be using the school's doctors? Why was Barry paying such a large health center fee? He felt bad that Sam was worried, but this was Franny's job. He ended the call before Sam could guess how furious he was at her. Barry would call Franny in the morning and demand she contact Sam. Hepatitis was scary.

Barry moved closer to the bar and eyed a new girl sitting three stools away from him. She was wearing a red dress and had on high heels. He sauntered over to her and used his best line, "Hi, Babe. You look great tonight."

Chapter 9

Liza felt the same way she did when she was fifteen, hopelessly waiting for a boy to call. What was taking Aurora so long to get in touch? After checking out a few other cottages and apartments for rent in the local paper, Liza was more convinced that this little house would be her next home. Most others requested long-term leases, were not pet friendly, or the renter had to vacate by June first. The on-line horror stories of renters who could not afford to live on the Cape in the summer scared her. She read landlords jacked up their prices for weekly tourist rentals. Year-rounders had to live in garages and tents. This was the underside of the local culture in this beautiful place. Although there was only a canal separating Cape Cod from the rest of Massachusetts, the mainland seemed a million miles away.

She needed to keep busy so she would not waste the whole day waiting for the phone to ring. "Okay, Licorice. I'm going to get out of here. It's time for a little shopping." Licorice yawned and stretched to her full length. Liza concluded that this was an affirmative response. Shopping always cheered her up in New Jersey when she was upset. Liza put on her coat and ruffled the kitty's fur. "I'll be back soon." Lucky cat. The pressure of anticipating a call was not getting to her. She should take a lesson in stress reduction from Licorice.

Liza drove to Hyannis and entered the Cape's indoor mall with branches of a few familiar chain stores. She looked around and did not see any of the high-end stores she shopped in at home. The mall could be located anywhere in middle-class USA. It should do fine to help her transform from a metropolitan New Yorker to a Cape Cod native. She knew it would take more than new clothes, but certainly, this was a good start. She studied the women walking through the stores. They appeared older, probably retired, and were wearing polyester clothes in pastel colors, with matching tops and bottoms. In deference to winter, many of these blue-haired ladies wore sweatshirts with the towns of the Cape embroidered on them. Clothing with Chatham, Dennis, and Provincetown had birds and flowers surrounding the names. If she became forgetful, these clothes would be useful. Now, where do I live? Oh yes, I live in Chatham. It is right on my sweatshirt. Twenty years from now, she might give a bright smile and rejoice she got through another day unscathed.

The younger women walking through the mall looked like they were on a perpetual camping trip. They mostly wore jeans, boots, heavy sweaters, and waterproof parkas with hoods and large pockets. She clapped her hands and decided this would be her new look. When a police officer walked toward her, she ducked into a store with tees and jeans piled on tables. She hid near the back of the store in case Barry had reported her disappearance. It would be terrible if her picture was on the bulletin board of the local police stations. Liza held her breath and glanced back until she was sure the officer was gone. She scooped a variety of pants and tops in a range of colors and sizes and selected three washable sweaters. She remembered Bonnie's instructions and added three white jerseys. This was the end of her ironing and dry-cleaning days, as she disdainfully recalled the grueling hours spent ironing Barry's good dress shirts. He had complained if she did not press them perfectly. She would never put up with crap like that again. Not from anyone.

After trying on an armload of clothes, Liza carried her purchases to the checkout counter. The saleswoman rang them up and commented, "My, you look like you're getting a whole new wardrobe."

"Yes, I needed something new to wear. I had to wait until the holidays were over." This sounded plausible as Liza handed over the cash. The saleswoman gave her a tenuous look and her stomach clenched. Was an all-cash transaction suspicious? She continued with chatty conversation, hoping the clerk would forget her. "You know how it is, as the money always goes for the kids. It takes a while to save up enough to treat myself to something nice." She smiled and decided in the future not to buy too much at any one store. It was crucial that she not make an impression on anyone.

With these purchases, she hoped to blend in better. Her life depended on it. The police officer came around the corner again and she turned towards a window display of purses to study his reflection in the glass. While willing herself to concentrate on the bags, she scrutinized the knockoff of a designer bag. The air felt stuffy as the officer approached. Trying to look nonchalant, Liza stood frozen with her hands clenched. Suddenly, he reversed direction and headed towards a group of men sitting on a bench. Liza counted to ten and sauntered toward the mall's exit. Sweat poured off her brow, leaving her hot and sticky. When she reached the parking lot, she walked as fast as she could toward her car. It was time to get out of there and back to the safety of her little cabin.

The phone rang as she drove along Route 28. Liza was reluctant to answer, as she did not feel safe driving, talking on the phone, and navigating unfamiliar roads. She did not want to do anything to cause an accident. When she arrived at the motel parking lot, she turned off the car and checked who called. Liza saw it was an unidentified missed caller. Could this be Aurora? Who the hell else would call? The Easter Bunny? She dialed the number.

A man answered. "Hi, Liza, it's Rick. I wanted to see how you're doing."

She forgot she promised her old friend she would let him know when she landed somewhere. He was the one person she trusted from her old life. He provided the car and her new identity. "I'm so sorry. I forgot to call you. You won't believe this. I wound up in off-season Chatham and working on finding a house-sitting position. I was hoping your call was from the woman who was looking for someone to live in her home and cat-sit."

"That's fabulous. Any word from Barry?"

"No, although I'm lying low. He may not have figured out I went to New England instead of Florida."

"Who's covering for you in the Sunshine state?"

"My cousin Lucy. She usually won't do favors for me, but I called in as many chips as possible."

"Tell me about your getaway."

"You and your old high school buddies were amazing. So many thanks for the new car and papers for Liza Kasner. I couldn't have gotten anywhere without them."

"I'd love to have seen Barry's face when he realized you left him," Rick chuckled.

"Me, too. Right before I drove away, I washed all his underwear with a load of new red towels. When he figures out how to open a washing machine, I'm sure he'll get the full benefit of my surprise."

The laughter from the phone was heartwarming. Liza realized her world had been grim over the past year.

"So. How are you doing?"

"I'm getting used to this new life, but I don't know anyone here. I'm so glad you called."

"What's off-season Cape Cod like?"

"It's pretty, if you like solitude. I sometimes feel like I'm on an indoor camping trip." She giggled.

"You've got to be kidding. What the hell is going on?" Rick sounded amused.

"It's hard to explain, but I wanted to blend in with the locals. You would not believe how I look. I just bought a boatload of camping clothes. It's very un-New Jersey."

"I can't wait to see you. Listen, call me on this number if you need anything. Let me know everything is okay."

"Don't worry, everything is fine. I'm here, safe and sound, and looking for a house to rent. Lucky for me, I've found a temporary job so I can make my money last. Get this, they call newcomers *wash-a-shores*."

Rick laughed. "On the Jersey shore, we'd need a hazmat team for anything that came in on the beach."

She laughed so hard that she shook. This was her first belly laugh in weeks. It felt magnificent. "True. I hope I can blend in and not look like I'm from another country."

"You're going to be fine," he reassured her. "I want you to call when you get a permanent address."

"Thanks. I love you, Rick. You're my oldest friend." She cried. It was so sad to hear his voice and not be able to see him. She was also glad that Barry never warmed up to him and would not even think of contacting her old buddy.

"Now keep in touch, you promise?" Rick added, "I love you too. Whenever I needed help, you were always there for me."

"Thanks, Rick." Liza disconnected and headed into the motel cabin.

"Hi, Ladybug, I'm home." Liza called out to Licorice, who opened her eyes and jumped off the bed to rub against her legs. "You must be hungry. I should have fed you before I left." Momentarily guilty, she dashed into the bathroom to check her cat's food dish. It was empty. "Oh, Licorice." She got teary again. "I'm so sorry." Everything was getting to her. Now she was apologizing to a cat. If she did not stop this behavior, someone might institutionalize her. Although that would solve her housing problem.

After she fed Licorice, Liza assembled a small lunch of yogurt and fruit. Carefully, she chose one new outfit and put the rest in the dresser drawer. She caught her reflection in the mirror, smiling at the pleasant-looking woman with green eyes. Although slightly heavy in the middle, her arms and legs were not too bad. If she lost forty pounds, she would look great. Maybe not twenty-five-year-old beautiful, but still not wrinkled. With her new blonde hair, she could pass for a younger version of herself.

She left the room to find Jeff and request he extend her time until either Aurora called, or she found somewhere else to live.

Jeff was in the yard, stacking firewood. When she approached, he gazed at her slowly and carefully. "New duds, I see."

"I needed to buy some warm clothes for the Cape weather. It's so raw near the sea." Liza shivered.

Jeff laughed. "I was wondering how long you were going to last in dressy clothes and high-heeled boots. It can get very icy here in the winter."

"So, I've noticed. I want to let you know I need to stay for a few more days. Maybe a week. It's hard finding a place to live with a feline companion."

"It's not exactly high season. Don't worry. You can stay as long as you want. No tourists are vying for housing this time of year."

"Thanks. I'll let you know when I'm leaving as soon as I can."

"No problem." He stared at her for a few more seconds, then turned back toward the woodpile, and continued to stack logs.

It was impossible to keep the conversation going. He was a hunk, but not very talkative. Liza rushed back to her cabin and donned warmer clothes. To pass the time, she explored some of the nearby beaches. Liza imagined the beach in the summer, with the smell of lotion and fresh air, and longed for warm weather. The thought of reading and lying in the sun made her happy. She sat on a rock, enjoying the aloneness and stark beauty of the winter sea. Maybe this place was not the luxury of the Old Cape Inn, but it would do just fine. Liza rechecked her phone. No messages. "Come on Aurora, call dammit."

Chapter 10

Barry

It was Wednesday morning, and Barry procrastinated. He was not ready to face the office at nine. Ten a.m. was a more fashionable hour to go to work. After checking the bedside clock, he reluctantly pushed the covers off and staggered to his feet. In the steamy shower, he remembered the call from Sam the previous night. Sam was always sick as a kid and the thought of hepatitis concerned him. The reality of not knowing where Franny was parking herself in Florida, and Sam's exposure to a disease, riled Barry. He called her cousin again to find out if his wife had shown her fat butt back at Lucy's house.

He figured Lucy was up and was probably putting on her makeup. Although she still had a tight body, she needed all the help she could get in the wrinkle cover-up department. After the phone rang four times, Lucy finally picked up. "Hi, this is Lucy." Her voice sounded gravelly. Maybe he woke her. He smiled.

"Hi, it's Barry. I need to talk to Franny today. Sam needs some help. Have you seen or heard from her lately?"

Lucy always had a soft spot for Sam. "No, I haven't. What's the problem?"

"Well, it's one of those medical things that Sam thinks only Franny can help him figure out. Lucy, it's important. Can you track her down?"

"Oh, well..." she dragged out. "I'm sorry, Barry," she finally said. "I'm not sure where Franny is."

This was not good news. Barry made a tight fist with his hands. "What do you mean?" he enunciated slowly and clearly, as if speaking to a small child.

"Well," she started slowly again.

Barry got impatient. "Lucy, I need your attention. What part of this conversation don't you understand?"

Lucy began again. "Barry, get off my back. I don't know where she is. I haven't seen her."

Barry was still foggy from last night's escapades at the bar, but he understood the meaning of her evasiveness. "Do you mean she isn't in Florida?"

"I'm not sure." Lucy tried to cover. "It's time for me to get to the club. I'm late."

Barry's hand shook. He would not let her go until he had an answer. He tried to keep his voice even. "I need Franny now. If you don't tell me where she is, I'm going to fly down there myself and drag her home."

"Do what you want, but I still don't know where she is. I bet she just needed some space."

"Cut the crap. She's either in Florida or not. Someone must know where she is." Barry raised his voice, although it remained very measured.

Lucy replied, "I heard one of the other cousins say Franny wanted to lose some weight to surprise you. I think she's at a health spa."

Barry laughed. "Oh come on. Franny hates to diet. Why would she go to a health spa? I think she would rather have her appendix taken out. Lentils and exercise? You can do better than that."

"Barry, she's my cousin, and even if I heard from her, I wouldn't tell you. I'm sick of your attitude and don't want to be interrogated, especially by you. Good luck finding her. Say hi to Sam. I'm getting off now."

Barry heard the click and stared at the silent phone. He was furious and his stomach clenched. Now, where was Franny? Lucy was a dumb broad. He punched the floral cushion on his wife's favorite chair. Wait until he found Franny. He would give her a surprise she would never forget. This made him smile, and he went to work with thoughts of revenge.

Chapter 11

After her late afternoon walk on the beach, Liza ate a quick dinner at another nearby restaurant. If not for the housing issue, she could have a great time exploring the Cape and finding the best beaches and experiencing the local atmosphere. By six, she was sitting on the bed, watching the news with Licorice. Her kitty was proving to be a great ally, as she never argued and always greeted her with a pleasant *meow* when she returned from explorations. She imagined herself in the pioneer days with a campfire and a faithful pet by her side. This cozy cabin was a much easier and warmer lifestyle for someone on the run. It was the twenty-first century, and she had her basic needs met, without having to worry about bears eating her while she slept. With no response from Aurora, she went online to check out more ads. She called a promising one that advertised a free room for home services. She knew how to clean. Picking up after Barry was a full-time job. After dialing the number with a Chatham exchange, she waited for someone to answer.

"Hello," a well-modulated voice responded. Liza could imagine the person on the other end wearing a twin set, stud earrings, and a double strand of real pearls.

"Hi, my name is Liza and I'm calling about your ad. Do you still need someone to care for your home?" She did not pause for a breath.

"I'm Mrs. Codman. I'm still looking for help."

Liza gripped the phone and tried to sound relaxed. "I'm new in the area and need a place to live. I'd love to exchange rent for cleaning."

"Cleaning? I need much more than that. I'm looking for a housekeeper to manage the staff." After a brief silence, the woman continued, "Do you have experience governing a large household?"

"No, but I took care of my parents for years and did everything for them." Okay, this was a stretch, but she would have done anything if they asked her.

"Let me take your name. We're looking for an experienced housekeeper. It's terrible keeping cleaners and chefs year-round. Every time someone leaves, a new person needs to be trained."

This was the first time she was interacting with the *haves* on Cape Cod. She did not know how to manage several employees or run a large home, but she needed a place to live. "I'm very reliable and would love to work for you." Her experience caring for Barry, who was impossible to please, should count for something. After living with him, this job would be a cinch.

The woman got off the phone as quickly as possible. "Thank you for calling. I have a few more candidates, and I'll let you know if we still need someone." Liza understood this was Yankee-speak for *when hell freezes over*. She was getting used to New Englander's civility.

Another dead end. Liza was so discouraged that she eyed the bag of chips on the dresser. She stared at the kitty. "No. I refuse to punish myself by trying to fix it with food. Licorice, I'm going to lose weight. You'll love the new me. Step one, take care of myself and get in shape." She contemplated step two and vowed to take charge. If she did not hear from Aurora by noon tomorrow, she would call her.

The next day was gorgeous, reflecting the rapid changes in weather on Cape Cod. It could be gray and overcast one day and sunny and bright the next. The winter sun felt like a good omen, and she took a brisk walk, trying to use up the energy created by her anxiety. "Please call." She begged the silent phone to ring. "I need this."

She shook her head, realizing she was speaking to and bargaining with an inanimate object. Great. Aunt Sylvia used to talk to Ed Sullivan on television. Maybe she was more like her aunt than she wanted to admit. Lucy and she used to make fun of her on Sunday nights when they visited and watched shows at her house. Aunt Sylvia would have one-way conversations with anyone on the tube.

At noon, she clenched her jaw and dialed Aurora's number.

"Hi, Liza," Aurora answered. How did she do this? Only the number came up on her disposable phone. No name. "I've been waiting to call you until Zeus and I finished meeting all the other applicants. Although he had some issues with Licorice, we both feel you'd be the best person to take care of him and live in our home."

Liza exhaled slowly. "Wow, I mean, great." That sounded awkward. "I mean, I'm thrilled to have this opportunity." Okay, now she sounded insincere. She hoped Aurora could understand her nervousness and relief.

"It's okay, Liza. I know you're under tremendous pressure. We think we can help you and Licorice find safety and peace."

"Aurora, you'll not regret your decision. I'll do everything I can to make this work for you."

"Can you come by tomorrow at two to go over the details? Bring Licorice."

"Sure. We'll be there... and thanks so much." She disconnected and thought about the call. At least she was not the only person who had meaningful conversations with her cat. The difference between Aurora and her kitty was Zeus appeared to answer her owner. She wondered what language he spoke. Maybe Greek?

She gave Licorice a quick hug. "Now be good when you see Zeus. We need this house." The day dragged on, and she could not wait until tomorrow. It would be her first day at work at the restaurant. Then she would complete plans to move to Aurora's house. She distracted herself with a short walk, mindless television, and an early bedtime. She would require a good night's sleep for her big day.

Chapter 12

On the first day of her new job, Liza woke at six. She needed to get to the Lobster Roll early to train with Bonnie, and she had a lot to learn. Dressed in her serviceable black jeans and a new white jersey, she felt like she was heading to the first day of school. She ate a quick bowl of cereal and left dry food for Licorice. Her kitty was her first customer of the day. So far, so good. She called out to her as she left the cabin, "Bye, Honey. Have a delightful morning. Keep warm." Liza was both frightened and excited about what today would bring. She almost shut the door before grabbing her keys off the dresser. She would feel like an idiot if she had to wake Jeff to let her back in for her car keys. "Get real, Liza. You need to stay focused. A lot is riding on today."

For someone who spent many years cooking and cleaning, Liza was unprepared for the pace of restaurant work. If this was representational of starting slowly, she was terrified of finding out what a normal day would be. Bonnie waited on the many regulars at the small cafe. They wordlessly sat down and expected to be served their coffee just the way they liked it. Bonnie was a better magician than Aurora in anticipating everyone's desires. Liza could barely remember any of their names. She observed a change in customers during her shift. In the early morning, contractors and plumbers came for breakfast. Later, shoppers and older adults showed up, looking for a warm place to enjoy a cup of coffee and be with other people. A hot drink and a muffin gave them hours of entertainment for just a few dollars. It was a great antidote for loneliness.

She noticed several people never spoke when they came in. Bonnie called out, "Eggs and coffee?"

"Yup," a burly man looking like he did not give a crap about his cholesterol replied. The food arrived with no other conversation, and Liza worried about how she was supposed to figure out who wanted scrambled or over-easy. This was not effortless.

By mid-morning, her feet were killing her, and her shoulders ached from carrying tray after tray of food. She had only earned $26.50 in tips and was wondering how many trays of food it would take to buy groceries for her and Licorice. This was not the life she dreamed about, but for now it was all she had.

Bonnie watched her carefully and suggested she stop at eleven. "It looks like you're pretty tired."

"I hate to admit it, but yes."

"It'll get easier. Why don't you take off and come back at seven tomorrow morning?"

Although Liza wanted to deny how exhausted she was, she was too tired to fake it. Bonnie was a person who specialized in reading people's expressions and moods all day. She could not bluff this out. "Thanks so much. I appreciate your time and help. I'll see you tomorrow."

"No problem. I'm not paying you yet and I know you're still settling in."

It was another magnificent day on Cape Cod, and Liza had time to explore the town of Chatham before she went to Aurora's house.

Chapter 13

Before driving to town, Liza went back to the cabin and shared another turkey sandwich with Licorice. Although her kitty avoided the bread and vegetables, she was happy to split the roasted meat. Liza took a shower and changed into a pair of clean jeans and a warm sweater. She headed along Route 28, taking in the sights along the way. The summer before, when she and Barry vacationed in the tiny seaside resort, they had to drive around for twenty minutes looking for a parking spot. Now she could find a space right on Main Street. With a cat in the car and sore feet, she was unsure how much walking she could do, but it was a shame to waste decent weather this time of year. Off-season, the town was quiet, with most of the stores closed for the winter. She peeked in the lit windows and caught the glances of mostly older salespeople who eyed her warily. Not too many sightseers shopped in town this time of year. Although she dressed more like a year-round Cape Codder, Liza was still an outsider. The best she could hope for was to be taken for a summer resident who was in town to check on her vacation house. When more people arrived in spring, she would not stand out as much.

Oh well, she needed to forgo blending in this time of the year. The few open shops had merchandise that was mostly geared to year-round residents and occasional tourists. The sale items on every shelf were enticing, and Liza felt a pang of wistfulness, wishing she had her old lifestyle with a disposable income. She would stock up on half-priced tee shirts with quaint embroidered flowers and sayings, pottery with shells in sea colors, and plaques to hang on her wall. It surprised her how few practical items were for sale. One variety store sported a limited collection of socks and underwear. She realized she would have to go out of town for most of her everyday needs.

The library, however, was an oasis. It was in a lovely old building. A reading room with soft leather chairs and periodicals beckoned for her to sit. If Licorice was not in the car, she might have given in to the invitation. Another room with computers was off a living room area with beautiful bookshelves and ornate woodwork. Every nook and cranny held a magical moment. Immediately, she felt a primal connection to the historic building, with the smell of leather furniture and a welcoming interior. Liza was determined to get a library card. With anonymous computer access, she could get in touch with the outside world. She approached the counter and faced an older woman wearing a blue jumper and turtleneck, who was checking in books.

The librarian looked up and gave her a kind, crinkled smile that went right up to her eyes. "Hi, can I help you?"

Could she help her? Sure. Get rid of her abusive husband and make her instantly thin. Solve these problems and Liza would be eternally grateful. Instead, she replied, "Hi, I'm new in town and want a library card." In larger cities, they often required patrons to bring in an electric bill or renter's lease. How was she going to produce any actual proof of residence? She wondered if Aurora was going to be a handshake type of landlord. Liza braced herself for the worst.

"Okay. Do you have a driver's license?" With shaky hands, she pulled out her newly minted license and held her breath.

The older woman continued, "What's your address?"

"I'm moving to 37 Seashell Lane." It was feeling real. She and Licorice were going to live here. Watching her busily complete the paperwork behind the desk seemed almost anticlimactic.

"Here's your card. Patrons can only take out books for three weeks. You can renew them online or in person."

Liza smiled and refrained from jumping over the counter to hug her. "Thanks." She tried to sound nonchalant. After a brief search, she checked out three books. It was a miracle that she had a library card and an address.

Checking her watch, Liza did not want to leave Licorice in the car too long or be late for Aurora. With a permanent address, Liza felt official. Now she could claim to be a year-rounder, the backbone of the town.

Chapter 14

Barry

Scrutinizing online bank statements was agonizing, and Barry found nothing. Franny was not using her ATM card. This seemed suspicious, as she was always shopping and spending his hard-earned money.

After work, he stopped at their neighbor's house. Julie was friendly with Franny, and he hoped she knew where his wife went. If nothing else, she was a nosy snoop and might give him a clue that would lead him in the right direction. He parked in his driveway and walked down the street to the white ranch-style home. Julie's driveway and walk were clear, and he imagined the inside of her house was also spotless. What made her friends with Franny was anyone's guess. He rang the doorbell and listened impatiently to its stupid chimes. Barry forced himself to smile when Julie appeared in the doorway. She was wearing tight black leggings and a large top that loosely flowed to her knees. He did not understand why dames with great bodies covered them up. It was just another idiotic move.

"Hi, Julie. I'm trying to find Franny. I heard she was going to a health spa."

"Oh, the secret is out?" Julie answered with a hesitant tone. "I thought Franny wanted to surprise you."

"Well, I need to get in touch with her before she returns. Do you know where she is? Maybe I'll send flowers or something." Flowers for her funeral would be a lovely touch. He continued, "Listen, Julie, this is important. It's about Sam. He needs her. You know she'd want you to tell me where she went." He was convincing himself that Franny wanted him to find her.

Julie looked down. "I think it was a place in Florida, near her Cousin Lucy's condo. I bet if you call Lucy, she could tell you where she is."

Oh crap. Where the hell was she? He kept it upbeat with Julie. "Okay, thanks. I'll call Lucy tonight. If you hear from Franny, please let me know right away. By the way, did you see her leave?"

Julie Goldstein, the detective at large, perked up. "Yes, I thought I heard the garage door open in the middle of the night last week. I thought it was late for her to be heading out to Newark Airport. I mean, unless she was going to Europe, who flies so late at night?"

"Well, maybe she got a hotel room to make an early plane."

Julie brightened visibly. "Yes, that makes sense. Some of the airport hotels will let you park for a reduced fee if you book a room before your flight."

He could not wait to get out of there and begin tracking Franny's car. He knew she had taken it, but what if it was not in Florida? She was so stupid she probably would not think that he could trace her from her E-Z Pass toll charges. It was a great tracking device. He was brilliant. He would find her and teach her a lesson. This made him smile.

Chapter 15

In Liza's rush back to the car, she slid on a pile of slush by the sidewalk. She caught herself on the door handle and grimaced. It would be disastrous if she had to go to an emergency room. Would they admit her without a health insurance card? She recovered her balance and wiped the perspiration from her brow. She was fine. After brushing off her pants, Liza got in the car and reassured her cat, "I'm back. I can't believe we left New Jersey a short time ago and things are falling into place. I want you to be good at Aurora's house. It's the start of our new life."

The car was still warm after her brief walk to the library and Licorice cuddled in the carrier with her favorite green fuzzy blanket. When Liza tried to pack Licorice into the cat carrier after lunch, her cat quieted when she felt the fabric. Liza wanted to leave her pet at the motel but worried it would be a deal-breaker if she did not comply with Aurora's request to bring the kitty for another visit. Unfortunately, Licorice hated being penned up, and Liza rubbed at the new scratch mark on her arm. Her hardly worn sweater also looked a bit frayed with her cat's attempts to claw it, but there was nothing she could do.

Licorice whimpered and meowed as she left town and followed Route 28 towards Harding's Beach. She tried to comfort her cat. "I know. You hate being cooped up in a box and taking car rides. Don't worry, we'll be there soon." Lately, she found conversations with the cat quite satisfying. The feline was a great confidant and friend. Best of all, Liza could count on Licorice to keep her secrets.

Turning toward Harding's Beach and driving down the road leading to the small unpaved lane, Liza felt so insecure it nearly paralyzed her. What if Aurora changed her mind? Then what would they do?

She glanced in the rear-view mirror and wished she heard a validating retort from Licorice telling her it was okay. "Franny or Liza, whatever you're calling yourself these days. You've done well so far. You have amazing possibilities for the future." Of course, glancing back again, the cat was restless and intermittently yowling from the drive.

Liza stopped in front of the cottage and pulled herself together. The cat carrier was heavy, and she balanced herself as she headed toward the door. She did not want a repeat of almost falling in front of her new landlord.

Aurora was standing there, looking as exotic as usual. Her crystal necklace sparkled in the sunlight. She gave Liza and her cat a warm, reassuring smile, and Liza relaxed. They were going to be fine. Inside the living room, Zeus lay across the top of the couch. His massive legs and paws hung down over the cushions. Liza wondered if she would find a seat on the couch with Zeus' appropriation of the entire space. Liza tried to sound upbeat. "Good afternoon. How are you today?" She picked her way around the assortment of packing boxes haphazardly scattered on tables, chairs, and the floor. Piles of clothes spread out on the couch looked a lot like her cabin's décor. Were they using the same decorator? Despite her discomfort, she giggled.

Aurora gazed at her. "We're overwhelmed with the mess. How're you guys doing?"

Instead of a reply, Liza let Licorice out of the carrier, who raced into the larger of the two bedrooms and jumped on the bed, regally ignoring Zeus. "I think we're doing much better. I'm working at the Lobster Roll restaurant in Yarmouth, on Route 28. Morning shift."

"Working in a restaurant is hard work. Have you done it before?"

"Well..." she began and continued with the truth, "Not really, but I'm learning fast."

"I bet you are." Aurora chuckled as they made eye contact and laughed.

Liza appreciated their similar senses of humor. If she did not want to live in this woman's house so much, she would want Aurora to stay and be her friend.

Aurora became serious. "So, let's get down to basics. I plan to be in LA for a while, at least until the fall. My mom needs a housing facility with twenty-four-hour support and nursing care. It's going to take time to convince her to pare down her stuff and move, but she can't maintain her house by herself. I plan to clean out her place and get it ready to sell. Mom's allergic to Zeus, so I can't bring him. He and I decided you would be the best person to live here and take care of him in our home."

"Have you figured out the rental price?" Liza held her breath until Aurora named an amount that she could afford.

Aurora added, "I know the rent is significantly less than the monthly rate and far less than summer rentals, but you also have an enormous responsibility. I need to know Zeus is happy."

This was a lot for Liza to process all at once, and she did not reply immediately. Financially, it was a great deal, and she knew it. However, what if something happened to the house or Zeus? She never had full responsibility for a home. The place she lived in with Barry was her childhood home. Until her parents died, they oversaw repairs. Barry managed the house in New Jersey. Or so he said.

Aurora looked at her and asked, "Do you have any problems with the rent or the time frame?"

"No...," she stammered. What was wrong with her? Why did this seem so scary?

"You don't have to be afraid. Things are going to work out for you."

Right. You don't have an irrational, angry bully who wants to kill you, and who happens to be your spouse. Liza cleared her throat and replied, "I'm sorry. Listening to you makes everything seem so real. So far, I've been able to pretend I'm on an extended vacation."

Aurora gave Liza a reassuring touch, and they went over the last of the details. It was going to be beneficial for everyone. Well, maybe not the cats. They would have to step up to the plate, or cat dish, and deal with their mutual dislike of each other.

Liza made plans to move. Today marked her one-week anniversary of freedom. She hoped her luck would hold.

On the way back to the motel, she felt exhilarated, excited, and scared. If she had known getting away from Barry was this easy, she would have done it forty pounds ago. Liza patted her jeans. Could they be a little bigger? That would be too perfect. She had found a job and a place to live. The last thing she wanted to do was to taunt the gods.

Chapter 16

Liza's next two days at the restaurant were less daunting. Learning the routines and habits of the regulars helped with keeping up with orders. Liza struggled to match Bonnie's pace, and by the middle of her shift, she was exhausted. It was hard waiting on customers, and she vowed never to tip less than twenty percent again. She almost dropped her tray when a woman called from the closest booth, "Is that you, Franny Blackman?"

Momentarily startled, Liza tried to identify the woman. The well-dressed lady continued, "Hi, Franny. Do you remember me? I'm Patty Rollins, the Harwich realtor who was celebrating my twenty-fifth anniversary with a weekend getaway. I met you at the pool last summer. It was so nice to meet you and your husband. If I recall, you were also celebrating your anniversary. Franny and Barry, right? I have your address and data at the office. You told me if I found a great buy, you might be interested in a second home... for investment." She said this all-in-one breath.

"You must be mistaken...," Liza stammered.

"Really? You look just like that English professor from New Jersey. She could be your double." Patty looked skeptical.

"No, my name is Liza," she paused. "So, what can I get ya?" She was desperate to change the subject.

The realtor gave Liza a long look and ordered, "I'll just have toast and coffee." After a few moments, she added, "So, are you from around here?"

"Nope. Just moved to the Cape. Be back with your order in a few minutes. I just need to get theirs." She pointed to two men in sweats sitting at the counter and rushed into the kitchen. Passing through the swinging door, she put her head against the wall and muttered, "What the hell am I supposed to do?" She needed to bluff this one out.

Bonnie looked at her as she flew in for more coffee. "Are you okay, Darlin'? You look like you saw a ghost."

Liza managed an insipid smile. "Oh... just the pace is killing me."

Bonnie placed her hand on her shoulder and patted it. "Don't worry, it'll get better."

If she only knew. Liza took a deep breath and whispered, "You can do this." With all her courage, she left the safety of the kitchen and brought out a tray with plates of eggs, muffins, and potatoes. She put food in front of the men sitting at the counter and grabbed the coffeepot and an empty plate for Patty, who was still staring at her and shaking her head. It was unnerving and Liza felt goosebumps. Forcing a smile, she took an order of toast from the toaster, put it on the plate, added butter and jam, and ambled to Patty's table. "Here's your food. Can I get you anything else?"

"How do you find Cape Cod in the winter?" Patty tried to engage her.

"I've just been here a short time. It's so quiet off-season." No other words came to her, and Liza realized she was a terrible actress. Unfortunately, her life could depend on convincing this woman that she was not Franny. Liza changed the subject. "So, you're a realtor. How's the market on the Cape?" It was feeble, but the best she could do under the circumstances.

"It's slow in the winter. Last summer it was wild, but you already know that." Patty smiled, took a small bite from one slice of toast, and left the rest on the plate. It was clear to Liza she ordered something to eat, just to spend more time with her.

"Can I get you a refill on the coffee?"

"No thanks," Patty answered, giving Liza another searching look. "I'm late for a meeting. If you're ever in the market for a new place, call me." She got up, leaving her business card on the table. Removing her coat from the rack, she glanced back again and muttered, "I'm sure that woman is Franny. I never forget a face."

Liza frowned as Patty walked out the door. It was a close call.

Bonnie observed her. "Are you getting sick? You look funny."

"I hope not. I'm just tired. Would you mind if I left a few minutes early today? I'll call later to let you know how I'm feeling." This sounded phony to Liza, but really, how many lies could she produce in one morning? She cleared the last of her tables and headed to her car.

Liza's hands were still shaking when she reached the motel. What now? Could this woman blow her cover? Did she bluff well enough? Did anyone even care? The worst was Patty had her personal information, including her address and home phone. Would she call Barry? Liza found herself wracked with anxiety and ate three chocolate chip cookies to calm down. She addressed Licorice sprawled on the bed. "Stop worrying. This can happen anywhere. Just get used to it and think of a plausible story." She shared a few more ideas with Licorice. "Maybe Franny has a twin? No... too canned. How about I've heard that before? I'd love to meet this woman. It'd be cool to meet my double." Licorice kneaded the bedspread, and Liza rubbed her cat's belly. It would be such a luxury to have the carefree life of a cat.

Feeling better, she headed over to the beach for a brisk walk. It was a choice between a walk or consuming an entire bag of cookies. Liza needed to do something physical to help her relax. When she returned to the room, she ate six more anyway. It was a very stressful day and there was no use trying to be perfect. Besides, they were good. For dinner, she regretted her earlier indiscretions and shared a bowl of cottage cheese with Licorice. She crawled into bed with her cat and watched television for hours. She felt fat, scared, and miserable. By eight, she called Bonnie to let her know she would make tomorrow's shift. She could not let Bonnie down and she needed the money too much to skip work. Later, Licorice and she scavenged through the fridge for a snack of sliced turkey and cheese. Although Liza fell asleep, she was restless and woke up a few times. Dreaming that Barry was hunting her, she woke in a cold sweat with her heart racing. It took her a long time to fall back asleep.

Another crisp, sunny morning renewed her optimism. This was just a minor setback, and she had to learn to deal with them. Although her body ached from carrying heavy trays, she could cope. Liza was determined to make a new life for herself. The restaurant was busy with regular customers. Anytime anyone she did not recognize entered, she wanted to bolt. If Patty returned, she would deny everything. Luckily, no one else from her past crossed the threshold. Relieved for the moment, she ended her shift and made plans to move into Aurora's house. She longed for safety and stability.

Chapter 17

Barry

The old-fashioned answering machine picked up just as Barry unlocked the front door. He listened to the first few seconds, "Hi, Barry... I don't know if you remember me. My name is Patty Rollins from Harwich, Mass. and we met last summer at the Old Cape Inn. I spent time with your wife. I'm a realtor with Smith and..."

Grabbing a beer from the fridge, he walked out of the kitchen, went into the family room, and sat in front of the TV. He could hear the woman talking in the background, but was not in the mood to stand there and listen to the rest of her yammering. "Blah, Blah, Blah. Shut up. I need somebody to just tell me where Franny went," he yelled to the machine.

Enraged, he pounded his fist on the coffee table. He did not want to be bothered by any of Franny's friends from anywhere, especially Cape Cod. A realtor, no less. What had Franny told her? Did this woman think they could afford a second home in a pricey town like Chatham? Anyway, he hated the place. Everything was too perfect. Green lawns and flowers everywhere. He wanted to go to Vegas, watch some shows, and play cards. Slots and bright lights. Now that was more his style. Too bad Franny made such a fuss. She begged for a pretty beach and romantic getaway for their anniversary. What a load of bull. The Old Cape Inn was too expensive, and the other guests looked like they had stepped out of an uppity magazine. However, the sweet young things in their bikinis were fine. The hot babes from Europe wore the smallest suits. Not like Franny with her oversized bathing suit and flab sticking out all over. He shuddered, thinking about her.

That last trip to Cape Cod had done it for him. He knew it would have to end soon, as he had enough of marriage. Sam was in college and Franny's folks were dead, so they would not be coughing up any more dough. That was the final anniversary trip, he reasoned, so he gave in to Franny's demands and wrote the big check to the resort. His last obligation.

He popped open the beer and flicked through the channels on the remote. Eventually, the call ended, and he peeked through the door into the kitchen and saw the flashing message light on the machine. He would erase it later. It was just one more crappy reminder that Franny was gone. Who needed her, anyway? After a few hours, he turned out the lights and wandered up to the bedroom, the machine still blinking in the dark.

Chapter 18

Moving day arrived. It snowed the night before and there was a white blanket over everything. Even the motel looked beautiful as the sunlight picked up small glistening patches of ice and reflected them like diamonds. Liza packed most of her stuff into the car and went outside to find Jeff to say goodbye. He was wearing heavy boots and gloves and was busy shoveling off the walks.

She greeted him with a sad smile. "Hi, I'm leaving today. The keys are in the room, and I'll try to be out before noon."

He looked at her with concern. "Are you okay?"

"I guess I'm nervous. I'm just moving to Harding's Beach, not another country. Besides, it's a sweet little cottage with an oversized cat. How bad can it be?" Too much information.

His eyes crinkled. "I'm going to miss you. It gets lonely here in the winter and it's been nice having you around."

It was surprising to hear this admission from such a stoic man. Jeff turned his back towards her and scooped up a shovel of snow. It must have amazed him, too.

"You can call and visit me after I get settled." Liza's eyes were getting wet.

He must have noticed her overly emotional response. "If you need anything, call me, okay?" he replied in a soothing tone.

He was her first friend on this new adventure, and she would miss him. "Thanks. You've helped me so much. I want to stay in touch." She was grateful for all his help. He even got her a job. After leaving Barry, she did not think she would ever trust anyone again. Liza knew it was going to take her a long time to get her confidence back in humans. She gave Jeff a big hug and went back to the cottage to pack the rest of her stuff.

It was funny how the place looked like home after just a brief stay. A feeling of comfort and peace replaced her initial reservations about the old-fashioned décor and vintage colors. This was home, and she felt safe here. With the last of her clothing tucked into the car, she looked around. Large garbage bags were a terrific way to carry clothes and keep them dry. The perfect suitcase. Later, she could reuse the bags to haul out trash.

Licorice was hiding under the bed. Since her kitty-brain was the size of a walnut, Liza was sure she could outsmart her pet and get her into the cat carrier. However, Licorice knew something was up and was determined to avoid her. "Hi, Sweetie," she cajoled and shook the treat box. The cat timidly came out and grabbed a tasty morsel. They smelled awful to Liza, but who was she to judge her feline's gourmet palate? Alas, Licorice proved she was still more clever than her owner and dashed back under the bed.

"Okay. Miss Kitty. We're moving today and I need your cooperation," She sternly reminded the cat, who was invisible beneath the only piece of furniture she could not crawl under. Liza shoved the bed a few feet to the left and grabbed her before she bolted. "It's for your own good." Licorice tried to scratch and wiggle away, but Liza wrangled her into the carrier. Licorice meowed loudly and fiercely. Feeling guilty for tricking her, Liza petted her cat through the metal crosshatched openings of the cage. "This is not normal." She did not have time to worry about the cat's feelings and said, "I need to make some more human friends."

After a slow start, Licorice and she began the journey to Aurora's cottage. The roads were a little slick, and she took her time driving up Route 28 toward Chatham. Although Liza felt excited at the thought of having a permanent place to stay, she was sad to be leaving Jeff and her first haven.

In a brief time, she totally changed her life. Liza was proud of her newfound resiliency. Barry had almost succeeded in completely demoralizing her with his constant bullying and dishonesty. She wanted to call him and tell him to go to hell, but resisted the urge. Someday she would face him and stand up for herself. "Not today, but soon the jerk will get what he deserves," she commented to Licorice. The cat interspersed, meowing with alternating moans of displeasure. Liza felt terrible about making her cat endure another drive. "I promise tuna when we get there." Licorice's plaintive cries escalated in the moving car.

After what seemed like an interminable ride, they came to the unplowed dirt road. Liza had to drive at a slow crawl around the curvy lane. When they approached the cottage, she smiled. It was lit up and welcoming, like a magical retreat. A long-lost princess should greet them at the door with cookies. Parking in the driveway, next to the car with a small, attached trailer, Liza made sure she left enough room to maneuver and carry her belongings into the house. She entered the porch with the meowing carrier firmly held in her right hand. It had been a long morning, and she was already exhausted.

"Come on in. It's open," called a voice from inside. Aurora was in the back bedroom, surrounded by boxes piled everywhere. She looked drained and Zeus was not in sight.

Liza stepped through the doorway, put the carrier on the floor, and opened it. Licorice jumped out and ran under the couch. Liza vowed to make all of this up to her.

"Hi, Aurora. Is there anything I can do to help?" Liza's stomach clenched because if Aurora did not move all her stuff out, she would have to return to the motel or live out of her car. Boxes and bags of personal items covered every chair and table.

Aurora apologized, "I'm running late and am so sorry the house isn't ready. I'd love to have help packing the trailer."

If she ever wanted to sit down or eat again, the cottage needed to be emptied. It took a few hours, but eventually, they loaded up the trailer, stacking the cartons first, and putting bags and bundles around them. It was well-organized; they were fast, and they got everything into the small trailer without mishap.

After they cleared the rooms, Zeus finally appeared. Liza almost hoped Aurora would reconsider and take him with her. No such luck. She could tell he was going to rule the place. Aurora and she exchanged last-minute information and Liza paid her in cash for the first month's rent. She was pleased they had taken care of all the major details the last time she visited because Aurora was not in any condition to manage much more. Liza tried to think of any other practical matters they might have missed. "Hey, before you leave, I have a question. What do you want me to do if something breaks? Do you have someone who repairs things?"

Aurora looked bewildered. "Oh yeah. I have a guy who fixes stuff. His name's Rocky. I think I have his number with all my other important documents." She opened a small drawer on one of the side tables and started rummaging through it. Pulling out a stack of varying-sized papers, she smiled. "Here it is."

After another hour, they finally completed everything, and Aurora was ready to leave. She hugged Liza and looked around the cottage. "Take care of my baby." Her voice broke with emotion.

"Don't worry. Zeus will be fine. Everything will be okay." Liza felt like she was doing a lot of reassuring today and wished she could muster up a more convincing voice. After Aurora left, she began the slow process of unpacking her car. Licorice finally came out of her hiding place, curled up on the couch, and studied her with watchful green eyes. Liza walked into the house with armloads of clothes. "It's okay, Sweetie. We're finally home. Safe and happy."

Chapter 19

Liza began the next week with a slight sense of dread. She glanced in the mirror and remarked, "Don't be so paranoid. What can go wrong? We have a wonderful place to live, and have escaped Barry." She shivered at the thought that Barry might have figured out she was not in Florida. The bastard was probably not even conscious that she left the house. What about Sam? Did he miss her? Would she ever speak with him again? A wave of sadness hit her, and she blinked away unexpected tears. It was a luxury talking to her son whenever she wanted to speak to him. Could she take a chance and make just one brief call? What harm could that do? She knew her location was untraceable through the burner phone, but she was still afraid Barry might force Sam to tell him where she was. Once her husband realized she was not in Florida, he would hunt her. She would wait another few days until she decided what to do. Life was getting more complicated.

Sitting on Aurora's pink and blue couch, Liza watched cars coming in and out of the driveways of the diehard neighbors who lived here all year. The street had twelve cottages arranged around a horseshoe-shaped dirt road. Aurora's cottage was right in the middle of the cluster, so she could see which places were lit up regularly. They were miniature Cape Cod houses, with weathered shingles and porches. Bright-colored trim was the only way to tell one from another. Aurora explained before leaving that most of the homes were unheated and people only occupied them for three to six months a year. The houses were so close together, Liza imagined it would be noisy in the summer. Right now, it was quiet and the light snow on the yards made it look like a scene from a New England Christmas card.

Aurora told her the summer people paid enormous sums of money a week to vacation in Chatham. It was shocking. Beach proximity was worth a fortune, and through a back path, she could walk to Harding's Beach in about fifteen minutes. Not for the first time, Liza understood she was lucky to live here for an affordable price.

Liza watched a woman get out of her car in the driveway of the next cottage and head towards her place with a bakery box in her hands. Moving purposefully, the neighbor looked to be in her mid-forties, tall, slim, and with short, dark hair. Liza predicted the knock on the front door and got up to greet her. "Hello." Although she was wary of strangers, Liza wanted to seem friendly.

"Hi, I'm Nora. I wanted to introduce myself and welcome you to the neighborhood. I brought a coffee cake." She had a wide, sincere grin and looked pleasant.

"Nice to meet you. I'm Liza. Thanks for coming over." She stepped aside so Nora could enter. "Come on in. I'll make tea to go along with your dessert."

Nora peered at all the unpacked boxes and bags. "It's tough moving into a new place. What happened to Aurora?"

"Her mom got sick, so I'm house and cat-sitting for a few months."

"I talked to Aurora in the yard, but never really got to know her. Wow, this place is amazing. I love all the bright colors in the rooms. Don't you just love it here?" Not waiting for a reply, Nora continued to look around. "I remember when I first moved to this neighborhood, how isolated I felt off season."

"It's quiet, but I'm sure I'll get used to it. How long have you lived here?"

"I moved from Boston ten years ago after divorcing my cheating husband. My teenage son mostly lives with his dad when he's not in boarding school in Concord. It was luck that I found a job in one of the few year-round retail places in town, the Shoreline Bookstore."

Liza felt a pang of envy. "I love to read and always wanted to work in a bookstore." She wondered how Nora could afford to live in such expensive real estate while making minimum wage. Her neighbor must have read her thoughts.

"My place doesn't cost much to run. I own it with my two brothers. It was our folk's summer home, and we came here every vacation as children. We had a wonderful time." She smiled.

It seemed like everyone kept reading her mind these days. What the hell was up with this place?

Nora continued, "When my parents died, no one wanted to give up the cottage, so we split the costs. In the summer, my brothers use it for a few weeks with their families and rent it out for the rest of the season. Every July, I move in with an old childhood friend in town. She enjoys making a few extra dollars, and we survive as roommates for two to three months. If it were full time, we'd probably kill each other."

"Wow, it must be a hassle moving out every year."

"Oh no. You wouldn't believe what people do in this town to keep afloat. Many families rough it at campgrounds every summer while they rent out their homes with everything in them. The kids get used to sharing their belongings with the tenants. We all sigh with relief when the tourists leave in September, and we can go back home."

"That sounds awful," Liza commiserated. This was a place with so many customs. Liza wondered if she would ever figure them out.

"Well, you do what you have to do to live by the beaches. It's wonderful here, especially off season."

Pouring tea, Liza asked, "Do you know many people who live in the neighborhood full time? Is it friendly?"

Her neighbor scrutinized her before answering, "I can see you're new. People who move here full time seem to either love it or hate it. They usually keep to themselves. Do you have a job?"

Liza wanted to be pleasant while not revealing too much. "Yes, I'm working at the Lobster Roll restaurant in Yarmouth."

"I bet you weren't a server where you lived before." Nora's sly tone sounded like a test.

Liza felt the first signs of a panic attack and she raised her cup with two hands so Nora would not see them tremble. Taking a large gulp of the hot liquid, she wondered how to respond. "No..." she hesitated. She was not sure how much to say but needed to tell the same story to everyone and stick to it. One thing she learned from reading suspense novels was to keep her story as close to the truth as possible. It made it easier to keep the details straight.

"I was mostly home with my son and did some volunteer work..."

"Where did you live? I can hear from your accent that you're not from Massachusetts. Your license plate is from New Jersey."

This was getting too close. She could not tell her the truth and tried to think of a plausible story. "I just moved from New Jersey, near Summit." That was a large enough town so Nora would not expect her to know someone's relatives, but close enough to Watchung so she could answer questions about the area. Tomorrow she would go to the Registry and get new Massachusetts license plates for her car. She did not want to be identified as a Jersey girl and have to explain her life history to anyone else. She had a rental agreement from Aurora, which should help her prove residency.

Nora was persistent. "What brought you to Cape Cod?"

Yikes, time to improvise. "I'm going through a messy divorce. I hate to even think about it."

"New Jersey, huh? I've got lots of family from New Jersey. Isn't Summit near Basking Ridge? My cousin lives in Basking Ridge and teaches at the regional high school in Warren."

Liza felt her heart race. Oh, no. Sam graduated from there a couple of years ago and Barry insured half the teachers. Liza resisted the urge to bolt from the room, smiled tightly, and took a deep breath before answering, "Yes, it's a well-regarded school. We played them in sports." She hoped Nora would leave it alone, as she felt the coffeecake rise. It was time to redirect the conversation. "So... do you see much of your son?" Everyone loved to talk about their kids.

"Messy divorces, ha. You don't know half of it. Let me tell you about my ex. He's such a bastard. He left me, fights over every holiday visitation, and then tries to get me to pay him for child support."

This was a great diversion from her earlier inquisition. Liza gave her a sympathetic look and Nora continued, "Can you believe it? He has more money than God and knows how to hide it in his business."

Liza nodded. Nora and she had more in common than she knew, including the parallels between their marriages. She still felt sick to her stomach. The earlier conversation unnerved her. She needed to make sure she said nothing to connect her to Watchung.

Nora began another sentence and then looked down at her watch. "I'm late for work. I have the afternoon shift today. We'll have to catch up later this week. Okay?"

Liza was both sorry and glad to have the conversation end. Nora seemed like a nice enough neighbor, and it would be great to have a friend, or at least, someone she could talk to who lived next door. However, trying to have a conversation while fabricating plausible explanations for everything was stressful. She was still shaking after Nora left. Had she said anything that could put her in danger? Should she keep moving? What about her promises to Aurora to care for her house and cat?

"Be reasonable," she said to both cats. "We're fine. Nora was just being friendly. You guys are the only ones who know the complete story. I wish I could tell everyone the truth, but I can't. Barry wants me dead." If he ever found out she was making a new life for herself, he would certainly kill her. She discovered his intentions when the mechanic told her she was driving with defective brakes. Barry assured her the Audi dealer told him there was nothing wrong with her car. She was glad to be rid of her old Audi. Her new Subaru might not be as prestigious, but it was safe. Liza had a lot to be grateful for. Her friend Rick and his buddies located a drivable car within her budget and supplied falsified paperwork. She glanced at Licorice and Zeus sleeping in front of the hearth. Neither of them would ever break her confidence. They were trustworthy.

Chapter 20

Barry

When Barry arrived home after work, he could not stop thinking about his wife. Was she surprising him by going to a spa? What would she look like when she came home? No matter what she did, she would still be Franny with her sloppy style and no class. Just thinner. "Loser," he yelled and continued to ruminate on the subject. Why hadn't she called to let him know where she was? Where was she? It was like a mosquito flying past his ear, and it irritated him enough to do something about it. He liked that thought and said, "She's a fat bug. I'd love to squash her, but first I have to find her."

He could track Liza through her electronic tolling system. At least he would know her route. After a quick dinner and two beers, he went back upstairs to the office, decorated in Franny's frilly style. He rarely used their home computer. Everything he needed was at work, but he was not going back there at this hour.

Barry tried to go online to check their accounts. He could not remember the password to her computer but knew the passwords were on a card in a small drawer with their banking and insurance documents. Rummaging through the desk, he found a piece of paper crumpled and wedged under a pile of note cards. It must have fallen out of the envelope where Franny kept their unpaid bills. He picked it up and smoothed it out. It was a receipt for a bank withdrawal. He looked at the number and blinked twice. It was for $63,000. Checking the date, he saw Franny took the money out right before her trip. What was she having, plastic surgery? How the hell had she gotten permission to take that kind of money out of their account? He remembered Carl Erickson's call about Franny withdrawing some cash to give him a surprise. He figured a few thousand dollars was at stake. Nothing like this.

Barry was so furious that he could hardly read the numbers. How did Franny get away with this? Carl should have told him how much money she withdrew. He needed to get to the bank. Too bad it was after hours and would not be open until tomorrow. This was outrageous. She could not take his money. He did all the work, and she stole his hard-earned cash. He would move heaven and earth to find the lazy slug. Barry shook with rage and hit the wall with his fist. Who the hell let Franny steal this kind of money? They would pay.

"Maybe it's a mistake," he reasoned aloud. He walked downstairs and took another beer from the fridge. He needed to track her car's toll route. When he found her, he would find the cash. Slowly, he returned to the den, scrutinized the E-Z Pass account, and found Franny had taken the turnpike and gotten off near Trenton. There were no other payments listed on the account. What the hell did that mean? What kind of spa would be in Trenton? That town was not near any resorts. No one could dupe Franny into going there for a few weeks of beauty. It was time to call the cops and report her missing. He wanted to find her and get his money back before she blew it on clothes and God knows what else. He went to bed and lay awake thinking of new ways to punish his wife.

Chapter 21

After a few weeks, Liza was finally getting the hang of waiting on people. She recognized most of the regulars and memorized their coffee orders. It was incredibly taxing, but she found it satisfying. Unfortunately, just as she was feeling at home at the restaurant, Bonnie was recovering well from her surgery and was already back part-time. The restaurant did not have enough work for the two of them. Until the crowd picked up, she would not have many more days working at the Lobster Roll. It was March, and the Cape was still noticeably quiet. One of her customers told her that anyone who had money left the Cape until late spring. Liza felt like she was still in the honeymoon phase, as it seemed fine to her. Although, everything about Cape Cod seemed great because she was away from Barry. She had new license plates on her car and had shed her New Jersey status.

After her shift, she arrived home, and Zeus eyed her as if he understood her dilemma. She knew she needed a new job and did not want a cat telling her what to do. She glowered back at him. "Okay, Smarty Pants, what am I supposed to do for work around here? Not much is open in town this time of year." Although the question was rhetorical, he continued to glare at her with an unnerving old man's stare. What was he thinking? The drive to Yarmouth from Chatham was also getting to her. The most direct route was over local roads and was often slow.

Liza found herself behind blue-haired drivers who thought the sign for Route 28 was the speed limit. It was even worse when it snowed, as the roads got slippery and the drivers were even slower.

She needed to go into town and find a job. Last summer, she and Barry ate at a small pub in town that catered to locals and tourists. It was down the street from the library, and she decided that getting a cup of coffee and sitting with the townies might give her courage. She wiped her sweaty hands on her pants, trying to figure out why she felt so nervous. Maybe because there was so much riding on her finding work. She entered the tavern, sat at the long wooden bar, and ordered a cup of coffee. The room was dark, paneled in old-fashioned knotty-pine, and decorated with Cape Cod memorabilia tacked on the walls. Many of the men seated on the bar stools wore flannel shirts, hoodies, jeans, and work boots. Unsuccessfully, she tried to guess which guy fished for a living. Liza gave up and studied the handful of ladies eating out in look-alike groups. She did not recognize anyone, and no one even gave her a second glance. Liza wondered why she thought she would meet someone here who could help her. She sat sipping her coffee, noticing that people seemed to keep to themselves. She left after one refill and strolled down the sidewalk looking for help-wanted signs in the windows. When she did not see any, Liza went into the stores and asked if anyone expected to need spring and summer help. A few shops with lights on brought her hope, and Liza noticed which clothing stores were open year-round. Judging by the window displays, some stores carried staid and conservative merchandise. Since she wore one of her better hand-knit sweaters, she felt confident enough to go into the snottiest of businesses to look for a job. By late spring, she might need a whole new wardrobe. An employee discount at a clothing store would be perfect. Lately, she noticed her clothes seemed a little looser, and she was curious about how much weight she had lost. She could market her new diet as a victim's food plan. It would include such wonderful recipes as tuna on the run and eggs over quickly.

Liza checked out the large window of Chatham Summer. The store, displaying elegant clothing, had a few racks of high-end merchandise near the door. She noted the brightly colored sweaters, interspersed with more somber winter clothes. They teased shoppers into believing that spring was coming soon. Everything looked expensive, and Liza wondered if she could even afford on-sale apparel. She crossed the threshold and heard a small bell tinkle. The store held tastefully displayed racks of clothes spread around the floor. She could see a few smaller rooms towards the rear of the place, but was not sure if they held merchandise or were for other purposes. Liza recognized luxury brands from her halcyon days of endless shopping. Fingering the fine fabrics, she felt a woman staring at her.

"Hello, may I help you?" the salesperson asked, eyeing her up and down. She was wearing a twin sweater set in blue wool and a pair of gray slacks. Her matching gray hair, cut in a flattering style, looked pricy, and her piercing blue eyes took in everything. The only jewelry she wore was a pair of diamond studs. To Liza's practiced appraisals, they looked like at least one carat each. Why was she dressed like this, and working in a store?

Even coming from an affluent town like Watchung, New Jersey, the woman intimidated Liza. She looked down. Were her underpants noticeable through her jeans? She had not felt so insignificant since Evie Jones got all the girls to peek at her under the door of the bathroom stall in sixth grade. "Why, um," she stammered. "I'm looking for a job. May I speak with the manager?" She would have loved to rise to the woman's level of haughtiness and outclass her, but knew it was hopeless. This lady was the alpha boss before she even started.

"Oh?" the woman questioned and examined her outfit.

"Yes...I think your clothes are terrific and I'd love to work here." That sounded feeble, but there were so few stores open in Chatham this time of year, and Liza was desperate for a job.

The salesperson stuck out her hand. "I'm Mrs. Woods, the hiring manager. This is a small family-owned group of boutique stores catering to a select clientele. They're very particular about their employees and the images they present. Are you new in town?" She looked at Liza with raised eyebrows.

"Yes... I just moved here and I'm looking for work." Well, of course she was. She just said that. Her face turned red, and even though it was cold, her hands were sweating. Liza had no choice but to shake Mrs. Woods' outstretched hand. How embarrassing.

"Will you live here year-round?" Mrs. Woods surreptitiously rubbed her hand on her slacks and examined Liza's face as if looking for a lie.

"Yes, I'm house-sitting out near Harding's Beach."

"Oh," she sounded brighter. "Will you be house-sitting through the entire summer?"

"Yes." Liza crossed her fingers behind her back. She was not sure what her plans were going to be. Only the cats knew, and they were not sharing.

"Can you work evenings and weekends?"

"Sure. Anything." Liza smiled, and the manager gave her a cool look that might be the warmest expression she had. She swore to herself she would never play strip poker with her.

The manager appraised her a while longer and said nothing. It tempted Liza to fill the silence. She dug her fingernails into her palms to keep quiet.

"Tell me about your experience in retail."

"Well," Liza drew out the word while trying to make up a plausible story. "I worked in a shoe store for two years and also sold hats and fine accessories in another store." She worked in retail in high school but figured it was like riding a bike. "For the past few months, I've been working as a server at the Lobster Roll in Yarmouth. I'm filling in for someone who needed surgery. "

"Good chowder," Mrs. Woods replied.

"Yes… I enjoy waiting on people," Liza added excitedly. "I intend to still fill in when they need me." Mrs. Woods frowned, and Liza added, "Don't worry. I'll work around your schedule." While the saleswoman waited again, Liza wondered if people ever made small talk around here. This Yankee-speak was getting to her.

Finally, the woman responded while giving her another X-ray look. "Okay, I'll try you. Can you come in later this week for a few hours of training? I'll put you on a regular schedule beginning next week. Your pay will be minimum wage and you will earn a five percent commission on what you sell."

Liza wanted to kiss her, but held back. "Great, I'd love to." She beamed her warmest smile.

Mrs. Woods did not return her enthusiasm. "Fill out these papers and we'll set up a schedule."

Completing the paperwork, Liza gave Mrs. Woods the social security card and license in her new name. On her way back to the cottage, she realized she did not even ask about hours per week or anything else. The manager must have known she was a novice, just by her omissions. Liza made a promise to be savvier next time. She hoped she would not blow her cover story but knew at some point someone was going to get suspicious of her naivete. Although it was a stressful afternoon, it thrilled her to land a job.

When she returned home, the house was quiet, and she assembled dinner with a cat at each side begging for pieces of chicken breast. They were comically racing across the living room floor to get the chicken. It was a moment of fun and she felt optimistic.

Returning to the Lobster Roll the next day, Liza could not wait to tell Bonnie about her new job. Bonnie looked relieved that she would not have to lay her off. "Oh, that's great. I hoped you'd find full-time work before summer. This time of year, it's tough doing enough business for more than one server. Do you still want to do a Sunday morning and lunch shift? I could use the help. Come summer, maybe you'd work a few days a week if you can spare the time."

"I'd love to help. I'm lucky to find something closer to home, too. This winter commuting is awful, especially when it snows."

Liza greeted her usual customers and said goodbye for now. The tips were generous, and she became a little teary as Jake the plumber gave her a sad smile. She would miss seeing him and serving him two eggs over medium as he entertained her with stories about broken furnaces and frozen water pipes. Even the electrician, who constantly reminded everyone about his high cholesterol, was less irritating today. Serving customers was intimate work. At the end of the shift, Bonnie and she hugged. They were friends and she would miss her. Liza knew she would not forget her aching back and sore feet at night.

On the drive home, she took a detour down Pleasant Street in Harwich. The weather was crisp and cold, and the sun sparkled on the water. On impulse, she called Jeff. "Hi, Jeff, it's Liza."

"Hi, how're you doing?" he replied quickly.

"I'm good. Do you want to come over tomorrow night for dinner?" Where did that come from? She must be lonelier than she thought.

"Sure. What time? What shall I bring?"

How about bringing the whole dinner, or taking me out to a cool restaurant? "Oh, just some wine. Come around seven." She gave him directions and hung up. So much for small talk. She sounded like everyone else around here. Minimal conversation punctuated with long silences.

After she arrived home, Liza peered inside the fridge to see what she had that would work for a nice dinner. Two potatoes, leftover chicken, and a half head of lettuce would not do. She needed to get some more food and clean up the living room. Should she change the sheets, just in case...? "Oh, give it up," she announced to no one. "You're not exactly his type. Besides, he probably has a girlfriend and just wants to be friends." She was trying to convince herself of something, but was not sure what.

The cats rubbed against her legs. "Listen. I've got to get Barry out of my head. Jeff's coming over tomorrow. He seems to be a nice person, so be on your best behavior." Licorice continued to purr as she jumped on her lap. One vote of confidence. She shared her meager leftovers with the cats and thought about what she could make for her dinner party. Tomorrow, she would buy special food to impress Jeff.

Chapter 22

Liza went to the local market and purchased a large brisket, potatoes, onions, and carrots. She remembered her mother's secret recipe for brisket and discovered Aurora had left a slow cooker in the basement. Once the meal was cooking, she rushed around, trying to get the house vacuumed and scrubbed. Her mother was a whiz at cleaning and putting a decent dinner on the table. She remembered her shortcuts, and soon the freshly vacuumed house smelled of Jewish comfort food. With the meat

simmering in the pot, the house reminded her of her aunt's Brooklyn apartment. All that was missing was her Aunt Molly, who used to take her into her bedroom for lessons on make-up, so she would look pretty and attract boys. Liza was wistful. She would have to repeat these sessions if she wanted Jeff to notice her. She tried to remember her aunt's advice, but lessons for a fourteen-year-old were not too relevant for a middle-aged woman.

Liza tried on at least ten outfits because her go-to black Eileen Fisher cashmere sweater was too big. She finally settled for a red V-necked cotton sweater, her tightest jeans, and boots. She looked as sexy as she was ever going to get.

"So, what do you think, Honey?" she asked Licorice. The cat purred and leaped onto her lap. "Thanks for all the cat hair," she commented while brushing off her clothes. "Come on

Sweetie," she cajoled. "Get down and I'll get you a treat." Liza stood so quickly that Licorice lost her balance and skidded over the hardwood floor. Just so Licorice would not accuse her of lying, she got the treat box and threw two across the room. One for Licorice and one for Zeus. They dashed for the delicacies and carried them into separate corners. So much for camaraderie.

Liza poured a glass of white wine and finished it in five minutes. She rationalized it was a small treat to take the edge off. The doorbell rang a half-hour early. Oh crap. Her hair was a mess, and her date was early. Liza peeked out the window. It was not Jeff. Her neighbor Nora was walking down the path carrying a plate of cookies. Did the woman think Liza should eat cookies? That was just cruel. She opened the door with a half-hearted smile. "Oh. Hi, Nora. How are you?" Was she just dropping off food? No such luck.

Nora entered and sat down. "I brought you these. They were for an open house at the bookstore, and I didn't want to keep them and eat them all."

Liza shuddered but said, "Thanks. I'd love to invite you for a cup of tea, but I have company coming soon for dinner."

Nora gave her an appraising look. "Oh, anyone special? You look hot. Nice sweater."

"No, just a friend." Liza looked pointedly at her watch.

Nora was not a quick read and appeared oblivious to her hostess' discomfort. Liza eyed the door, knowing it was rude. However, she was desperate. Nora looked like she was prepared to stay for a long visit. Liza chewed the cuticle of her right index finger. What the hell did her neighbor want? When she could not take it any longer, Liza stood and walked toward the door. "Hey, thanks so much. Can we save these for teatime tomorrow evening? Say around five? I've got to finish making dinner before my friend arrives."

"Oh." Nora looked disappointed and put the plate on the coffee table.

This was incredibly awkward, but Liza did not know how to get Nora out without insulting her. Feeling embarrassed, Liza covered it with a friendly smile. She understood that the best part of living alone was freedom. This was the first time in her life she did not have to worry about unwanted social visits. However, she needed to make friends, and being courteous was the price she had to pay. "I'm so glad you came over. I guess I'm nervous about tonight. It's a guy I'm trying to impress." Now that she admitted it, she realized she was telling the truth.

Nora gave her a tepid grin and headed for the door. "I hope you have fun. Sorry to bother you." After she left, Liza felt both uneasy and guilty.

What a lousy way to start an already difficult evening. She ate two cookies and finished her second glass of wine. Sitting by the fire waiting for Jeff, Liza shed a few tears. Only a short time ago, she was in a charming house with a routine. She filled her day with predictable situations, despite living with a bully. Everything in this new life was so complicated by the uncertainty of uncharted waters. She dried her eyes and walked into the bedroom. The mirror above the mahogany dresser reflected a woman with messy hair. Her frizzy ringlets would not stay tamed, even with her new hair products. The picture of a girl with lovely waves on the bottle was a lie. She finger-combed her hair and returned to the couch, pretending to be relaxed. The wineglass in her right hand was barely helping.

A few minutes later, Jeff's truck pulled into the driveway and her guest sauntered up the walk. He strolled nonchalantly and was wearing his usual flannel shirt and jeans. His hair and beard were neat. "Please God, make me a boy next time," Liza said to her cats. It looked so much easier. She frowned at the unfairness of putting in hours of effort with makeup and clothes. Jeff just combed his hair, jumped in his truck, and drove over without even worrying about impressing her. She put on a broad smile and greeted him at the door. Jeff walked in and glanced around.

"Nice place. It's great to see you." He smiled.

They stared awkwardly for a few seconds and her hostess role kicked in. "Nice to see you, too. Can I take your jacket?" Without answering, he tossed it on the couch, and she left it there. What the hell, this was not a formal dinner party. She went into the kitchen, and he followed.

"Yum. The place smells like my Aunt Rosie's house at Passover."

Liza found herself amused. Her parents would be so happy she had brought home a nice Jewish boy. "I didn't know you were Jewish."

"Yeah, well, it didn't come up in our previous conversations," he replied.

"I spent most of my childhood in a town where being Jewish was a curiosity."

"Not me. I'm originally from Long Island. Most of my friends went to the same Hebrew school as me. Where exactly did you grow up?"

This was dangerous territory. Liza handed him a glass plate, and he carried the appetizers back to the living room. They sat on the couch, and she ignored his question. She served a piece of spinach pie and spoke about her high school days. "Being different wasn't easy, especially in high school."

"What do you mean?"

"When it came time for my senior prom, I hinted to Chris, a boy in math class, that I was still available. I didn't know he already asked Ally, a cute blonde, who went to his church. She bragged Chris asked her and looked right at me when she said it. All the girls knew I had a crush on him. I can still hear them snicker." She paused, recalling the details like it was yesterday. Her face must have reflected those long-ago feelings of betrayal because Jeff took her hand. "It devastated me because I thought Chris liked me. I'll never forget how I felt when my friend Eloise told the kids he wasn't allowed to date girls like me."

"That must have been awful. What did you do?"

"I asked someone from my Temple to go with me." It was Barry, but Liza could not talk about him either. Why did she even mention this? Distracting Jeff was one thing, but this was not a light conversation.

"Did you have a good time?" Jeff looked concerned.

"The night wasn't perfect, but at least I didn't sit at home." She forced a small laugh. "So, tell me about your family. Do you have brothers and sisters? I'm an only child."

Jeff sounded empathetic. "Hey, Liza. You must have had a tough time growing up."

She responded with a light answer. "It's okay. I've moved on." She shifted her weight and gently extricated her hand from his. "Oops, I better check the food." That was lame, but Liza could not think of anything else to do to break up this line of conversation. It was getting too personal, too soon. She went into the kitchen, lifted the lid on the slow cooker, and poked at the meat. Pretending she had done something, she returned to the living room. Jeff was staring at her with a thoughtful expression. She smiled and tried to steer the conversation away from herself. "So really, tell me more about your childhood."

"I was one of six, two brothers and three sisters. It was a zoo."

"Lucky you."

"Usually, it was great. I always had someone to hang around with and watch my back." His eyes crinkled at the memories.

"Are you still close?"

"I see them a few times a year. I have fourteen nieces and nephews. My parents still live in the same house where I grew up. Most of my siblings live near them."

"What made you move away?" She noticed he looked away and wondered if she was treading on questions that were too personal.

He paused and looked pensive. "I'm the black sheep of the family because my brief marriage didn't work out."

"How difficult. Do you have children?"

"No, that didn't work out either." He had a sad expression on his face and stared out the window.

Liza was even more curious about his past, but knew when it was time to change the subject. "Did you ever go to Jewish summer camp?"

"I went to both day and overnight ones. I still keep in touch with some of my friends from the overnight camp." He hummed a camp tune.

"I know that one. I only attended a Jewish Day camp. However, when I was older, I returned as a counselor in training. That was an awful experience."

"How come?" Now that they were making casual conversation, Jeff sounded more engaged.

"The youngest kids were around five, but sometimes they accepted four-year-old campers if their siblings went to the same camp. The little ones spent a lot of time missing their parents, crying, and napping. Parents shouldn't send their kids so young. It can ruin the experience forever for them." She thought about Sam. She had not allowed him to attend camp until he was six. After his first year, he loved it and begged to go every year. She was not ready to talk to Jeff about Sam and Barry. They were too difficult for her to discuss with someone she hardly knew. "So, what's the Jewish population on the Cape?"

"More of us are in Hyannis, closer to the bridge. Out here it's pretty isolated, but even in the off-season, there's a small group of Jewish adults who meet regularly. If you're interested, I can call my friend Myra in Orleans and find out who you should contact."

"Thanks. That'd be great. It'd be nice to meet some other Jewish adults."

He laughed and explained, "This part of Cape Cod has a lot more churches."

Liza poured another glass of wine. So far, so good. She must be getting better at small talk or ignoring that tipsy feeling.

"So, how are you doing, Liza?" He looked straight into her eyes.

This was it. She took a deep breath and considered her options. She liked him, but should she tell him the truth? Could she trust him? Her logical side kicked in and she remained silent. Without telling an outright lie, she could not think of a plausible answer. Thoughts bolted through her brain. Why the hell did she invite a man she just met over for dinner? She knew she had to say something. "Oh, you know, some good, some stressful days. I found a new job in Chatham."

"Where?"

"Chatham Summer. It seems like a nice store."

Jeff whistled. "Expensive clothes. A little resorty."

She had forgotten he was in the fashion business before he came to the Cape and laughed at the accuracy of his description. "I know. Maybe I'll bring in a whole new crowd."

They smiled. Another awkward silence followed this comment. Jeff asked, "Do you think you'll feel comfortable working in a store where a lot of the patrons are super-entitled?"

"I came from an area of New Jersey where status was important. Once I went into a store to buy some tiles for my remodeled kitchen and the saleswoman ignored me for almost a half-hour. When new shoppers came into the store, she rushed to help them and disregarded me. When I was the only customer left, she came over and asked me if I needed help."

"What did you do?" Jeff looked amused.

"I asked her if I was invisible."

He threw back his head and laughed. "You didn't."

"I sure did. When she looked confused, I explained how long I was waiting, and I was sure I must have been invisible."

"What did she do?"

"She looked a bit embarrassed, but not embarrassed enough in my book. I had enough money in my checking account to cover any of the tiles in the store, so I made her drag out all her sample sheets."

"Did you buy your tiles from her?"

She gave him a look of mock horror. "Of course not. I know how to play the passive-aggressive shopper when I need to. I went to her competitor and found just what I wanted. However, I stopped in from time to time to buy grout and other small purchases while letting her know I'd finished the kitchen project."

"Remind me to never get on your bad side."

"Why don't we eat?" she suggested. She certainly did not want him to think she was an awful person, but she would not be a pushover. Jeff followed her into the kitchen and helped her carry the food to the table. The wine left her feeling buzzed, but a little scared.

He took a bite of the brisket and gravy. "This is amazing. Where've you been all my life?"

She wondered the same thing. "Do you want any more?" He already ate two pieces. She was cutting hers into small bites, so she did not appear too anxious.

"Sure."

Liza stood to carve off another piece. She remembered picking up the long stainless carving knife, but after that, she was not sure what happened. The knife slipped, and she experienced a searing pain across her left palm. She felt almost detached as blood ran down her arm. "Oh, crap. My hand...it hurts."

Jeff must have been a Boy Scout. He ran into the bathroom for a towel. After wrapping the wound and making Liza sit in a chair, Jeff banked the fire, grabbed Liza's purse and coat, and rushed her outside towards his truck. He practically hoisted her into the passenger's seat.

It was happening too fast. "We're going to the hospital." He buckled her seatbelt. "Keep your hand up," he commanded.

"No, I'm really fine," she argued. What happened to the delightful dinner party she planned?

"Yes, you will be fine. I'm taking you to the emergency room now."

Her face contorted in horror.

He misinterpreted her frightened expression. "Don't worry. I checked the house before we left and locked up. Everything's going to be okay."

Silent hot tears fell down her face. Her stomach was tight and her hand throbbed. How could she go to a hospital? She had a fake name and no health insurance. What was she going to do?

Before she could even think of what to say, Jeff started the truck and peeled out of the driveway. The road was slippery, and they skidded around corners. Liza broke into a cold sweat and took deep breaths to calm down. Time crawled. She watched individual fat snowflakes plop on the car windshield and panicked. When Jeff stopped at the intersection at the end of Barn Hill Road, she attempted to open the latch to the door. Liza tugged with her free hand but could not open the seatbelt. Frantic, she tried to get out of the truck, but her seat belt was stuck.

"What are you doing?" screamed Jeff. He pulled over to the side of the road, turned on the interior light, and idled the engine. His face looked stricken.

Liza took some satisfaction that Jeff appeared as terrified as she felt. "I can't go to a hospital," Liza yelled. "You're not listening to me." She got the door partially open.

"Okay, okay, calm down." He struggled to reason with her, but she was behaving like a six-year-old and he looked flustered. Jeff attempted to de-escalate the situation. "Close the door and I'll think of something else. You need to see someone to sew your hand up. This can't wait."

Liza watched the snowflakes and tried to concentrate on being reasonable. She sat in the seat, ready to spring at a moment's notice. Despite her attempt to listen to Jeff, she could not relax. Her breaths were shallow and fast, and she knew she was a mess.

Jeff stared at her and placed his arm over her shoulder. He took a deep breath and said, "Okay. Who do I know that can help you?" Jeff pulled out his cell and made a call. "Yes, a deep cut, but she's alert and not in shock. Okay, I owe you, buddy...we'll be right there."

Jeff explained in a voice that was deliberate and calm, "I have a friend who's in the medical field. He sometimes helps people who can't go through regular channels." He waited until she nodded and continued, "He'll see you at his house. Right now."

Tears of gratitude ran down Liza's cheeks, and she gave a weak smile. "I'll make this up to you. I promise."

Jeff responded with a reassuring comment, "Look, it's going to be okay. My friend's a great guy and an amazing doctor. He's Ivy-league trained, but you can't tell anyone about him. He had a little trouble a few years ago and doesn't practice medicine anymore. At least not for most people."

"Is he licensed?" Liza could not stop worrying about his qualifications. What had the man done to lose his license? Should she have taken her chances and gone to the hospital? She hiccupped and promised, "I won't ever mention your friend to anyone. I swear."

Jeff looked at her for a few seconds, turned off the interior light, and started the truck. He did not say a word.

Liza understood she may have overstepped the bounds of their brief relationship, but she was desperate and needed help. She was not in any position to question Jeff's friend's credentials. Her hand felt huge, and she sniffed back tears of pain as they sped along the quiet back roads of the Cape.

Chapter 23

Liza closed her eyes and tried to concentrate on anything but her hand. The large snowflakes on the window were pretty but not distracting enough. Her mind raced, and she thought about Barry discovering her location because of a medical procedure. Life sucked. Just when she was feeling safe, this showed how vulnerable she was. Just one minor mistake and she could be in danger all over again. The trees grew thicker as they drove further down Route 137. Liza heard gravel and ice crunch under the truck's tires. Where the hell were they? Slowing down and turning onto a snow-crusted lane, she was grateful they were in Jeff's four-wheel drive. She could see lights coming from a house set far back from the winding road. She shivered as the truck slipped along the unplowed ruts. What kind of place was she going to? A large cottage appeared, and she gritted her teeth. This must be the doctor's house.

When they were in front of the house, Jeff stopped the truck and unbuckled her seat belt. He opened the door and stepped closer to help her get out. Liza tried to decide what to do next, and Jeff noticed her hesitation. "It'll be okay." He patted her arm. "Just don't ask questions."

"Is this guy an actual doctor?" Liza was panic-stricken that she might get hepatitis or something terrible.

"I already told you about him. Just trust me. He knows what he's doing."

If she had not left New Jersey, none of this would have happened. Barry ruined her life again. Jeff walked her up to the front door and knocked. It opened and a man wearing jeans and a work shirt greeted them. He had a beard and was over six feet tall. She looked up to inspect his face. Did Jeff tell the truth about him? No way did he look like a doctor. Maybe a fishing guide. Was she so desperate that she was ready to risk her life by having this man stitch her hand?

He looked at Liza with amusement. "So…this is your latest adventure, Jeff? She must be incredibly special." He met her gaze and continued, "Okay, let's get you inside."

She took a few small steps into the foyer. The house was warm, and the decor looked like a hunting lodge. Leather couches surrounded an enormous stone fireplace. A deer's head hung over the mantel. The large folk-art rug on the floor was beautiful. Jeff knew his way around and took her right arm to guide her through the living room into a hallway. The small room on the right surprised Liza. It looked like a doctor's office. The walls were white and there was a paper-covered table in the center of the room. The glass-fronted cabinets appeared full of medical supplies. What the hell?

Her amazement must have shown on her face because Jeff whispered, "No questions, remember?"

Liza took a deep breath. "Okay," she whispered in reply.

Jeff's friend entered wearing a lab coat, washed his hands in the small stainless sink, and put on vinyl gloves. At least he looked the part. He looked at her with a half-smile. "You can call me Doc." When she nodded, he turned toward Jeff and said, "Hey Bud, why don't you wait in the living room, and we'll be right out."

Panicked to be left alone with Doc, she looked at Jeff with a plaintive expression and wondered how he could leave her alone with this man. She still had serious doubts that Doc could repair her hand. Jeff squeezed her arm, planted a light kiss on the top of her head, and left.

Doc peered at her and said, "You're going to be just fine...."

"I'm Franny...I mean Liza. Everyone calls me Liza." She felt her stomach lurch at her mistake and promised herself she would never let her old name slip again.

He gently took her hand in his. "Now, Liza, let's see what you did to yourself."

She tried not to look when Doc unwrapped the bloody towel and threw it into a plastic bucket. "Can you wiggle your fingers?" She complied, and he nodded his head.

"Wow...looks like Jeff did a great job keeping this together. I'm going to numb you, clean the wound, and stitch this up. You're one lucky girl. It looks like you didn't cut through any tendons. Are you allergic to any medications?"

"I'm not allergic to anything," she replied in a small voice. Oh boy, was she a lucky girl? Her husband was trying to kill her, and she had a nice guy over for dinner and ruined it with an accident. She sobbed in pain and self-pity.

Doc ignored her tears and continued to repair her hand.

Did this guy even have a heart? Couldn't he see how upset she was? At least he did not ply her with whiskey and give her a bullet to bite. She tried to distract herself from what he was doing and recalled the time she went to a very famous surgeon who was abrupt and dismissive of her complaints. When she grumbled to her girlfriend, she answered, "Well, do you want to go out to dinner with him or have him perform excellent surgery?" She had the surgery, and it was successful. Point well-taken.

Liza tried breathing exercises to manage her anxiety. She recalled they did not work very well during childbirth either.

After what seemed like hours, he finished stitching and bandaging her hand. Doc did not say a word throughout the whole procedure. When he was done, he called Jeff into the office and gave him the follow-up, including written instructions. "I think she's going to be fine, but she needs to keep it bandaged and elevated, and take these pills." He handed him a pill bottle and pointed to the paper. "Call me and let me know how she's doing. I want to see her back here soon to make sure everything's healing like it's supposed to, and remove the stitches."

Although he treated her as if she were invisible, Liza responded. "Yes, I understand your directions. Any precautions on the medicine?" What kind of person dispenses prescription drugs without knowing the person? He asked her about allergies. That was something.

"They're antibiotics. You can take them with or without food."

She wondered where he got them, but tried to keep her face expressionless, so she did not make him angry. "How often do I take them?"

Doc rolled his eyes and pointed to the paper. "It's all written."

Jeff smiled and ignored her. "I owe you one, Doc. She'll be fine. How about we return at the end of next week?"

"Just text and let me know when you're coming. I might fish if it warms up."

That was it. Jeff rushed her out of the house and back into the truck.

"Who is he? I mean, really?" she asked.

"Now, Honey, if I told you I'd have to kill you," Jeff replied.

Get in line. A nice Jewish girl from New Jersey. Who would believe there was more than one person ready to kill her? The ride home was uneventful, and Jeff walked her into the house and helped her into the bedroom. This was not the bedroom event she had anticipated at the beginning of the evening. She wriggled out of her boots, kept her clothes on, and lay on top of the spread. Jeff brought her the first pill with a glass of water and pulled a multicolored crocheted blanket over her.

"I'm going to put the leftovers in the fridge and clean up a little. Remember, Doc says no washing dishes for a while."

"Thanks so much. I can't believe this is happening... I need to...."

He cut her off. "By tomorrow morning, it'll be much better. Can you put on your pajamas by yourself?"

"I'm fine. I think I'll just lie here for a while. Later, I might get up and finish getting ready for bed." If Jeff thought she was going to put on nighttime sweats while he was in the house, he was nuts. She was not senile, just injured. Liza reached for her latest novel sitting on the nightstand and tried to read a few pages. She could hear Jeff puttering around the kitchen, clanking pots and dishes. The house became quiet when she heard the front door close. Still dressed, Liza got up, brushed her teeth, climbed into bed, and pulled the covers over her face.

The next thing she knew, the cats were meowing for food, and she was under two of Aurora's purple and red quilts. It was light outside, and she was groggy. It was the opposite of her imagined dream date. Clothes on and alone. Bleary-eyed, she squinted at the clock. It was eight-thirty, and she was late for the first day at her new job.

Liza's head was pounding, and her injured hand throbbed. She needed to get out of bed without using her left hand. To make things more complicated, her legs were tangled in the quilts, making it difficult to stand. After a few minutes, she was finally upright. In full panic mode, Liza inspected the room for something clean to wear. Then it hit her. Liza realized she had on clothing suitable for work. Could she go to the store like this? Why not? She studied her attire. Good thing her shirt was almost wrinkle-free. Should she change? Did she have any pride left? She stared at the clock and decided that just this time, she would wear yesterday's clothes. She promised never to do this again. It was scary how easy it was to recalibrate her dress standards while living alone. Before she could change her mind, she reassured the cats, "Don't worry. I'm not becoming an eccentric old lady. I'll change into clean clothes from now on. Just this one time." Zeus rubbed against her leg, looked at her in disbelief, and stalked out of the room.

Liza struggled to feed the cats, wash her hands and face, and attempt to make coffee. After two tries, she gave up and decided she would pick some up in town. Doing everything with one hand was unbelievably hard. Everything took so much longer than she imagined. After much effort, she rushed out the door with half a peanut butter and jelly sandwich in her hand. She was late for work and would have to wait to get coffee.

Chapter 24

Barry

After a few more beers, Barry fell into a deep sleep. When he opened his eyes, the sun streamed into the room and blinded him. He squinted at the clock. Eight-thirty. "Damn. Late again."

Caught in the powder blue blanket Franny bought during a decorating frenzy, Barry regarded the gray suit pants he wore yesterday. Beer cans clanked as he turned over. "Franny, where are you? What the?" Barry yelled until he realized he was in his bed and was rolling onto an empty can. He threw it across the room, stood, and fell back onto the mattress. The wallpaper was moving, and he could not see the bathroom door on the opposite wall. "One more time," he stated and pushed himself away from the bed. "This is better," he continued as he stood on unsteady legs.

Barry thought about the missing cash. He needed to get that money back before Sal acted on the threats he made when Barry spoke to him on the way to Hartford. His chest felt tight just thinking about his debts. "Oh crap, Franny, what have you done to me?" he yelled. This was enough to refuel his anger, and he wobbled to the bathroom. Inspecting the stubble on his face, he spoke to his reflection. "I need to look good and impress the jerks at the bank. Then I'm going to sue their asses off." He chuckled.

After shaving, he found his last clean shirt, took a suit from the closet, and scrutinized the bedroom. Clothes piled on every surface and beer cans strewn all over the floor caught his eye. The room was a pigsty. Did Franny think he was going to work like a dog to keep her in style if she did not take care of his home? She needed to get back here and put this place in order. Then he would kill her. This made him feel better. Before leaving the house, he went into the study and grabbed the computer printout of the missing money.

Making a quick call to the office from his car, he left a message with his assistant. "I've got an appointment with a client this morning and I'll be a little late." That should keep his idiot boss happy. Barry drove to the bank and scooted into a parking spot right in front. It was a good omen. He got out of his well-maintained sports car and entered the building.

When he approached the front desk, a girl wearing a gray suit and frilly blouse greeted him. She sauntered over with a smile. "Hi, I'm Shirley." The desk plate identified her as a Customer Service Representative.

Barry put on his best land-selling smile. Shirley could service this customer anytime. "Hello, Shirley."

She looked into his eyes. "How may I direct your business?"

"Are you new?"

"With whom did you want to meet?" she continued.

"How about you and me grabbing a glass of wine and a long lunch?"

Her smile wavered, and she looked down, saying nothing.

"Okay. I get it, you're being watched. They do this all the time at my place with the gorgeous dames. So, for now, how about you find Carl Erickson for me? We'll talk later."

Shirley hurried away and returned with a young man in a designer suit. It was not Carl, but the cut of his suit and his confident stride screamed, *I am important.* The man put his hand out in greeting.

"Now we're getting somewhere." Barry grinned. He liked this sign of respect and gave him a big, toothy smile. "I'm Barry Blackman and I usually do business with Carl Erickson. Is he around?"

The man noticeably took a step back. "No, Mr. Blackman, Carl's not here right now. He just got married and is off on his honeymoon, I believe."

Barry felt his face turn red. The jerk was celebrating using the profits from his investments. He waited until the younger man introduced himself.

"My name is John Dowler, and I will be happy to help you." He steered Barry into a large office. They sat in plush chairs on either side of an impressive desk. It was empty except for a large computer and a pad with an expensive pen.

"Nice digs." Barry rubbed his hand on the glass-covered top. "I should decorate my office with stuff like this."

John looked at Barry with a frosty but polite expression. "So, Mr. Blackman, what would you like to discuss today?"

Barry did not like to make small talk. He wanted the bank to understand the severity of the problem and not gloss over the error. He drummed his fingers on the desk. "We need to talk. You guys made a big mistake and I want it fixed today. You gave my wife $63,000 without asking me." Barry thrust the printout and receipt for Franny's bank withdrawal at him.

John took the papers and looked over the figures. He narrowed his eyes and did not respond. He peered at his computer screen, inputting data, and remarked, "You both signed up for an equity loan two years ago and your wife co-signed the loan as a homeowner. Each of you can borrow money from it." He looked at Barry to make sure he understood. When Barry did not comment, John continued, "I see a large withdrawal last February to your wife. Hmm, it also looks like you took $100,000 out of the bank over the past two years on your own." He gave Barry a tight-lipped smile.

"Yeah, well, that was different. I needed the money for the business. Who'd give so much money to my wife for no reason at all and without calling me first?"

"I'm sorry, sir, but we did nothing wrong. She may legally take money out."

Barry screamed, "What idiots would give her that kind of dough?"

John was silent for a few seconds and then answered in a quiet voice, "What we did was completely legitimate. I also see a note from Carl Erikson in your file. He called you about an overdue loan payment. Your minimum amount would be..." He handed a slip of paper to Barry and continued, "Would you like to take care of that today?"

Barry stood, shook his fist, and hissed, "I'll move all of my business out of here and tell everyone you are incompetent morons."

"I'm sorry, Mr. Blackman, but you'll have to leave now."

Barry bellowed, "You won't get away with this. I'm going to fry your asses in court."

He did not see Shirley duck into an empty office as he moved through the reception area and stomped out the door. He loosened his tie, feeling rage. "Incompetent thieves, all of you," he screamed as he left the building. "I'll find Franny and make her pay back every red cent. She's not going to get away with this. I'll get all of you." He got into his car, slammed the door, floored the gas, and just missed hitting a man walking across the street. "Get out of my way, you lazy bastard," he yelled out the window as he gunned the engine and sped away.

Chapter 25

Liza ate the peanut butter sandwich in the car, wiped her face with an old tissue, and made it to work five minutes after nine. Not a good start to her morning. Crossing the threshold of Chatham Summer, Mrs. Woods walked over and peered at her watch. She was not smiling. "You're late. I hoped you'd be here on the early side, so we would have time to go over a few things before the store opened."

"There was a problem at home. It won't happen again, and I'm so sorry." This was not a great way to impress her.

The manager inspected her bandages. "What did you do to your hand? Are you okay with working?" She was not the compassionate type. Not even an attempt at sympathy.

"I cut myself and got a few stitches. I can move my fingers. It's fine." It was throbbing, but Liza certainly would not share her story with her.

Mrs. Woods must have had a heart of stone, as she showed no empathy. "Okay. We still have time to review some store procedures and policies."

It was early in the season, and very few people were shopping in town. Liza learned how to replace sold items from the stockroom and use the cash register. The computerized register managed inventory and was much more sophisticated than the one at the restaurant. Liza hoped for robust sales, as even her small commission would boost her minimum wage salary. It was difficult using only one hand for most tasks, but she prided herself on being an adaptive person. Moving a pile of patterned sweaters to the front was almost satisfying.

Mrs. Woods came by and commented, "We target our merchandise towards Chatham customers. The other stores carry stock aimed at their clientele."

Liza did not know what she was trying to tell her, but used this as an opportunity to make conversation. "The clothes in this store are so beautiful, and I love the way you display them." She had to search for a glimmer of a half-smile. Mrs. Woods was a tough sell.

"We're all about customer service. A well-organized store creates a pleasant shopping experience."

Liza fingered a price tag on a cotton dress. At $250, the customers had better have an enjoyable time. After what seemed like forever, she snuck a glance at her watch. She could not believe it was only eleven and would not be lunchtime for another hour. Mrs. Woods set her up in the back room, ticketing new clothing. After the fast pace of the restaurant, this was interminable. With too much time to think, she worried about Sam at college. How was he doing? Was he upset because he had not heard from her? Was there a way she could contact him without alerting Barry? Liza had not spoken with anyone from New Jersey in a while and the isolation was getting to her. What the hell was she doing here? Was she making a colossal mistake?

Maybe she could send him an untraceable email from a library computer. Liza contemplated the possibilities. Did she trust anyone enough to help her? What about Jeff? Who was this guy and how did he know someone like Doc? Was Doc also hiding? Did he have a criminal past? After another hour of tagging clothes, her imagination soared. Liza tried to ignore the pain of her swollen hand and concentrate on something else. When could she go home and read a book? Her stomach rumbled. How soon was her lunch break? She missed the cats. Did they have enough food? Were they getting along? After another ten minutes, she had to get out of there. Soon.

Mrs. Woods startled her. "Are you almost done tagging those tops?"

"Oh, hi. I finished most of them and was not sure what to do next."

"Why don't you come back to the floor and wait on customers for a while?"

Thank you, God, for answering her plea for help. If she had to tag one more Oxford cloth shirt, she was going to put size eight labels on the sixteens. Although that might make a larger-sized person thrilled, it would be the end of her retail career. She followed Mrs. Woods to the front of the store.

A tall lady with long, shining blonde hair came through the door. She was wearing a fur-trimmed blue wool coat, well-tailored slacks, and leather boots. Her understated clothing was simple yet classic. Liza tried not to pounce on her too soon. The customer appeared more interesting than the typical weathered Cape Cod native.

"Hello, may I help you?" Liza used her perkiest voice and smiled.

The customer eyed the mannequin nearest the front door, attired in a pale green wool dress. "Do you have anything like this in size eight? I'm staying in town and want to wear something special for dinner." She added in a quiet voice, "I met a very distinguished gentleman yesterday."

Liza's stomach tightened in a flash of jealousy. How could she find a guy so easily? Life was not fair, but she put on a big smile. "Of course. You'll look lovely in that dress. It'll be fabulous with your coloring." Was she allowed to undress the mannequin? Probably not. She scanned the store to find the same dress. After a quick search, she found the woman's size on a rack near the back, and the customer tried it on. It looked perfect. Liza was so envious of the woman's easy ownership of good looks and grace.

Wouldn't it be great to be a tall blonde who could wear anything and look great? Liza's dream was to be a sophisticated, lanky woman who walked down the aisle of a plane, perfectly put together with one small carry-on. She was the overweight woman with a large purse, a rolling suitcase, and an extra plastic bag full of food who banged into everyone as she stumbled to her window seat. The sight of people cringing, probably hoping she was not their seatmate, was a common occurrence. When she arrived at her assigned place, she often spilled the contents of her bags over the other passengers. She was anything but a cool, classy blonde like this stranger.

The customer handed her credit card over, and Liza requested her license. She was Melody Parks from Basking Ridge, New Jersey. This was the second time someone from this tiny area of New Jersey crossed her path. She started shaking. This was too close. They could have met while shopping back home.

"So, do you enjoy living on Cape Cod?" Melody asked.

"It's beautiful this time of year. The beaches are quiet, and the stores and restaurants are opening. What brings you here?" Liza wanted the customer to keep talking.

"I needed a break. My boyfriend broke up with me, and I wanted to go on a getaway. I remember coming here as a child with my parents. It was a blissful time with band concerts and beach days."

Liza smiled and encouraged her to continue. "Did you grow up in Massachusetts?"

"No, did you?"

While pretending to play with the credit card receipt, Liza responded, "Oh, it's your lucky day. Do you know that there's no sales tax on clothing in this state?" This was not an exceptionally smooth way to change conversations.

"Has there ever been a tax on clothing?"

How the hell would she know? She just moved here. "Not for a long time." She hoped it was true.

"So, where are you from? You know, originally," the woman continued.

"My parents were in the service. So nowhere and everywhere."

"Oh...That must've been hard. I lived my whole life in New Jersey. Do you know Basking Ridge?"

Liza's doctor was in Basking Ridge. Of course, she knew it. "Not really. I'm sure it's lovely. Anyway, your purchase is all set. Is there anything else I can help you with?" Poor grammar, but what the hell? She looked away from her. Liza wanted the woman to leave before she accidentally revealed something that might blow her cover.

Mrs. Woods snuck up behind her. She must have heard her last sentence because she gave Liza a tepid smile and the customer a broad fake one. She glanced toward the accessory display. "A nice scarf will complement your dress," gushed Mrs. Woods.

Liza got the point and added, "The green and blue paisley silk one matches your new dress perfectly."

It was too late. Melody Parks glanced at the scarves and eyed the door. It was clear she wanted to leave. Her interest in sticking around and shopping was over.

After she exited the store, Mrs. Woods moved closer to Liza and spoke in a tight-lipped, sarcastic tone. "The purpose of a salesperson is to sell as much merchandise as possible. Before you ring up a customer, you need to discuss the possibilities of matching accessories and shoes. Once they pay, they rarely buy more items." She glanced around the store and continued,

"Why don't you straighten up the clothes on the display tables in the sweater area?"

Hot tears of anger came to Liza's eyes. She just sold a dress in March, the dead season. Instead of feeling good about her first sale, the woman reprimanded her. Her stomach rumbled and her hand throbbed. This was unfair. Mrs. Woods sauntered away to greet a new customer.

Liza took a deep breath and organized piles of soft cashmere sweaters in an array of pastel colors. They looked like the inside of an Easter basket with layers of pink, green, yellow, and blue. She finished stacking them and checked her watch. It was twelve-thirty, and she was desperate for lunch and a bathroom break. She knew there was a law about break-times, but Mrs. Woods did not seem to care.

By one, she inspected her watch in five-minute intervals. Mrs. Woods snuck up behind her and Liza knocked a whole pile of men's sweaters onto the floor. "When you finish with the sweaters, you can take your half-hour lunch break."

The need to get out of there was overwhelming. Liza picked up the sweaters, refolded them in record time, and walked over to her boss. "I'm finished. Can I go for lunch now?"

The dragon lady nodded. "I'll see you promptly at one-thirty."

Thirty minutes was not enough time to drive home, eat, and return. Unfortunately, she had brought no food because she ran so late this morning. To get away from the store, she wandered through town looking for an open restaurant. Halfway up the street, the sounds of a lively lunch crowd spilled out of the open door of the old-fashioned bar. She crossed the threshold and immediately spotted a familiar face. It was Doc sitting on a barstool with three men, all wearing jeans and rough wool sweaters. Who were these guys? Certainly not a local welcoming committee from the Chamber of Commerce. Now, what should she do? Should she ignore him or say hello?

He spotted her by the time she was five feet away and solved her dilemma by shouting out, "Hi, mystery girl, how's your hand?"

"I'm fine, thanks." She was indignant but had to chuckle. Mystery girl? What about him? Who the hell was he?

"Great. Remember, I need to see you guys soon to check my masterpiece." He turned back to his buddies, and she heard peals of laughter. The thought that they were making fun of her made her furious, but she owed Doc for helping her.

"Sure, thanks," she mumbled and rushed down the narrow aisle, escaping further conversation. At the back of the room, she sat at a small red Formica-topped table. Her face burned at her embarrassment. Liza could not avoid running into familiar faces in this small town.

After a quick bowl of chowder, she returned to the store. The afternoon was just as boring, although folding and tagging pale pink and green clothes reminded her that spring was coming soon. By five p.m. she was exhausted.

Mrs. Woods approached without startling her. "So, how was your first day?"

"Perfect." She lied with as much enthusiasm as possible.

"I have you on for tomorrow, will schedule you for three days next week, and then I will assess our needs. Until the summer crowd starts in May, there isn't enough work for more than a few salespeople at one time. This week I needed more help to set up the spring merchandise."

"That's fine." Although she needed the money, she wanted to get out of there as soon as possible. "How many more staff are you hiring?"

The manager paused before answering. "At the end of May, the college kids arrive. We have a few returning from last year, and we'll hire a couple more."

Could she hold on for two more months with no other companions?

Mrs. Woods prattled on, "A few year-rounders work during the winter, but you probably won't overlap with them."

Liza did not want to be responsible for her actions, spending the next two months alone with Mrs. Woods. However, she had to cope for now.

Heading out the door, Liza struggled to keep her balance. The slushy sidewalk was freezing, and it was gloomy. She could not wait to get home to her warm cottage and adoring felines. Despite the weather, her fatigue, and a throbbing hand, she smiled. She called the cottage home, and it felt good.

Chapter 26

Exhausted from her first day of work, Liza struggled to secure a plastic bag over her bandaged hand. Jumping into the shower, she relished the hot water cascading down her shoulders. Afterward, she took an aspirin and wrestled into her go-to outfit of black sweatpants and an old extra-large tee-shirt inscribed *The World's Best Mom*. It was the perfect antidote to Mrs. Woods and her stylish fashions. Sam gave her the shirt last Mother's Day and she would never put it in the giveaway pile. After the pain lessened, she ate dinner made up of the leftovers from her previous night's disaster meal. The cats begged for scraps of brisket from her plate. At least they appreciated her hard work.

"You darlings are special," she crooned. Liza knew she was not supposed to feed them from the table, but they were her dinner companions, and she did not want to be rude and eat in front of them. After an inhaled meal, she cleaned up the kitchen. Keeping her hand dry was almost impossible and routine chores were difficult. She promised herself that when she was done, she would watch television and do nothing. That sounded like paradise. The ringing phone broke her quiet reverie. Only a few people had this number. She ran through the list. Mrs. Woods, Jeff, Bonnie, Aurora, and her old friend Rick, the mastermind of her escape plan. She forced herself to remain calm.

"Hello?" It came out as a tentative question.

"Hi, Liza." A guy's voice boomed, and she did not recognize his number. This was not Bonnie or Mrs. Woods. It could be Jeff, but she did not want to admit she was unsure who it was. If she kept him talking, he might provide a clue to his identity.

"Hi. How are you? What are you doing?"

"Just great and talking to you." So far, no hints. Who was this? Did he think everyone knew him by his voice? How arrogant.

"What's up?" She still did not know who he was.

"I heard from Doc. He said you were in town at lunchtime. How're you feeling?" The mystery man was Jeff. She should have recognized his voice, but they had not spoken on the phone much.

"Oh, I'm fine. Sorry about the dinner last night. I'll have to make it up to you." Maybe in a hundred years.

"No problem. It was fun in a dysfunctional way."

Perfect first impression. She had to omit this from her book titled *How to Impress a New Date*. "Thank you for everything. Doc seemed competent." She hoped this would lead to an expanded description of Doc's credentials.

"Yeah. He does a decent job. My buddy nearly sliced off his finger gutting a fish, and he's doing great."

That was not the medical endorsement she was expecting. "Is he a genuine doctor?"

"Now Liza, you know I can't discuss the details. Let's just say he has a prestigious medical background with an unorthodox practice."

What the hell did that mean?

"Anyway," he continued, "I'm out and close to Chatham. How about I drop by to see how you're doing?"

"Tonight?" She glanced at her stained tee and sweatpants with frayed hems.

"Yeah. I can be there in about ten or fifteen tops."

Was he stupid? Maybe tomorrow or the next day. No way could she handle drop-in company. Especially a guy. She wanted to decline, but after last night's heroic rescue, she owed him a personal thank you. "Sure. It'll be great to see you again."

Liza was angry with herself that she agreed to let him come after an exhausting first day at work. Anyway, who would drop by without an invitation? What was she thinking to have said *yes* to this? After hanging up, Liza rifled through her closet for something clean she could get on easily. She inspected her black elastic-waist pants and oversized blue cotton sweater thrown on a chair. She sniffed them, determined they were clean enough to wear, and struggled one-handedly into the garments. They required major straightening to look passable. She walked to the full-length mirror and observed a pale-faced woman with dark shadows under her eyes and unruly blonde curls. Too bad. He would have to deal with her the way she was. Running a brush through her hair and skipping makeup, she did not have the energy or time to recreate date night.

Twelve minutes later, Jeff's headlights appeared in her driveway. He must have been close when he called. Did he think she was such a loser that she was available on such short notice? Her face turned red with anger.

Jeff seemed oblivious to her irritated expression. He walked in smiling, with a tray of cookies and a bottle of wine. "We skipped dessert last night." He grinned.

This was an extremely sweet gesture, and she went from stressed out to a crinkly smile. It was so easy for him. How did he know that this would work? "Thanks so much. They look delicious. Did you make them?"

"No. I got them at the Angel Bakery in Dennis."

They tasted heavenly. An angel must have baked them. "Did they just come from the oven?"

"Yes. Angela was putting away her last batch when I dropped by."

Who was Angela? Oh, who cared? They were chocolate chip cookies. Her favorite kind. Warm cookie smells filled the room, and it was close to being an aphrodisiac. Sexy man. She carried the wine glasses in her right hand and put the corkscrew in her pants pocket. When the cookies and wine were on the coffee table, they sat on the couch, not touching.

"Would you like a fire?" he offered.

"Sure." Why was he here? Did he have a hidden agenda?

Jeff went out to the porch for logs and kindling. After ten minutes, there was a steady flame and a familiar woody smell.

"So, what's up?" Liza did not know what he wanted.

"I feel bad about last night. You went to so much trouble making a delicious meal and then things kind of went out of control."

"Yeah," she cut in. "I'm sorry to wreck the evening."

"Let's start over and pretend last night's accident never happened."

They stared at her bandaged hand and laughed in unison. It was hard to miss. How could they pretend it was not real?

Liza began, "Okay. Let's continue with the pleasant part of the evening. Cape Cod life in the winter."

His expression became serious. Jeff looked into her eyes and responded, "Liza, what is going on with you? Are you in trouble? Maybe I can help."

So much for light conversation and gooey cookies. Jeff had an agenda and expected an answer. She sat in silence. Her face flushed, and she regretted eating two cookies. Could she trust him? He seemed careful with Doc's secrets. She needed a friend, and he was so nice last night. Should she tell him? "It's a long story," she began. She considered delaying enough to think of a reasonable explanation for her hysteria about going to the hospital.

He matched her silence, and they perfected one-upmanship. Liza needed time to figure out a plausible and truthful explanation without revealing too much. "Look, Jeff, I need to sort things out. I promise I'll tell you everything when I can." She placed her hand over his and gave it a small, reassuring squeeze.

Jeff looked disappointed and said nothing for a moment before answering. "I thought we were more than acquaintances. I'd like you to trust me. That's how friendships work."

"I want to explain what's going on, but I'm really confused and it's incredibly complicated. Please give me a few days." She fixed her gaze on the cats to keep from crying or blurting everything out. The evening was not going the way she hoped, and her anxiety took over. "It might be better if you leave." Did she really say that?

Jeff gave her a concerned look and planted a gentle kiss on her cheek. On his way out, he turned around for one last comment. "Okay, Liza. I'm coming back tomorrow night with some takeout, and I'm going to help you. Just trust me."

The door closed behind him, and Liza did not know whether she was relieved or disappointed that he did not try harder to get her to talk. Gulping the last of the wine from both glasses, she banked the fire and headed to bed. Nightmares of being caught by Barry interrupted her sleep. She woke even more tired the next morning. It was time to confide in Jeff.

Chapter 27

Occupied with conflicting thoughts about how much to trust Jeff, Liza barely made it through the workday. She was positive if she did not tell him what was going on, any possibility of a relationship would be over.

Arriving home a few minutes past five, Liza put a few candles on the coffee table to set the mood. Jeff would have to light them when he arrived, as it was impossible with one hand. The place looked as neat and as inviting as she could make it. An hour later, he arrived with a grease-covered brown bag and a six-pack of beer. Jeff lit a fire and the candles. The place was warm and glowing in the darkness of the winter's evening. When he opened the bag, Liza took a deep breath and salivated at the smell of fish and chips. The man was brilliant, as he figured out how to impress her and make her talk.

Sitting on the couch, balancing paper plates on their knees, the cats surrounded them, meowing and begging for their share. Liza put some fish on an extra plate, and they pounced on the food.

When all was quiet, Jeff gave her a serious look. "Well, Liza. Are you ready to come clean? I want to help you but I need to know the truth."

It was time Liza trusted someone, because it was impossible to continue without help. "Okay." She took a deep breath. "I'm married to a horrible man. We met when we were young, and I didn't know any better. At first, Barry was considerate, and my father gave him a job in the insurance business. After my dad passed away, Barry found a new job. That's when our problems began. Barry got into business deals with some criminals and has become secretive. He's angry all the time and blames me for our money problems. I can hear his voice change when one of them calls. The way he begs for more time to repay the loans, I can tell he's desperate. Right before I left, I discovered Barry was stealing money from our home equity, having an affair with his personal trainer, and plotting to kill me."

Jeff gave her an incredulous look. "That's unbelievable. Does he know where you are?"

"No. I snuck out one night after he..." She shuddered thinking of the times he hurt her. "He hit me. A lot."

"No wonder you've been so afraid to trust anyone."

"He threatened to kill me if I told anyone that he hurt me. When my parents died, they left me their house in Watchung, New Jersey. Other than that, and a small trust left by my aunt, I don't have anything in my name. He took my paycheck every week. I had almost no money and nowhere to go."

"What made you finally leave? That must have taken a lot of courage."

"I knew I had to get out when Barry lied about fixing the brakes on my car. After I sailed through a stop sign, I spoke to our mechanic. He said the brakes were almost gone and that he'd told my husband months before. That was the last straw. I knew my husband was behind the faulty brakes. That way, he'd inherit the house and collect on my life insurance."

"Did anyone help you escape?"

"An old high school friend set me up with new identification papers." Telling Jeff, tears streamed down her cheeks. She wiped them away with her sleeve and finished with, "If my husband finds me, I'll be dead for sure."

"Do you think there's any chance he could find you?"

"I've been covering my tracks as carefully as possible. I haven't even called my son, Sam, to let him know where I am."

"Don't you think it's time you went to the police? I have friends in the department, and they'd be able to get a restraining order so you wouldn't have to worry all the time."

"No police!" She felt the contents of her stomach rumble. What was this guy thinking?

"I'm sorry. Of course, no police. Just go on." He was gentle and encouraging.

She described the details of her escape from New Jersey, talking nonstop for the next thirty minutes. When the story was over, she was sobbing.

Jeff went into the bathroom, brought out a box of tissues, and looked at her with compassion. "You're safe with me. I understand why you didn't want me to take you to the hospital when you sliced your hand." He touched her arm. "You must be terrified. I don't even know your real name."

The tears kept coming. She blew her nose with a loud honk and wished she were a dainty crier. "My name is Franny, but I'm Liza now. It's so…hard." The tears gushed out faster than her words.

He moved closer and hugged her. It was a deep hug, and she melted into his scratchy wool-sweater embrace. It was not romantic, but this was better. They sat intertwined for an hour. Liza talked, and Jeff mostly listened. Sometimes he asked a leading question, and she responded with a torrent of words. It was cathartic. Both cats jumped on the couch, and it was cozy with the four of them all huddled together. The fire died down, the embers glowed, and the room took on a golden aura.

"What can I do to help?" Jeff asked.

"I need to know how my son Sam is doing. He's in college." She hiccupped. Could Jeff help her get in contact with Sam without alerting Barry? "I'm worried about him. It's been so long since we last spoke. He must feel I've abandoned him."

She paused and felt the muscles in her face tighten. "Oh crap, I hate putting Sam in the middle of this mess. He needs both parents. It's not fair."

"Hey, Liza…don't jump to conclusions without the facts. If he's a typical college student, they usually don't call or even think of their parents unless they're in trouble." He planted a kiss on her head and continued, "Why don't I set up a Facebook page with a false identity and try to *friend* him? College kids have hundreds of friends. Most of the time, they'll accept anyone who asks. It can't hurt to try. I'll use the name Jonas Fishinger, and we can sign in with the same password."

"That'll be incredible. Can we set it up from your account?"

"Hell, no problem. I'm happy to help. This way, no one can trace it back to you."

"Do you think that'll work?" She needed reassurance.

"Sure, why not? Other social media platforms may be more popular, but this is the easiest for us older folks."

Liza exhaled. It thrilled her to follow Sam's life and see what he was doing in school. For the first time in a while, she relaxed. The beer, warm fire, and Jeff beside her lulled her into a feeling of peace. Close to midnight, Jeff left, and she felt convinced that everything was going to be all right. She could not imagine her life on Cape Cod without Jeff's support. She prayed her positive state of mind would last.

Chapter 28

The next morning, Liza woke with a pounding headache. Licorice was curled into her bent knees, pinning her into an awkward position. When she tried to move her legs, the cat stretched out her body and arched her back. After giving her a disdainful glance, the cat moved to her original position and looked at her with half-closed green eyes.

"Oh, Licorice. What have I done? I told Jeff everything. Can I trust him? Should we get out of here and find a new place to live? We promised Aurora we would take care of her cottage and Zeus." She could not bail on her responsibilities. Licorice remained quiet and snuggled closer toward her legs. This gave Liza little comfort, as she needed answers. She disconnected from her cat, untangled the pink sheets, grabbed her gray sweats from the chair next to the bed, and stood. Walking toward the bathroom, Liza caught her reflection in the wall mirror. She wrinkled her nose. She looked old, with her puffy eyes and pale pallor. Liza whispered, "No more drinking for a while." She thought about Jeff's visit. The beer and fire must have destroyed her inhibitions. She told him so many personal things. What had she been thinking? Recalling how much she had disclosed, her stomach lurched, and she felt vulnerable and afraid. What should she do?

Explaining herself to Licorice and Zeus, she declared, "I'm not stupid. Jeff's a good man. He said he'd help us contact Sam.

Why would he want to hurt me? Not all men are jerks like Barry." Zeus sauntered into the bathroom. He gave out a loud meow, being much more communicative than Licorice. "See, you agree, don't you, Zeus, my man?"

The oversized tabby followed her into the kitchen, purring and rubbing against her legs. He was most affectionate right before mealtime. Just like a guy. Hearing the commotion, Licorice joined them. Out of habit, the petite tuxedo waited in the doorway for Liza to throw her a morning treat. It was their routine. Appetizers always came before the meal.

Cats fed, coffee made, Liza went outside to pick up the morning paper. It was a typical weekly Cape Cod paper that was news-heavy on local events. She enjoyed reading about the best places to eat and which beach had the nicest sand. Local news clips and a calendar section of what to do all over the Cape were her favorite sections.

"I should go to a gallery," she announced to the cats, who were back in bed and curled up together. "Yes, something intellectual. I need to meet new people and enjoy some artwork. After being cooped up here in the winter, I need to get out. Spring is coming."

March on Cape Cod was misleading. It was not like a typical New Jersey spring, with flowers poking up and noticeably warmer weather. Here it was still dreary and rainy, punctuated with cold, sunny days. Pelting sleet and gray skies were the norm this time of year. The occasional warmer days tried to sucker the locals into pulling out their spring clothes. She was still wearing sweaters and jeans and did not see any chance of donning summer attire soon. The beginnings of early crocuses were poking through the dirt yard outside her window, but their blooms might not show for a while. They were the first flowers in Aurora's garden, and she was looking forward to their presence. Liza wondered what other perennials would bloom in the next few months.

The phone rang and pulled her out of her reverie. "Hello?" Her voice was croaky after crying so much last night.

"Liza, it's Bonnie. You sound froggy."

"Yeah. I just woke up."

"Can you do an early shift tomorrow? I'm short-staffed."

"This weekend? I'd love to help, but I have a bandaged hand that I need to keep dry and clean. Can you work around that?"

"Sure. I can get Johnny to clear the tables and take care of any dirty dishes. What happened to you? Are you okay?" Bonnie's voice sounded concerned.

"Sort of. It's a long story. I cut my hand, slicing a pot roast. Jeff was here for dinner."

"Are you sure you're able to handle this? I can try to get Sandy to help. She's a lazy slug, but will work for beer money."

"If I'm careful, I'll be fine."

"You know, the customers prefer you."

"When do you want me?"

"Tomorrow morning at six-thirty for the early rush. Now that it's almost spring, the summer owners are starting to re-appear. Families like to go out for breakfast. It's a good value for the money as far as eating out is concerned."

"I'll be there."

"What about you and Jeff? What gives?"

"Nothing." Things were too new for her to come up with anything else to share.

"Oh, come on. Are you two seeing each other?"

"Just friends. Does he have a girlfriend?" Where the hell did that come from? Was she hung over?

Bonnie laughed. "You know better than that. Just because he hasn't made a move doesn't mean he's in a relationship with someone."

"I know, I know. I'm feeling odd today. Ignore almost everything I say. I'll be at the restaurant first thing tomorrow."

"It'd be great to see you. Take care and thanks so much."

"Bye." Liza hung up the phone. Speaking with Bonnie left her feeling at ease. The woman was such a good person, and this was the first time since school she had a new girlfriend.

Happy that she had no plans or pressing errands, Liza declared it a Liza Kasner day. The problem was, what did she want to do? Dressing in her favorite indigo jeans and striped turtleneck sweater, she noticed gaps at the waist, and fabric bunched at the hips. Should she buy a scale? Liza shook her head and relived the dreadful memories of being weighed at school and the school nurse calling her mother to let her know she was overweight. Her mom would drag her to Doctor Golden, who regaled her with a stern lecture on changing her habits. After that, she promised to do better and exercise, but she would find a shady place to read and eat cookies.

It was not until her freshman year of college that she skipped lunches, walked to class, and lost thirty pounds. She discovered long-lost confidence and a new body. Her social life improved, and she started dating with some regularity. Her roommate, Trish, filled out a dating service form, and they agreed to only go on double dates. Whenever someone called, they told the prospective man that he needed to bring a friend for the other. It worked well, although there was one week when they went to the same movie two nights in a row with different partners. It was a popular comedy. Every time something funny was going to happen, they laughed in anticipation. The guys were too busy groping their breasts to be suspicious.

Liza kept her weight down until she married Barry. On each anniversary, she noticed a few pounds came to visit and stayed. By the time she left New Jersey, she was seventy pounds heavier than her college weight and was miserable. Barry tormented her about getting fat. He hated her body and never lost a chance to insult her.

She tried every diet published in the last ten years. She could recite from memory foods allowed in the grapefruit, high fat, low carb, high carb, liquid, fruit, and brown rice diets. The problems came when she combined them. Eating high-fat and brown rice together did not work and she fast-tracked by gaining five more pounds.

Since being on the Cape, she had lost weight without trying. Should she worry if she had cancer or diabetes? Liza forced herself to stop thinking like that. The run-away, the victim-free-from-Barry diet was working. She liked that name. Maybe she would write an article on how to lose weight and feel better without having to follow a food plan. Just dump the jerk and find some self-esteem. The rest would follow.

She pulled the waist of her pants once more to gauge how many inches she might have lost, put on her blue ski parka, and laced up her black hiking boots. Not a Jersey girl fashion statement, but warm and dry. She smiled at her new look in the mirror as she walked out the door.

Where should she go and what did she want to do? Barry would have grabbed her throat by now and told her to make up her stupid mind. She relaxed. No Barry, no threats. Just her and a day to herself.

While it was cold, the skies were blue, and the sun was peeking through the clouds. It was an unexpected, pleasant day for March, and the beaches on the bay were lovely. Heading to the Northside beaches, Liza enjoyed the new vistas. Retracing part of the route to Doc's house in Brewster, Liza wondered if she could locate his driveway from her adventure in the night. Nothing looked familiar, as she followed the straightforward route from Chatham to the Brewster beaches. Cutting across the peninsula on Route 137, heading towards Brewster, Liza took in the rural landscape. Brewster was a long, thin village surrounded by lush woods, with the Old King's Highway running through the length of the town. Views of marshes and beaches were visible between historic sea captains' homes and iconic buildings. Last summer she enjoyed exploring antique stores, gift shops, and galleries along Route 6A. Today, most of the stores had discreet signs announcing they were closed for winter. *Back in April,* plaques hung off mailboxes and on entrances to large studio barns. Well, it was almost April, and where the hell was everyone? She was told that after mid-April, the solitude ended with the week of school vacation. The quiet would disappear, and she would yearn for closed stores, empty roads, and privacy. Driving through Brewster, she recognized a few familiar landmarks. She prayed Doc was not exploring 6A, too. It was enough to run into him in Chatham. She laughed at being afraid of meeting him and realized he probably did not want to see her either.

Reassured, Liza continued her journey. A large sign caught her attention. Colonial Books, New and Used–Open. Excited for a place to go, she headed into the almost empty parking lot. The store's sign was small but lit by a carefully placed spotlight. Although it was daytime, the sun was weak, and the light was effective in catching people's attention as they drove by. She entered the crowded room with books piled on every surface. It was warm and inviting and she expected to spend lots of time there. Liza was a sucker for all things in print.

"Good morning." The older woman behind the register brightened at the sight of a customer.

"Hello. How are you?" She gave the woman a big smile. Liza knew how lonely a store could be without shoppers.

"Can I help you?"

This was a reversal of her job at the clothing store. Liza responded politely, in the expected conversation dance of off-season Cape Cod. In New Jersey, she could say, "Just looking," and browse with no hurt feelings. Here, during the quiet months, salespeople wanted to talk to shoppers. At Chatham Summer, she talked to anyone just to get out of folding sweaters. Even comments about dogs were an appropriate conversation starter. "Nice day," she replied. It was a light-hearted cocktail party exchange.

"Are you from around here?"

Here we go again. What story should she give her? She was not about to share personal information with anyone, especially a stranger.

The shop owner ignored her silence and nattered, "Thanks for stopping in. Are you vacationing?"

Liza had an epiphany. While she was worried about not revealing too much, no one cared what she said. Taking a deep breath and exhaling, Liza did not want to talk to anyone. She just wanted to sit on one of the leather couches in front of the gas fireplace and look at books. A small surge of exasperation made her end the conversation with some vague pleasantries and leave. It was not the experience she had hoped for, but she knew she was an outsider and had to learn the customs.

Liza continued to explore the length of 6A, stopping in a few of the places open for business. It took up the rest of the morning. Most of the open shops were in large antique barns and sea captains' houses, set far back along windy driveways. Only a few, clustered together in small walking areas, were in town centers. She had heard that in the summer months, the road would back up with traffic for twenty-five miles from Sandwich to Orleans. Liza was glad she was here now. The thought of endless traffic was incredibly unappealing.

A gallery sign with brightly painted letters caught her eye. She parked in front of the old barn and walked down a brick walk to the entrance. When Liza entered the building, the contrast between the antique barn and the modern interior flabbergasted her. Large shafts of light emitted from skylights and twinkly lights scattered on the wooden beams. The brightly lit studio was awash in color from floor to ceiling.

"Wow, these are beautiful," she exclaimed. The pictures were wall-sized, with vibrant colors, depicting fishing scenes. Men in cherry-hued boats hauled translucent multi-colored fish from aquamarine water.

"Isn't she an interesting painter?" A voice behind her announced.

Liza jumped and almost lost her footing. "Oh, I didn't see you back there."

"Sorry. I didn't mean to startle you."

The clear voice came from a woman who was at least eighty years old. She wore a sweater with missing buttons and there was butter-yellow paint on her white hair. Her wrinkled face had clear blue eyes that gave her away. They were alert and amused. If she did not look so at ease in the gallery, she would have passed for a homeless person.

"Are these your paintings?"

She answered with a smile. "You caught me. I like to hear what people say about my paintings before I introduce myself. I guess the paint in my hair is a dead giveaway."

"You're an amazing artist."

The artist presented her with a Cheshire smile and walked away while Liza scrutinized the paintings. The men and their fish looked like they could leap off the canvas and join them in the room. They were unbelievable. She strolled the perimeter of the barn. After she circled the entire room, the artist joined her. Saying nothing.

In awe of the majesty of the artwork, Liza was silent for a long time.

"They are my life's work. My name's Midge."

Liza was so swept up in the raw emotion of the paintings, she almost collapsed onto one of the polished wooded benches.

"Sometimes my paintings hit people that way. They feel small beside nature." Midge smiled as if she expected Liza's response to the painting.

Liza nodded and stared at the brilliant artwork. "Where do you show them?"

"One is at the Smithsonian, another at the Met, and a couple in Europe. I have a major show in Boston this summer if I live that long."

"Are you not well?" Liza noticed the woman appeared frail.

"I'm fine, however, I'm almost ninety and one never knows." She looked into Liza's eyes with a perceptive look. "Are you okay?"

Liza's breath hitched, but she sensed that this woman was trustworthy and would understand. "I don't know what's going on..."

"It's going to be alright. I can tell." Midge moved closer and hugged her. It surprised and comforted Liza.

"Thanks." No words could describe the roller-coaster of emotions Liza was experiencing.

The woman released her and hobbled out of the room.

What a strange experience! Liza slowly composed herself and exited the gallery. She was calm and reassured. What just happened? Could this woman tell her future? She hoped so. Tomorrow she would spend the morning with Bonnie and have a chance at a routine day. Although working in a restaurant was demanding, it was predictable, and she needed that.

Chapter 29

Barry

Barry left work so enraged he almost forgot his wallet. Where was Franny? What had she done with his money? He stopped by the police station to see if they had any updates on his case. He thought about his first visit when he filed the missing person's report. A *case*, that's what they called it. This was not an incident of a missing person. It was a theft. They refused to see it that way.

The young officer told him when he first went down to the station, "Sir, the money was also in your wife's name. We'll file it as a missing person since she's been gone for over a week."

"Missing person my ass," Barry snorted. "She up and stole my money and sneaked off in the middle of the night. You flunkies better find her soon, and I mean yesterday."

The officer grimaced with tight lips. "Yes, Mr. Blackman. We'll do our best." That day, Barry stomped out of the police station. He would never give up. Never.

Today he entered intending to play the devastated husband, miserable over the loss of his wife. Maybe this would get better results. "Hi, Doll. I'm Barry Blackman, and I filed a missing person's report a few weeks ago about my wife, Franny." The woman at the desk was a looker. She had blonde hair and a pert figure, accentuated by her tight uniform. Barry moved closer to check her left hand for a wedding ring.

"Sir, I'll get Officer Wilson to review the case and give you an update."

"What time are you finished here? We could grab a beer."

She ignored him and picked up the telephone.

Oh well. He tried. Barry looked around the room. It was almost empty.

"Why don't you sit down and wait in a chair over there?" She pointed to a bank of gray plastic chairs. "Officer Wilson will be right out."

Barry sat in a chair and concentrated on his sad husband's story. He wanted to get it right.

"I'm Officer Wilson. Can I help you?" A large woman stood in front of him. She had short, cropped gray hair and wore a police uniform with buttons bursting at the seams. A stern expression on her face added to her no-nonsense demeanor.

She must weigh over 200 pounds. Just like Franny. Barry unintentionally scowled and cleared his throat. "I'm still looking for my wife, Franny Blackman. She's been gone a long time, and you found her car in Trenton with no sign of her."

"I checked the updates from the report, and we have no new information."

Barry forced tears. "You've just got to find her. I'm getting desperate."

Officer Wilson hiked up her tight black polyester uniform pants and moved closer. Barry shrank back in his chair. "We're doing our best, sir."

Barry lost it. "No, you're not doing your best. You're all incompetent morons. This is your job. The fat cow stole money and took off. For all I know, she's in Vegas, gambling my money away. You need to find her right now!" he shouted.

Officer Wilson lowered her voice and enunciated each syllable. "Mis...ter Black...man." Her tone was icy. "Get it together and calm down. Unless you want to spend the night in jail, I suggest you shut up and leave the station. Do I make myself perfectly clear?"

Winking at the blonde on his way out, Barry left without another word. When he arrived home, he spotted his neighbor taking out the trash. Her little dog was nipping at her heels. "Hi, Mrs. Ames." He called out with faked cheer.

"Hello, Mr. Blackman. How are you? I've not seen Franny in a while. Is she okay?"

Mrs. Ames was a retired teacher, formal, bossy, and nosy as hell. Although she was an eccentric old bat, questioning her was worth a try. The police told him they canvassed the neighborhood, but they were so lazy they probably skipped half of the people and went out for donuts.

"Franny's been missing for weeks. Do you remember seeing anything that might help me find her?"

"Franny looked pretty as a blonde," she answered.

"Franny has dark hair," he retorted. This woman was blind and stupid.

"No. She dyed her hair. I saw it through the window way back in… I don't exactly remember. It was winter."

"Blonde, huh?" Another clue. She changed her hair color. "Did you see anything else?" he prompted.

"After she dyed her hair, I heard a car drive away in the early morning the next day. I always get up at four a.m. to feed and walk my little Bootie." When the dog growled at Barry, Mrs. Ames pulled at his leash. "Quiet, Baby." She petted his head. "When I looked out the window to check the weather and decide what coat to put on poor Bootie, I saw a strange car coming out of your garage. It wasn't yours or Franny's. My late husband, Gary, may he rest in peace, taught me a bit about cars. I pay attention. Anyway, it was freezing, and I needed to get Bootie back home, so I didn't get a good look."

"Did you tell this to the police?"

"Not really. They didn't ask me much. They wanted to know if Franny told me she was planning to take a trip. I told them no. I hardly see her during the winter to have a conversation. It's too cold to go outside, except to walk the dog."

Barry was impatient. "So, tell me about the car." This old biddy would keep talking until he fell over.

"It was like the one Mr. Melrose drives. I don't know much else. It was too dark to see the color."

Mr. Melrose drove a small Subaru SUV. Where had Franny gotten a car like that? Barry mused.

"Well, I've got to get back in and feed Bootie." Mrs. Ames walked up her stairs, pulling her dog into the house.

Barry was livid. Franny had planned to leave him. He knew for sure. Blonde hair and driving a SUV. Who had helped her? He would punish them all.

Chapter 30

Liza fumbled for her phone, trying to make the ringing stop. The cats shifted, moving to the other side of the bed. They wanted to avoid the noise. Smart cats. Who was calling at this hour? Especially on a Sunday. It was her day off and she planned to sleep all morning.

"Hello." Her voice cracked. Morning voice, her mom used to call it.

"Hi, how are you doing?" It was Jeff's usual game of *guess who was calling*. Why did he think she would automatically know his voice or remember his number?

"Hi. How are you?"

"Great. Are you ready to get the stitches out today?"

"Jeff, no way. It's Sunday morning."

"Rise and shine. Your doctor doesn't keep bankers' hours."

"Do I have to go today?" Was this guy a doctor? Why couldn't he work regular business hours?

"Yup, and I'm going to take you to the best bagel place outside Boston if you're a good girl."

"You can find bagels on Cape Cod that don't taste like donuts?" That could be worth getting into clothes at eight a.m. Liza had not had a decent bagel since New Jersey. Although they looked authentic, they did not taste like real bagels. New York bagels were crispy on the outside with soft chewy dough.

Cape Cod bagels were bready, soft, and squishy. No self-respecting Jewish girl would call them a bagel.

"Do they have cream cheese and lox at this place?" She was not going to all the trouble to wake up and get dressed without the works.

"You're impossible. Of course, this is the land of smoked fish."

"Okay. I'll be ready in an hour." Liza looked at the pile of dirty laundry on her bedroom chair and wondered what she had that was clean enough to wear. She had to do laundry soon, so she had clothes for the week. It was just too hard to do it with one hand.

"No dice. I'll be there in twenty minutes. Doc said he's going fishing later this morning."

Jeff was smart. He knew she would cave for a real bagel. "I concede you win. See you in a few."

After the call, she leaped out of bed, covered her hand with a plastic bag, and took a quick shower. Liza called them lightning showers when she was a child. Growing up in a one-bathroom home, they did their business and got out fast. There was no lingering in a luxurious tub for anyone.

The cats followed her into the bathroom, meowing. They were hungry. "Don't worry, I won't forget you." Two pairs of eyes watched her finger-brush her curls, grab a clean pair of jeans, and, with heroic effort, go through her closet to locate a clean white blouse. She flattened out the collar and selected a yellow sweater that would cover the rest of the wrinkles. Boots finished the outfit, and she added lipstick, but no other makeup. Surveying herself in the mirror, she looked passable. Liza had no time to fuss this morning. Jeff's early-morning call annoyed her, and she was too tired to put in the effort to look great. Jeff may have won the match, but he had not won the game.

After feeding the cats, she put a slice of bread in the toaster. She did not want to be too hungry for a first-date bagel breakfast. Liza was devouring the toast when Jeff's car pulled into the gravel driveway. She was furious. It was only seventeen minutes since he first woke her. He must have called from the road, not understanding how long it took a woman to get up, shower, put on make-up, and eat breakfast. She laughed at the realization he undoubtedly skipped the shower, put on yesterday's clothes, and jumped in his car. What a simple life. She wished she were clueless or confident enough to get away with doing that.

"Hi. How are you?" He walked in with a bright smile and was wearing one of his usual flannel shirts and jeans. Nothing he wore ever needed ironing.

"Let's get this show on the road," she replied, refusing to be chipper or make small talk. He expected her to rush on his terms, but she would not give him any satisfaction.

Jeff opened the door to his truck and helped her in. It was difficult, as she was too short to hop into the high cab. Liza wished for a step stool so he would not have to boost her. It was both embarrassing and intimate and she was not ready for either.

"So, are you ready for the big day?"

"Huh? What big day?"

"Getting your stitches out. Don't worry, it won't hurt, and you'll be good as new. Afterward, we'll have a delightful treat."

"I'm not a six-year-old. I've had stitches out before. Sometimes it does hurt."

"I'm just trying to have a pleasant conversation. You don't have to bite my head off." Jeff looked upset.

She relented. He was doing her a favor. What was wrong with her? "I'm feeling off this morning. I'm sorry." He fell silent, which was the last thing she wanted. She needed someone to hug her and make a big deal of getting her stitches out.

He was not that enlightened as he replied, "Wait till you taste the bagels. They're terrific."

Why was he avoiding a discussion of her feelings? She wished he were savvier; however, the thought of wonderful bagels overrode her mild annoyance. " I appreciate your help." Liza had spent the last ten years mastering how to be nice and capitulate. This was the only way she could keep her husband from taking things out on her.

Jeff noticed the change in her tone and sounded apologetic. "Look, I should've called last night to tell you Doc wanted you in early this morning." He gave her a small grin. "I didn't think it would be a big deal."

"Thank you for doing this. I need coffee before I wake up and face the world. Sorry, I've been rude. You're just trying to help me."

The tension broke, and they traveled to Doc's house in comfortable silence. This time, her visit with Doc was quick and painless. He pronounced her hand was healing well, removed the stitches, gave her last-minute instructions, and a reminder to call him if it became red or painful. He was efficient and professional. No money changed hands.

"How much do I owe you?" She broached the subject with Jeff in the truck.

"Don't worry about it. Doc and I exchange favors all the time."

What the hell did that mean? Was Jeff involved with something illegal? Better not to ask. "I can pay you back on an installment plan." In twenty years, she should own her hand. When he did not respond, she shut up. It was clear Jeff would not tell her more.

"It's okay, Liza. You don't owe me anything. Now let's get those hot bagels."

Not for the first time, Liza wondered if the man ever thought of anything besides his stomach. She could live with that as she remembered the taste of a typical New York Sunday breakfast. The thought of fresh-cooked bagels piled high with lox and all the fixings roused her. "How did you ever find a decent bagel on the Cape?"

He pulled into a small strip mall and answered, "You're about to find out."

Approaching the tiny coffee shop, Liza thought this was not even close to a real New York deli. Once inside, however, she reconsidered her first impression. This place smelled authentic, and a yeasty garlic odor filled the room. Along one wall were racks of fresh-baked bagels labeled with her favorites. Garlic, onion, poppy seed, and everything bagels competed for her attention. The menu on a sign with black movable letters described the offerings, bagels, eggs, and many ways to combine them.

They sat at a small Formica table in the corner and Liza perused the other customers. They did not look like Sunday morning New Yorkers. At one of the other tables, two men in plaid flannel shirts and worn jeans were drinking coffee and eating plates of eggs and bagels. A tired-looking young woman came over to take their order.

"Hi, Guys. What'll you have?"

"I'd love a bagel with the works. Lox, cream cheese, onions, and tomato on a poppy seed bagel and a cup of coffee with cream." Liza ordered fast, anticipating an amazing feast.

"Hi, Jenny. How are you doing?" Jeff smiled at her. "I want you to meet Liza. She's never been here before."

Feeling like a child being rebuked for rudeness, Liza's face burned. She had almost forgotten the New England reserve and should have waited to order.

Jenny gave her a tepid smile. "Hi, Liza. Glad to meet ya."

Responding with the perkiest smile Liza could muster this early in the morning, she realized there was nothing else to say.

Jeff continued as if nothing had occurred. "I'll have one of your fantastic cheese omelets, a plain bagel, and a cup of black coffee."

When Jenny headed into the kitchen, Liza questioned Jeff, "How do you know her? Are you a friend of every woman on the Cape?"

"Whoa, calm down. She's Doc's girlfriend and I've been friends with them since I moved here. What's the matter with you?"

Liza blushed again. Hunger made her ill-mannered, as well as stupid. She kept quiet until Jenny arrived with their coffee and bagels. "Oh look, the food is here."

All appeared to be forgiven. Jeff spoke as if nothing had happened. "It's surprising how many transplanted New Yorkers stumble onto this place and feel right at home."

"Sometimes I miss my old metropolitan New York life, minus Barry, of course." Liza blushed. She never meant to bring him up. It was like another person showing up at the table. And not a welcome guest either.

He smiled. "Oh, Liza. It's okay."

"I'm sorry...."

"Don't be. We all miss the excitement of the big city and our earlier lives. Give it time. Cape Cod has its charm."

Liza took a huge bite of the bagel, and the cream cheese oozed out the sides onto her cheeks. "Wow, heaven." This made up for everything. Maybe not her unbelievable journey to get here, but fantastic bagels with a nice guy were better than she ever expected.

Jeff stared at her face and chuckled. "You sure get into your food, don't you?"

Liza knew she was not a pretty sight with cream cheese smeared on her face. She attempted to wipe herself with the thin napkin she had pulled from the stainless-steel container on the table and laughed. This was going to be another date where she failed miserably to make a good impression.

"That's what I like about you. You're so real," he roared. The men at the other tables looked over and watched them wiping their faces and laughing. One tipped his fishing hat and smiled.

Where did she find this guy? He was almost perfect. "Thanks for being so nice." They ate in silence until Jenny returned with the check.

"Anything else I can get you?"

"No," they answered simultaneously.

Returning to Chatham on the Old King's Highway, Liza felt the hint of spring. For the first time since coming to Cape Cod, she felt optimistic.

Chapter 31

The year-round Chatham residents who shopped at Chatham Summer off-season bought mostly practical items. They shopped for Yankee basics, such as jeans, oxford shirts, and sweaters. By April, the store targeted the burgeoning tourist crowd. The inventory included sundresses, pastel sportswear, and brightly colored beach clothing. The weekenders who vacationed early in the season could purchase the newest summer styles.

Liza remembered the previous summer when she stayed at the grand hotel right outside the town center and was one of the resort shoppers. She remembered the crowded aisles and patrons jostling for dressing rooms. Liza was still reminiscing when a young woman with a doublewide stroller entered the store.

"I'm sorry, but it's too tight in the store for strollers. You can park it safely right outside the entranceway." Liza stood with her arms crossed.

The woman gave Liza an imperious look. "It's early in the season and there's no one else in the store. Let me speak to the manager. I'm sure she'll make an exception. I can't leave my stroller unattended. It's worth a fortune." She gave a winning smile, as if she had already won the argument. "Don't worry. My children are incredibly well-behaved, and I won't need much time."

Liza peered into the stroller and scrutinized the toddlers. They were identical twins, dressed in matching white embroidered dresses and sporting runny noses. She feared they would be a walking germ factory. Reluctantly, she agreed to let the woman leave the stroller near the door and emancipate the kids from their seats. "Okay, please keep a careful eye on them. Make sure your adorable children aren't too close to the merchandise." The last thing she needed was to have them grab the hanging dresses with their grubby hands. However, she lost the first round by letting the woman bring in the stroller and understood this was likely to be a long summer if she did not get better at saying no.

The young mother tried on three dresses and handed one to Liza. "I'll take this." It was a delicate silk dress in cornflower blue. Liza had a moment of clairvoyance as she imagined spaghetti sauce down the front, but pushed it from her thoughts. She needed to make a sale.

"Great. It matches the blue in your eyes." Liza watched the toddlers grow restless and tried to move her customer along. She was desperate to get the family out of the store before other moms with strollers arrived and demanded in-store parking, too. "We have some lovely shoes that would make it a great outfit." Although she wanted the young mother to pay and leave, she still smarted from the reprimand her boss gave her when she did not push accessories. Liza carried the dress to the shoe section and pointed to a pair of flats in blue. They were a close match.

Pursing her lips, the customer frowned. "I'm not sure. Do you have these flats in black?"

"Not anymore. We have blue, beige, and off-white. How about black flats in another style?"

"No. I don't know why I came in. The styles are for old ladies." With that, she tried to exit, but pushed the stroller into a rounder of dresses. The children wailed. "I can't believe this place. If you expect my business, you better make more room for my babies." She freed the vehicle and left in a huff.

A dumbfounded Liza held the unwanted dress. Who the hell did the woman think she was? Before she could calm herself, an older well-dressed woman entered wearing a gorgeous designer suit. Liza was so distracted by her lovely outfit; she did not register that she recognized the wearer.

"Why, Franny, what are you doing here?"

"You must be mistaken. My name is Liza." She felt her stomach lurch as she tried to turn away. It was her old neighbor in New Jersey, Mrs. McMillan.

"Don't be silly, Franny. I'd know you anywhere."

"No, really, my name is Liza. I live on Cape Cod."

"Hmm...well, whoever you are, I'd like to try on the dress on display in the window. The one with pink flowers. Size ten."

Size fourteen was more like it. They were both liars. "It runs quite small. I'll bring you a range of sizes."

Mrs. McMillan emerged from the dressing room wearing the larger-sized dress. "Do you think this is too big?"

"No, it fits you well across the back."

"I guess it runs small."

"Or you've been eating too many donuts," Liza muttered, too low for anyone to hear.

"So, Franny or Liza? Did you know that the whole town is looking for you?"

"I'm not sure what you mean. I live here on Cape Cod. Where are you from?"

"New Jersey, but you already know that." Then, in a quiet voice, she said, "It's okay, Honey. I can keep a secret. By the way, you've lost weight and gone blonde. You look good."

She must have thought flattery would make Liza confess. The woman was the biggest gossip in Watchung, and Liza could not count on her discretion for over five minutes. She gave her an innocent smile. "I've no idea who Franny is. I hope you find her."

Mrs. McMillan paid and left with the dress wrapped in tissue and in a bold-lettered Chatham Summer bag. When the door closed, Liza felt her hands shake. What should she do? What if her neighbor told Barry that she found his missing wife? She would be in serious trouble.

Liza called Jeff and left a message. "Hi, Jeff. This is Liza. I need to speak to you. Please call as soon as you get in." She did not want to say it was an emergency in case he panicked that she had re-injured herself.

After silently repeating, "Deep breaths, calm down...calm down," Liza spent the rest of the day in a daze. She waited on a few customers, mostly lookers. The browsers usually headed for the sale rack and fingered every item before walking out with a guilty glance at her.

After work, Liza returned to the cottage. How safe was her secret? How many days did she have until she had to get out of here? She chewed her nails, something she had not done in months. She examined her cozy home. The cats were curled around each other on the bed, beginning to get along. Licorice had bonded with Zeus, and Liza had promised Aurora she would take care of him. She could not let them down. She loved it here and was not leaving. It would be impossible to start over again. She was desperate to talk to Jeff and get his advice. What should she do? Why didn't he call?

Sharing a tuna sandwich with Licorice and Zeus, she anxiously waited for Jeff's call. By six, she was furious. How could he be so insensitive? She left another message. Where the hell was he? It was not until eight that the phone rang. She answered before the second ring.

"Hi, Liza. What's up?"

He sounded so upbeat she wanted to scream at him. She willed herself to remain composed. "I need your help."

"Did you cut your hand on a bagel?"

"No. Just. Listen." Her voice rose as she spoke to him. "One of my New Jersey neighbors came into Chatham Summer and recognized me. I don't know what to do."

"What did you say to her?"

"I denied being Franny. She didn't believe me."

"How do you know?"

"Are you even listening to me? She looked me in the eye and called me Franny."

"Maybe she won't tell anyone."

"She's a big loudmouth and I'm sure it will get back to Barry. Should I find another place to live?"

"First, chill. We'll figure something out."

"Can you come over now?"

"Now? It's after eight and I just got in and all I want is dinner and a beer. What are you planning tonight that can't wait for tomorrow?"

His sense of logic overrode any recognition she needed emotional support. He was obtuse because he wanted a beer and dinner and did not understand how scared she was. She wanted to be held and reassured right now. "Okay." She forced herself to sound reasonable. At least the cats would cuddle tonight. Even Zeus had more heart than Jeff did.

"I'll be at the cottage first thing tomorrow and we'll think of something."

"Sure. Gotta go." She did not want to prolong this conversation. This was an emergency. After they disconnected, she held the phone for a long time. She needed a safety plan. Not tomorrow, but right now.

She was awake most of the night. Every time she stared at the clock, it was only one hour later than before. Her restlessness was contagious. The cats shifted in bed while Liza tossed and turned. She could not stop thinking about Mrs. McMillan. Was there anyone who would believe her? What were the odds she even spoke to Barry? He hated their neighbors, and they avoided him. Maybe this would blow over and turn out to be nothing. If Barry found out and she had to move, where could she go and who would help her? Would she ever be safe? These issues occupied most of the next eight hours. When morning finally arrived, the stress of worrying all night exhausted her. She had almost no sleep, accompanied by hours of anxiety. The phone rang at seven forty-five.

"Hi, Liza. How are you doing today?" She recognized Jeff's voice before she even looked at the screen to see who it was. "Good news. I *friended* Sam on Facebook yesterday."

Her heart raced. "What did he say?"

"Nothing yet. I'll let you know when he responds."

Momentarily excited and then immediately disappointed, she wanted to discuss yesterday's events. "Remember what I told you last night? I was working at Chatham Summer and my former neighbor came in and called me Franny. Maybe I need to get out of here. There's no way I'll ever be able to avoid my husband." That came out without a breath.

"Whoa, slow down. Of course, I remember our talk last night. I figured everything would look clearer this morning."

She gulped for air. "What do you mean, clearer? What do you think changed overnight?"

He responded, "A neighbor thought she recognized you, and you didn't admit to being Franny. Maybe you convinced her she was mistaken."

"No, because she persisted in talking to me like I was Franny and said she didn't believe me."

"So, what's she going to do that requires you to leave your life here and run away again?"

In the morning, logical questions made more sense than the runaway thoughts she conjured at two a.m. "Well...she could tell Barry...."

"Do they talk regularly?"

"No, but what if she tells someone else and they tell Barry?"

"How likely is that? Who does Barry talk to in your old neighborhood?"

"Well, no one really...."

"So, it's a non-issue. Let's go out and do something fun today."

"Are you kidding? I'm stressed out."

"I'll be over in twenty minutes. Dress warmly." He disconnected, and she stared at the phone for a long time.

He was ridiculous if he believed all she needed was a diversion to make everything better. She crawled back into bed with the cats. They snuggled close to comfort her, or maybe to get warmer. Twenty-five minutes later, Jeff was pounding at the door.

"Come on, Liza. Where are you?"

She considered not opening it. She had asked for help, and he offered a fun day. What was that going to do? Nothing. She relented and answered the door. "I'm coming."

He gazed at her rumpled sweats and uncombed hair and rolled his eyes. "Did you go back to sleep after I told you we were going out?"

"Well, I was up most of the night."

He looked concerned, pulled her close, and stroked her hair. Tears puddled down her cheeks. He murmured, "It's going to be okay. I promise."

"Are you sure? I'm so scared."

"I'm here for you."

She collapsed into his embrace and hugged back. When Liza caught his smile, she understood he was warm-hearted and trying his best to console her. She shivered, thinking about her last relationship. It was impossible to compare Jeff to Barry. This man was kind.

"Come on, get dressed, and wear something warm. I have something planned that will take your mind off your problems."

She left him standing in the living room and headed back to the bedroom. The cats studied her and shifted on the rumpled covers. "Okay kids, I'm going out with Jeff. You can have the bed to yourselves." They did not answer.

She put on clean underwear and considered wearing yesterday's clothes. They were good enough. Liza cared less if she impressed anyone this morning. Today was going to be a fuss-free day. After finger-combing her curls, she brushed her teeth and splashed water on her face. No makeup. He was going to get the real Liza.

"Liza, come on. Did you eat breakfast?"

"Not yet."

"Have you got something that's quick?"

She grabbed a bagel from the counter and offered him one on a paper plate. "These are from yesterday, but shouldn't be too stale. Want one?"

"Thanks." He pinched it to see if it needed toasting or not. They smeared the bagels with cream cheese and drank fresh-squeezed orange juice from paper cups. "Yum. These are good. Now put your jacket on. We're going to have a great time today."

She threw the dishes in the trash and frowned. Liza did not want fun. She wanted him to calm her, but this did not appear to be on his agenda. She grabbed her parka and red hat.

"You need gloves."

"They're in my pockets."

"Do they have grippy palms?"

Liza removed them and held them out. They were thick red wool gloves. "They have suede palms for driving. Will they do?"

He scrutinized them. "Do you have any thin leather ones?"

"Why?"

"Well, do you?"

She went into her room for dressy leather gloves. They were from a small boutique in New Jersey and were elegant. The last time she wore them was for a formal party, her birthday dinner. That was when she caught Barry with another woman. She grimaced at the memory.

"Oh, these are perfect." He ignored her stormy expression.

Approaching his truck, Liza spotted two bicycles in the bed. "Oh, no...."

"You'll love it."

Dare she admit that she never really learned how to ride a bike well? She did not want to look stupid. Everyone rode a bike. Well, almost everyone. She had terrible balance and would need time to practice before she could steer or remain upright long enough to go in a straight line.

"It's early in the season and the bike path should be practically empty. This is the best time to ride and explore the beauty of Cape Cod."

"I'm not sure this is a good idea."

"Come on, Liza. You need to think of something else besides Barry. You're not thinking straight. It's time you got out of your cottage and had something to get your mind off your problems."

He was right, but killing herself on a bike was not the way she intended to die. It could be a slow and painful process. He took her silence for acquiescence and drove toward the town dump and playground.

"We can park here and ride towards Harwich."

She wanted to brunch at a restaurant but understood it was not happening until she rode with him. How was she going to get the courage to get on the bike and stay on long enough to satisfy his idea of a bike ride? Liza walked her bike to the two-lane asphalt path and stood with her body barely touching the seat. No one was coming in either direction. That was good. At least she would not make a fool of herself in front of a large audience.

"Liza, just get on and ride. You'll love it."

"I need to practice."

"Everyone does this. Even old people."

Liza took a deep breath, gripped the handlebars with her gloved hands, mounted the bike, and pushed off with her right foot. Miraculously, she grabbed the pedal with her left foot and moved forward. This was not bad. She was riding. She continued to progress at a slow but steady clip. Jeff was ahead of her, but turned his head to make sure she was keeping up. Things went smoothly until a stop sign appeared at a street crossing. She pulled hard on the hand brakes and stopped so fast that she fell off the bike. Jeff turned around and approached her, looking concerned.

"Get the damn bike off me and help me up."

"You're doing great."

"Well, not so great. Look at me. I fell."

He laughed. She could not decide whether to laugh or sob. She knew she looked ridiculous. What was he thinking of her?

"Are you okay?"

"No, I probably broke something." Like her pride. Even little kids rode better than she did.

He lifted the bike off her and gave her a hand. She took it, struggling to stand.

"No more." Liza felt hot tears and sniffed to keep her nose from running.

"You're doing well. You just need a little practice. It's like riding a bike...."

"Hilarious. I'm so done with this." She lost it and sniffed back tears. It humiliated her, and she was angry and scared.

Jeff held her tight and stroked her back. "It's all right. You're going to be okay. Everything's going to be fine."

With renewed determination to prove she could do this, Liza broke away from his embrace, walked her bike across the intersection, and climbed on again. Keeping her balance and praying to the Bike Goddess, she whispered, "Please let me stay on." The Goddess granted her wish, and she half-stopped at the next intersection with the brakes and her feet. Not elegant, but functional.

"You're doing great. Isn't this fabulous? You haven't thought about your problems all morning." Jeff was riding next to her, staying close, in case something else happened.

How could he know what she was thinking? She had to admit, she just wanted to stay alive, and her problems with Barry were secondary. "No, it's not wonderful. I want to eat brunch at a fancy sit-down restaurant."

"You drive a hard bargain. Another breakfast out."

"You promised me a fun morning if I tried biking. Eating out's my idea of a good time." He drove into town, and they headed to a swanky hotel. It was lovely being warm and having someone bring them food. Liza sipped her hot chocolate, keeping her hands wrapped around the mug. They were almost numb, as the thin dress gloves were not warm enough for the weather.

"So, Liza. Didn't this get your mind off your troubles?" Jeff reminded her for the second time. He really should give up on this one.

"Not really. It just added a new anxiety to the pile. Now I'm sore and freezing, too."

"Come on. You know you were having a fabulous time. Admit it."

Liza shot him a frosty look. Did he think falling off her bike was fun? How was this going to solve her problems? Sitting across from him, Liza thought of Barry and panicked.

Jeff noticed the change in her expression. "Everything is going to be alright." He took her hand and kissed it. "I'm here for you. No one is going to hurt you. I promise."

Liza felt some of the tension leave her shoulders. Maybe he was right.

Chapter 32

Barry

Barry arrived home before five p.m. Staying at work any longer was useless, since he did not have enough to do to fill an entire day. After a long lunch, he checked in with five clients. No one was interested in buying insurance. Leaving, he called out to the department administrator, "See you later, Babe. I'm going to stop at a few clients' houses on my way home tonight." He ignored the look of disgust on her face. Despite being reprimanded for calling women Babe, he did not care. When he collected Franny's life insurance, he would be out of there. It was getting more difficult to think of plausible excuses to leave early, but so far, no one had called him on it. Barry smiled as he got into his car. He was smarter than any of his co-workers. He would not work in a place like this until he dropped. It was a deadly existence. To prove his point, last week Toby Forest keeled over at his desk. The guy came in every morning at seven-thirty and worked until six. He even ate his one-slice turkey sandwich while making cold calls to prospective customers. Barry could not think of a worse way to spend the rest of his life.

Approaching his house, Barry spotted Mrs. McMillan and Mrs. Ames gossiping across the street. Her small dog, Bootie, was running around in circles.

"Maybe I could run over the stupid dust mop," he murmured. "Nah, I'd just mess up the street." Still, it was tempting....

He opened his garage door and noticed the two women coming down his driveway. How was he going to get out of talking to them?

"Hi, Barry," they said in unison. Their phony smiles told him they had bad news to report.

He opened the car window and called out, "Hi, ladies. I gotta run. Got a conference call coming in at...." He looked pointedly at his watch. "Right now." With that, he drove into his garage and closed the door. That was close. Barry entered the laundry room and heard the doorbell ring. What the hell? Those broads did not listen. They reminded him of Franny. He peered through an opening between the living room drapes and saw both women standing on the front stoop. He opened the door a crack and yelled, "Catch you all later... gotta make that call."

Barry watched them through the curtains as they crossed the street. Relieved that they were gone, he entered the kitchen and pulled a beer from the fridge. He popped open the top, sat on the couch, and turned on the TV. The beer was cold, and he relaxed. Now, this was more like it. If only someone would bring him corned beef on rye. Yup, that would be perfect.

The phone rang, and he ignored it. The machine picked up. "Hi, Barry, this is Sonja McMillan from up the block. I know you're busy, so I thought I'd leave you a message. Call me back. It's important. I wanted to talk to you about Franny...."

Barry hit the erase button and canceled all the messages on the machine. He did not want to see her, talk to her, or hear from her. Some people did not take hints. Unless they could get his money back, he was not interested. They just wanted more stuff to gossip about, and he was not about to talk about Franny to them. Just thinking about Franny made him angry.

Tonight, he just wanted to have a few beers and rest. Was that asking too much? He put his head on the green plaid couch pillow and stretched out. If Franny were here, she would be nagging him to keep his feet off the furniture. He paid for this couch with his hard-earned cash and if he wanted to lie down, then he would.

After three beers, the phone rang again. He woke up in a daze and reached for it. Thank God it was Sam. He was done with the neighbors.

"Hi, Dad."

"Hi, Sam. What's doing?" What did the kid want? He hoped it was not money. He did not have any.

"It was my birthday, and I hadn't heard from you in a while."

Crap. He felt a small prick of guilt for forgetting the kid's twenty-first birthday. Well, no one remembered birthdays when Barry was his age and he turned out just fine. "So, what'd you do?"

"I went out with my buddies and drank legally."

"I bet that wasn't the first time you were in a bar."

Sam chuckled. "Caught. Have you heard from Mom?"

"No, she's still missing. She stole some money, so she may be on the run."

"What? Did Mom rob a bank?" Sam was laughing.

"No, she stole our money. Family money."

"I don't believe you."

"Your mom had lots of problems. I didn't want to tell you about them."

"Like what?"

"She lied and stole. Isn't that enough? Listen, Sam, if you hear from her, you gotta tell me. Okay?"

"Yeah…sure." Sam sounded reluctant.

Barry persisted, "I'm not kidding. She could be in real trouble, and we may need to help her."

"What are you talking about?"

"The police are looking for her and if they find her, they could put her in jail."

"Oh, my God. Dad, you got to work this out with Mom. I really miss her."

Barry did not want to be lectured by his kid. "Sam, I gotta go. Just call me if you hear from her. It's important."

Barry chuckled. The kid might lead him right to Franny. He was so tied to her apron strings. She would call him for sure; and when she did, he would find and kill her. This was sweet. Barry smiled and resumed his place on the couch. He popped the top of another beer.

Chapter 33

Sam

Disconnecting, Sam closed the door to his dorm room. He wanted privacy and time to think about what his dad had told him. How could his mom steal? She was a stickler for honesty. When he was little, they found a wallet with hundreds of dollars in it on a sidewalk. Mom insisted they take it to the lost and found at the police station. No, his dad was lying, and she did not take their money. If he heard from her, he would not tell his father. Mom might be in trouble, and if she contacted him, he would help her.

He went to his computer and checked his social media accounts. He hardly posted on Facebook, but gave it a quick glimpse. Maybe his mom would try to message him. If she knew how to do that. He had opened an account for her, but she did not log on very much. He had 750 friends. A new friend request came in with a name he did not recognize. Who was Jonas Fishinger? Maybe someone he met at a party? He looked at the picture and thought the guy looked old. At least thirty. Maybe a professor at Brown who was trying to be cool? Oh hell, he accepted him as a friend. After 750 friends, what was one more?

"Got wasted last night. Thanks for the birthday party." Sam posted on his wall.

"Sam, my man, loved when you took off your shirt and danced on the table." His classmate Bill commented.

Someone tagged him in a photo with his girlfriend, Heather. The picture of him half-naked and swaying on a table with his friends around him was incriminating. He worried his mother might see this. She would not be happy.

"Great time last night," added Sarah.

He felt a moment of panic and hoped Heather was not reading this. Sam had not dated Sarah in a year. Did he have sex with her? He could not remember much about the evening. It started innocently enough with music and a keg. He remembered everyone singing to him, blowing out candles, and eating cake. After that, it was a blur of hazy images of people dancing close and groping. What had he done last night? Did he have fun? His head was pounding. He was so wrecked. Sam wished he could recall the evening. Oh hell, it was his birthday, and he could be wild occasionally. His whole life, he had been a good boy. His dad was mean, and he saw that his mother suffered from his bullying. It was great to be out of that miserable house. Maybe he could find a summer job and stay in New England. Some of his friends were going to Cape Cod to work in restaurants. That would be fun. He would check with the guys tomorrow. He needed a job and had to get away from New Jersey. An entire summer with his dad would be dreadful. Besides, there was nothing to do in Watchung. It was dead.

Sam checked out Jonas Fishinger's posting. The dude did not post his birthdate, but Sam was sure he was much older than his friends. Who the hell was he? His picture was blurry, and it identified him as living in Yarmouth, Massachusetts. Was that on Cape Cod? What an odd coincidence. He was just thinking about finding a summer job there. Jonas listed his occupation as a fisherman. Ha, ha, another coincidence? Moby Dick would've been a better name. Jonas had three friends and there was not much on his wall. Just some postings about tides and fishing limits. Was this dude a stalker or a phony Facebook friend his friends made up? He checked the name through two search engines. Nothing came up like this guy. One older man in Ohio and another in Virginia. He debated about *unfriending* him, but who the hell cared? Sam posted *like* on the size of the bass that Jonas had caught, deciding to check on his new friend.

Sam loved how easy it was to get information on the web. He found a listing for summer jobs on the Cape. Last summer, he and his folks went to Chatham. It was a swanky town with lots of small stores and restaurants. He answered a few ads for Chatham jobs, mostly waiting on tables and parking cars. A few even had housing. That would be critical unless he could rent a small cottage with some guys. Party time. Now that would be a great summer.

Chapter 34

Spring came in increments to Cape Cod. Although it was June, some days were drizzly and cold. Liza woke to a chilly morning. The two cats were sleeping peacefully. Their collective weight kept the quilt on their side of the bed. She tried to pull the comforter back over her, but the pair of felines was too heavy. "Move over, you guys. I'm freezing and you're hogging the blankets." No response. They looked at her with disinterested green eyes. She decided it called for drastic action. With all her strength, she yanked the quilt up with the cats in place. They looked startled, then rearranged themselves, and stretched out to find new positions. She envied their adaptability.

It was one of those days when staying in bed with a good book would be perfect. However, she needed to get to Chatham Summer before ten. It was almost summer, and the population of the town was swelling. New stores were opening, and more people strolled the sidewalks every day. Lighter skies in the evening and flowers blooming hinted at the promise of warmer weather. Liza threw off the conquered blankets and checked her wardrobe for clean clothes, which looked presentable and still fit. She had lost enough weight to have dropped at least one size. Although some of her older clothes were still passable, she went from the just poured-into-them look to looser fitting. Recently she bought a few sale items from the store. Even with her store discount, most of the clothes were outside her budget. Splurging on her Chatham-bought chinos and a pastel sweater gave her the *Chatham* look. Liza wanted to fit in with the early tourists who dressed in spring wear no matter what the weather.

After grabbing a quick cup of coffee and a half muffin, Liza ran into the bathroom to check her hair. The humid weather made it so curly that she rarely needed to comb it. Studying her reflection in the mirror, Liza felt a moment of astonishment at the attractive blonde with a slimmer body staring back at her. She was doing well by ignoring Barry's insults, that were stuck in her head. She was almost pretty. "Bye, guys," she yelled to the cats in an upbeat voice and left for work.

When she entered the store, a smiling Mrs. Woods greeted her. Was her boss going to fire her? Why else would she look so happy? "Hi, Liza. I want you to meet Rebecca."

She looked around but did not see another person in the area. Was she hallucinating? "Sure, I'd love to meet her."

A few minutes later, an older teen came in and approached them wearing a pretty spring dress with pink and green flowers and flats. "Oh, don't you look pretty," fawned Mrs. Woods. "How's your mom? I haven't seen her in church for a while." The church lady connection. Liza should have known. People who came from one of the old families or attended one of the large churches in Chatham all seemed to know each other.

"She's good and says hello. Gram's been sick and Mom's taking care of her."

"I'm sorry to hear that. I hope your grandmother gets better soon."

"Thanks. Ever since Gramps died, she's had a hard time."

"I know. She's a lovely lady and we're all looking forward to hearing her sing again on Sundays."

Who was this lady and what did she do with Mrs. Woods? Liza had never seen this side of her manager. What was going on? Her suspicion meter ran high.

"Oh yes, Rebecca, this is Liza." Mrs. Woods eyed her like a cat stalking a mouse. "Rebecca works here in the summer and on school breaks. She goes to college in Boston."

"Hi, glad to meet you." Liza extended her hand.

Rebecca did not take it. She barely looked at her and glanced back at Mrs. Woods, giving her a pert smile. "When do you want me to start? I'm so excited to be back. Mom said she'll send me to France on break next year if I make enough money for the airfare. She'll match whatever I earn this summer. Isn't that great?" She beamed.

This was going to be a long summer. Mrs. Woods would have someone to spy for her. Longer lunches and late morning starts were over.

"So, Liza, I'll divide the hours between you and Rebecca. She gets the first choice since she has seniority."

Liza was positive Mrs. Woods would give anyone a first choice over her. "Sure." She smiled with tight lips. She was going to lose money because of this girl. Did she always have to come in last? It seemed so unfair.

Rebecca and Mrs. Woods went into the backroom to work on the schedule, leaving Liza excluded from the conversation. Rebecca left after thirty minutes and waved to her on the way out. No conversation, just a hand gesture. Liza had some other ideas for hand gestures to express her feelings, but refrained. She was proud of the fact that she was the consummate professional.

"Liza, dear, you'll work early mornings, some evenings, and weekends. Rebecca requested time for the beach and to see her friends. You know how kids are."

"Okay." Liza remained noncommittal. She did not want to do anything to jeopardize her job. She was lucky to be working in a place that stayed open all year, as not too many stores in Chatham had vacant positions in the winter. Although she agreed to the schedule, she did not have to be happy about it. Liza walked across the floor and began folding and stacking sweaters on a table. Keeping busy was her best way of coping at work these days. She believed she could manage anything if she just kept moving.

Mrs. Woods left on an errand, and the store belonged to her again. She enjoyed the quiet time with mannequins and racks of beautiful clothing. After an hour of peace, customers started coming in and browsing. Every time the door opened, she had a flash of paralyzing fear. What would she do if Mrs. McMillan or some other person from her previous life came in? How many days did she have left in paradise before Barry found her? She willed herself to stop over-thinking. She needed the job and did not have the luxury of staying home in her safe cottage. However, there were few customers this time of year and the odds of another person from New Jersey who knew her were incredibly low. Unfortunately, because much of her money came from commissions, the small number of patrons meant her paycheck would be scanty.

Liza was so lost in her thoughts; that she did not notice that two women had entered the shop until she heard them commenting on the merchandise in quiet voices. "This is pretty," one woman said to her companion as she picked a dress off the racks. They wore expensive clothing and shoes that probably cost a week of her salary. Maybe they were knockoffs. Could they be posers, trying to look like rich tourists? Probably just middle-class women looking for bargains.

"You know, you could get it cheaper online." One of them commented a bit too loudly. She did not seem to care if Liza overheard her.

"I'll just try it on and see how it fits." Her companion picked up a designer dress in two different sizes.

Liza knew the game. The customer would try it on for size and then go home and order from an online discount store. She would have to put the merchandise back in sale-ready condition, knowing there would be no commission for her.

"I love this dress. Where are your changing rooms?" She gave Liza a bright smile.

"Over in the corner." Liza pointed to the discreet sign. "Do you need help to find anything else?" She understood she had to be gracious, no matter what the circumstances. Unfortunately, any chance of a sale to this woman was nonexistent.

She and her friend traipsed to the dressing area and came out with a dress over her arm, while her friend discreetly took a photo with her phone. She handed it to Liza and announced, "I love it, but want to come back later with my husband. You know how that is. He likes to see me in something before I buy it."

With a tight smile, Liza was solicitous. "Do you want me to hold it for you, Mrs....?"

"Oh no. That's okay. I'll see you later." The customer did not make eye contact, a sure sign that she was lying. Everyone wanted to keep up appearances. When she was Franny, that never occurred to her. The new Liza was more understanding of frugality. Unfortunately, she needed the commission.

Mrs. Woods returned to close the store, and Liza had sold only two sweaters and a pair of shoes. If business was this slow all month, she was terrified her boss would reduce her hours until the crowds arrived at the end of June.

The manager pursed her lips as she reviewed the sales. "Not a great day, Liza. What's going on?"

Did she live in a box? "Not too many people came in today. The rain must have kept them home." That sounded plausible.

"Hmm, I'm going to keep a close watch on sales this month. I don't want to report poor earnings to the owners."

Liza did not care about the store's problems unless they affected her, or resulted in decreased hours, and ultimately her paycheck. "I'm sure we'll do better tomorrow." What else could she say? She exited the store and drove home. Did she have enough money to get by? She knew that these were ridiculous worries because she had saved most of the $63,000, she borrowed from the bank. However, she continued deliberating in panic mode. Should she look for another job? Would Mrs. Woods give her a reference? She realized the thoughts of Mrs. McMillan talking to Barry added to other terrifying thoughts. "Stop thinking like that," Liza shouted into the empty car and forced herself to breathe in and out. "I'm in charge and safe." When she reached the cottage, she remained in the car until her heart stopped pounding. The incessant worrying was making her irrational. It was time to stop.

After she plopped on her living room couch, twenty-five pounds of fur surrounded Liza. "Hi, guys. Did you have a lovely day?" They purred and rubbed her legs. Feeling more relaxed, she thought about a getaway plan. She would find a new place and go back to waiting on tables if all else failed. She could take both cats and go to Lake George or even Maine. Places with a tourist economy should have plenty of pickup work. With summer coming, vacationers would pay top dollar to rent Aurora's house. She smiled at the simplicity of her idea. It just might work. She would make it work, as the alternative was too scary to contemplate.

The next morning, the sun was bright and the sky clear. It harbored the beginning of better weather, and she laced up her sneakers and went for a walk. The back path to Harding's Beach was empty, and she roamed the quiet landscape. From a crest, the beauty of the ocean and the sight of seagulls on the beach made her smile. Liza never ceased to be awed by the crashing waves and the picturesque road through the dunes that led to the abandoned lighthouse. It was all hers, at least just for this moment. Her irrational worries were gone. She knew this would be her home for a long time. It felt right.

It was finally her turn to do what she wanted. Barry's needs had always come first, or living with him was a waking nightmare. Why did she stay with him for so long? What was wrong with her? She had questions, but no answers. When she was young, she wanted a career, kids, and a beautiful house in the suburbs. Unfortunately, it came with a big price tag, her integrity. She swore she would never compromise again. The soothing sounds of the ocean and the quiet of nature made her realize how lucky she was.

Returning to the cottage, she made breakfast, sharing an omelet with the cats. Liza kept up with a modicum of deportment and resisted the urge to let them eat at the table on her fancy dishes.

It was a pleasure having the morning free, as she was not due at work until one. Unfortunately, she would not get home until seven-thirty for dinner.

The phone rang, disturbing the harmony of the moment. Who was calling so early?

"Hi, Liza, this is Nora." She had given her friendly neighbor her number, in case she spotted anyone prowling around.

"Hi, how are you?" Nora lived right next door. Why didn't she come over if she needed something?

"I wonder if you wanted to go out for breakfast today. A new restaurant opened in Harwich, and I thought we could try it." Her neighbor sounded upbeat and cheerful, a little too sweet.

Could she eat another breakfast? No, she was full. "I'm sorry. I just ate." No response from Nora. Silences made Liza nervous, and she resumed speaking, "I guess I could get a cup of coffee and something light."

"Great. I'll drive. See you in fifteen minutes?"

"Sure." Why couldn't she decline politely, like everyone else? She was too much of a people pleaser and now she was stuck eating a second breakfast. Since she would not be home until after dinnertime, she wondered if two breakfasts could count towards dinner.

Nora arrived in fourteen minutes. Liza looked down at her legs and noticed the briars from the beach walk covering her jeans. She did not have time to change her clothes, so she discreetly picked them out and put them in the tiny bowl she used as a change holder near the door. She would dump them outside later.

"So, how do you like your first spring in Chatham?" Nora asked.

"It's nice." Liza was not sure how much to say.

"We need to stick together when the summer folks come. It gets noisy and crowded."

"Tell me about summer in the neighborhood." People who had enough money to own two homes intrigued her, especially owning a house that sat vacant for most of the year.

"Well…first the owners come, and they clean out their cottages and stay for a week. Then the renters show up around July fourth."

"Are most of the cottages rented out?"

Nora pursed her lips. "About half. The renters are a wild card. Some arrive in multiple cars with seven or eight people for these two-bedroom cottages. Two families can cut their costs if they rent together. It's cheaper than a motel because they can cook in and save money on food. Although it's crowded, everyone spends hours outside. The kids wander through the neighbor's lawns looking for playmates. The parents drink beer and hope their children stay out as long as possible. I call it a zoo."

"It sounds awful." Liza shuddered at the thought of lots of cars parked along the unpaved street. The road must be impassible.

Nora required little affirmation to continue, "You have to drive slowly because the kids are on bikes or playing baseball on the dirt road."

"How do you get through the summer?"

"I'm not around. I rent my place, too. If it gets too loud, you can call the police."

"Let's hope that doesn't happen." This would certainly interrupt Liza's peaceful reverie; however, she did not mind families and crowds. It was easier to stay anonymous. She would keep her mouth shut no matter what they did. Making a complaint was a public record.

They arrived at the breakfast place, and she felt at home. It reminded her of Bonnie's, with ten small tables and a breakfast bar for a quick cup of coffee. The server was a perky twenty-year-old wearing black pants and a white polo shirt. With her auburn hair tied in a ponytail, she seemed nervous. Probably a college kid in her first week. The restaurant displayed a handwritten menu posted on a whiteboard. Eggs benedict with lobster, vegetable omelets, and breakfast wraps. Everything looked delicious. Liza forced herself to look away from the food and address the server. "Just coffee for me, please. Are you in school?" She felt empathy for the young woman and wanted to put her at ease.

"Yes, I just finished my junior year at Brown. This is my first job on Cape Cod."

Liza wondered if she knew Sam and studied her name tag, Christie. The next time she went on Facebook, she would see if she was one of Sam's friends. Liza willed herself to stop thinking about him and getting upset.

Nora ordered a lobster omelet and a blueberry muffin. The food arrived promptly. "Want a taste?" Nora shoved a forkful of her omelet at her.

"No, thank you. I really did just eat." Of course, she wanted to eat her food. All of it.

"So, tell me about the other cottage owners. Will any cute men be coming to the cottages this summer?" She had to get Nora to talk and distract her from the enticing smells.

"No. Mostly families and children. A few older women and grown kids. They're nice enough, but I keep my distance. We year-rounders don't mingle with the summer folks. They just clog up the roads and make our lives impossible."

"It's already getting crowded on the roads. I suppose that's a minor inconvenience for a boost to the economy. Since I work on commissions, I look forward to more people shopping in town." Liza figured that she would have to be independently wealthy not to rely on tourists. However, she had not lived through a summer in Chatham. Maybe by next year, she would complain, too. "So, besides Chatham Summer, what other stores are open all year and have nice clothes?"

"Why do you ask? Are you thinking of quitting already?" Nora's tone was sharp.

She did not want to tell Nora she was worried that Mrs. Woods might fire her. "Of course not." Liza sipped her coffee and added, "No, just wondering about the competition." She was proud of herself for her quick-thinking response.

"A few stores stay open all year on 6A in Brewster. Hyannis is your best bet. It has year-round chains and department stores," Nora responded.

"Driving to Hyannis would be impossible in the summer traffic."

"Are you kidding? I rarely go past Dennis and never travel over the bridge until fall."

"Don't you go to Boston for museums and culture? It's only two hours away."

"You'll see. The Cape has plenty to do. We even have a town band."

Liza feared she would become this provincial, but realized she had not been over the bridge since she got here. When they arrived back at the cottages, she was content. Nora just might become someone she could confide in on Cape Cod. "Thanks for the invite. I loved the restaurant."

"Yeah. We'll need each other when the madness starts," Nora replied.

The definition of madness varied. After living with Barry, summer people would not even make it to the bottom of her list. Liza smiled in agreement and crossed the yard leading to her place. Then came a flash of anxiety. Until she was sure Barry had stopped looking for her, Liza would never let her guard down with Nora. It would be impossible to be real friends with anyone. Maybe someday that would change.

This turned out to be a day of delicious choices. Nothing on her schedule until one. The decision of what to do next was easy. She headed into town to the Chatham Library, her new favorite place. The notice on the bulletin board caught her attention. It was an invitation to a party honoring its volunteers. Liza would love to go, or at least volunteer, for a library function. The town had tastefully renovated the library, keeping the original architecture while being modernized. It was free, warm, inviting, and available to everyone. Even the bathrooms were decent.

Liza approached one of the gray-haired ladies behind the desk. Her tag identified her as Mary Walsh, a volunteer. She smiled and encouraged Liza to sign up to use the computer. Thirty minutes a session, although no one cared this time of year.

"The place is mostly empty this morning. Stay as long as you like." Mary was polite and helpful.

Liza headed for a small room with wood-paneled walls. If it became too crowded, she would grab a book and move to the reading room with a large bay window and leather wingback chairs. Only three other people were in the library. A man wearing a plaid sports shirt and jeans sat at the big wooden table with a laptop computer. He was well-dressed and smiled when she entered. Was he a sales rep for her store? She liked to think about why people went to libraries. An older couple was at another table reading the newspaper. This place was a cure for loneliness, and if you came every day, you could get the paper for free.

The old-fashioned parlor had five computers on small tables that were available to anyone. It was the perfect juxtaposition of modern life in yesterday's space. Liza sat at the computer and signed into Jeff's fictitious Facebook page. She used the library computer in case she wanted to write something on Sam's page and did not want anyone to trace it to her personal computer. Signing onto Jeff's page, it amused Liza that he only had three friends. This must be the record for the most unpopular person with a Facebook account. She clicked on Sam's wall and read what her son had posted.

Last week, Sam wrote, "Finished up with finals. Thanks for the party. Have a cool summer." A friend tagged him in a picture, dancing on a table with a girl who was wearing a ridiculously small bikini. This was not what a mother needed to see. His newer entries asked for information about summer jobs. "Anyone out there working at a place looking for students? With housing? I want plenty of action."

Yikes. Action was also not something she wanted to know about. She would rather have him work at a nice summer camp with a tight schedule and only one day off a week. She wrote on his wall, "Have you checked out summer camps?"

No immediate reply or *likes* from anyone. Liza thought this was a perfectly respectable idea.

A comment three days before caught her attention. "Hey, Dude. What about the Blueberry Street Inn in Chatham on

Cape Cod? It's a huge beach resort with lots of great-looking chicks working there. Ben and I were there last summer, and we had a blast. They have co-ed bunks in a building for all the staff. You'd love it. We met with kids from all over and earned amazing tips parking cars."

She glanced around the room to see if anyone noticed the change in her breathing. It was coming in gasps. Was Sam on Cape Cod? Here? She worked in downtown Chatham. What if she ran into him? Would he tell Barry? She willed herself to breathe and stop panicking. With thousands of tourists coming to the Cape every summer, why would her son go into a clothing store targeted at the older crowd? The thought that she might see Sam overrode her fears. Liza forced herself to relax her muscles. She missed him so much and was desperate to know he was okay. What if she never saw him again? What if he got married and had a baby? Nervous thoughts ran through her head. "Whoa, you're going overboard." Did she say that aloud? She was not sure. A man entering the room looked startled. Did he think she was another weird lady in the library? Liza forced a smile and kept her eyes on the screen. He looked away, and she tried to remain calm. The library was quiet again.

Sam's latest entry read, "Thanks, Chris. See you at the Blueberry Street Inn soon."

Chris replied, "You can stay at my cottage."

Sam answered, "Great. I love Chatham. We can make serious money."

That was Sam's last post. Sam might be on the Cape for the entire summer. Liza had planned to hide out in a quiet village on Cape Cod, but things were spinning out of control. She realized the summer might turn out differently than she first imagined, but needed to make the best of it.

She sent a text to Jeff. "Lots to tell. Want to come over tomorrow night for dinner?" Liza hoped this meal would not include an emergency trip to Doc's house.

He replied immediately. Didn't he have anything better to do than live on the internet? "Sure. I'll bring wine and be over around six."

Jeff was his usual oblivious self. Shouldn't she decide on the time? Oh well, no big deal. "Okay, see you then." Liza shut down the computer, went home to eat lunch, and change her clothes. This was going to be a long afternoon, and she was having trouble getting focused on anything besides Sam working on Cape Cod.

Chapter 35

Barry

Barry rolled over in bed, tangled in sticky sheets. Where was Lacey or Macy or Gracie? Whatever her name was? She was so hot. He remembered almost nothing about last night and forced his eyes open. Through half-closed slits, he saw both the girl and the hundred bucks on the dresser were gone. Too bad she left. He took a swig from the beer can on the nightstand. It was flat, but he drank it anyway. What day was it? Did he have to work today? Oh crap. His eyes registered on the hands of the bedside alarm clock. It was Tuesday, and he had a ten o'clock appointment with a new customer. It was already nine. Just a few more minutes and he would get up. He closed his eyes and tried to make the room stop spinning. A bell rang nearby, and Barry desperately wanted it to stop.

He reached for the phone and knocked over the dregs of the beer can on the bedside table. Liquid dripped onto the carpet. Good thing he drank most of it. He sopped the rest up with yesterday's boxers. "Hello," he croaked. This better be good. Who was calling at this hour?

"Hi, Dad. Is this a good time?" It was Sam. What the hell did he want?

Barry sat up gingerly on the side of the bed. "You caught me on the way out to work. I have an appointment and can't be late."

After a long pause, Sam replied, "I have a job on Cape Cod, so I won't be home this summer. I wanted to make sure it was okay with you, with Mom gone and everything up in the air."

Barry smiled. No kid around to cramp his style. "I'll miss you, Sam." Never hurts to take the high road. "So, I won't see you at all? That's too bad." He enjoyed spending time with Sam but relished a summer of freedom.

Sam answered, "Well, I have a small favor. Could you drive me to the Cape from Providence? Chatham isn't on a direct bus line. It'd be impossible to get all my stuff there. I want to bring my guitar and sports gear."

Barry could not think of a place he would rather avoid. When he left the Cape last summer, he vowed he would never return. The one major highway, jammed with cars, ran along the center of the peninsula. He remembered traffic crawling while he sat two exits from the bridge. During that time, Franny prattled on about how lovely it was at the Old Cape Inn. Too bad. He should have thrown her off the Sagamore Bridge. Barry regretted missing the perfect time to kill her. "I don't know...." He trailed off, trying to think of a good excuse to say no to Sam. The kid hardly asked for anything, and he did like his company. It could be a bonding experience, kind of like a fishing trip without mosquitoes and camping. They could go out looking for girls. Sam was so handsome, maybe they could find some sweet young things.

Sam begged, "Oh Dad. You can drop me off and go right back home again. Please. I need to get there in time for orientation."

"Orientation? Where are you working?"

"Remember the Old Cape Inn where we stayed? I'm working near there, at the Blueberry Street Inn. They hired me to clean the grounds and maybe even park cars. The kids who worked there last summer said the tips were amazing," Sam answered in an enthusiastic rush of words.

Barry thought about the college kid in a blue blazer who parked his car and stood around when he returned it. The boy expected a tip. For what? He had not even brought him a drink. He stiffed the kid. What kind of money was parking his car worth? Barry replied, "When do you have to be there? I'm busy at work right now."

"I need to get there before Saturday. Can you drive me up on Friday? After I meet some of the other guys, I'll try to get one of them to drive me back to school. You won't even have to come back and pick me up at the end of the summer."

Barry thought about it before agreeing. "I work hard. How do you think you can afford to go to such a shmancy, fancy school? I just can't take off a day so easily." Let the kid grovel. It would be good for him to learn his dad was the boss.

Sam answered with a slight edge to his voice, "Yeah, sure, I know. It's tough out there with the economy and everything. I promise, just drive me there and I won't bother you again for rides. Please?"

Barry was just getting used to being alone and living the good life. Taking the kid to Cape Cod would give him a chance to hit the beaches, but he did not want to give in too fast. "I don't know...."

Sam continued, "I bet I'll earn enough money, so I won't have to hassle you for anything next year."

Now, that was more like it. Sam argued like a man. He really loved that his kid could stand up to him. "Okay, I'll try to clear it at work. Remember, I said try. No promises. It'll take a lot of convincing to get a day off on a Friday." Barry could not think of a Friday in recent history, when he did not arrive at ten and leave by noon.

"Thanks, Dad. I knew you'd come through. What time will you get here to pick me up?"

Barry gave in. "I'll be there around three. We'll be in Chatham for dinner. Do they give you free meals?" Barry figured he should get something for this deal.

"I don't know about food, but I'm staying in a cottage with a friend of a friend. You can meet some kids. The girls are supposed to be fantastic."

That could be interesting. An evening with a bunch of lovely twenty-somethings. "See you later, Sam."

"Yeah, back at you, Dad."

After he hung up the phone, Barry sprawled on the rumpled sheets. He had to meet a client at ten and stick around for at least a few hours. Getting any more demerits for mediocre performance would not be good. Although he was mad that he would have to give up part of his weekend to drive Sam to Cape Cod, he would make it worth his while. After dumping the kid, he would find a cheap motel closer to Hyannis on Route 28 and have some fun. Chatham was too expensive and uptight. He would spend time at work online and find a place to stay near some action. Barry smiled at the thought of a well-endowed college babe, a beach, and a couple of drinks. Not like last year. He frowned at the memory of sleeping in an overpriced hotel with people watching every move. It was Franny's kind of place, but not his. He hated Chatham. It was a quaint village with bars filled with upscale tourists. All the women were wearing pants and shirts covered up to their necks. No short shorts or low-cut tops. Kids and babies were all over the place. It was impossible to get away from the noise and ritzy atmosphere. He wanted a quiet life, a few girls, and a couple of beers. That would be a real vacation. He rolled over. Just a few more minutes of sleep and he would feel a lot better.

Chapter 36

Barry

Barry appeared at the office every day for the rest of the week. He was polite to everyone and even made a few sales. By Thursday night, and exhausted from working so hard, Barry opted to stay home and get ready for his trip with Sam. He thought about the previous summer when Franny required three suitcases to hold all her stuff. What should he bring? He remembered the toiletry bag Franny kept with his extra toothbrush and shaving kit. He looked around but could not find it. Another reason to hate his wife. What had she done with his stuff? He needed a nightcap to help him relax. After three drinks, he was exhausted and put off packing until morning.

The next day, he woke to incessant blaring from across the room. Who was calling this early? Barry rubbed his eyes and put the pillow over his ears. It would not stop. Then he remembered today was the day he was picking up Sam and driving him to Cape Cod. He had set the alarm for seven-thirty so he could legitimately get into work before nine. Barry would leave the hell-hole office by eleven to avoid rush-hour traffic through Connecticut. Leaving at eleven was about the same as leaving at noon. Why not?

Barry dragged himself out of bed and sauntered to the bedroom chair covered with clothes. He smelled the armpits of the shirt he wore to work two days ago. After a few minutes in the bathroom to get rid of the wrinkles, it would be fine. He was desperate to find someone to do his laundry. A new chick who would clean up this mess. Even Franny was looking good.

More awake, he staggered to the bathroom, put his shirt on the door hook, and turned on the shower to steam it. Fifteen minutes later, he dressed and got ready to leave. He was almost out the door when he realized he had not packed his suitcase.

Barry pulled his gym bag from the floor of his closet and dumped last week's workout clothes and a wet towel on the rug. He repacked it with the last two pairs of clean underwear from his drawer, a pair of jeans, and another shirt from the chair. Before he closed the bag, he added a bathing suit and threw his toothbrush on top of everything. The latest in resort wear. He wanted to look good in case Sam's friends had a party. He licked his dry lips, drank juice from the carton, grabbed a muffin from the freezer, and heated it in the microwave. It was one of the last muffins that Franny had baked before leaving, and he ate it in the car, spilling crumbs all over his jacket and front seat.

The morning was uneventful. Barry moved piles of papers around the desk and made a phone call to the police. When he got through, he demanded to speak with Officer Wilson, "Miz Officer Wilson, if you please."

After a few seconds, a woman got on the phone. "This is Officer Wilson. How may I help you?"

"Hey, remember me? I'm Barry Blackman and am still looking for my wife, Franny. I haven't heard from you guys in a while, so I thought a call from one of your employer-taxpayers might refresh your memory."

Dead silence on the other end greeted him. Ten seconds, twenty. Finally, he heard a throat clear. "Yes, Mr. Blackman. What can I do for you?"

"I just told you. I'm looking for my fat old lady. Why haven't you called to let me know about the investigation? I told you I wanted a weekly update. Instead, I bet you're just sitting around eating donuts. You have plenty of time to call a worried husband."

Another pause. "Mr. Blackman, we have nothing new to report. Do you have any information that could help us?"

Barry fumed, "Listen, you idiot. My taxes pay your salary. You work for me. I want regular updates. Do you understand?" His voice rose.

She answered quietly, "We are following police protocol. I have nothing new to tell you. I'll call when I have something. Please let me know if you have any other news. Goodbye."

Barry was enraged. His wife was missing, and the *Keystone Cops* were in charge. He should hire a private dick. Maybe his homeowners would cover that. Stomping around the first-floor offices, Barry opened and slammed file drawers to make his presence known.

"Mr. Blackman. Mrs. Rollins is on line two. Can you take it?" The pretty young chick in the next office called out to him.

"Sure, Babe. Anything for you."

"Hi, Mrs. Rollins. This is Barry Blackman. How can I help you?" Racking his brain to remember who the hell she was, he hoped she was tall, with an impressive body. He liked them young, too.

"Hi, I'm Patty Rollins from Harwich Realty. We met at the Old Cape Inn in August, and you looked at some properties with me. I called you at home and left a message but haven't heard from you. I kept your business card from last summer and wanted to follow up about Cape Cod real estate. It's a great time to buy. You and your lovely wife seemed so interested...."

Barry cut her off mid-sentence when he heard her pitch. He could smell hustlers. "No, we're not in the market for a beach house. I don't know what Franny told you last summer, but she's not buying a house in Chatham. I'm the one who decides and there's no way I'd buy a house on that sandbox loaded with traffic. Besides, Franny's missing, and I'm busy trying to find her."

"Oh my. I'm so sorry and hope your wife's okay. I thought I saw someone who looked just like her the other day around here, but she said her name was Liza. Too bad it wasn't your wife."

"Look, lady. I don't know your game, but this isn't funny. I don't need another house, and I'm in the middle of a very important deal here at work." Barry had a thought as he was brushing her off. Could Franny be calling herself Liza on Cape Cod? He changed to his worried husband's voice. Soft and whiney. "You thought you saw Franny? Where was she? She could be in big trouble. Her brother's in the mob. Some men are out there threatening to kill the whole family. I need to find her. She needs protection."

Mrs. Rollins was not biting. He must not have convinced her. "Oh sorry, I just can't recall. I'm all over the Cape this time of year. If I remember more, you'll be the first person I notify." She hung up quickly.

Barry mused after this call. Franny on Cape Cod. Calling herself Liza? Hmm, this weekend could be very promising. If he found the lying slob, he would permanently get rid of her.

Right on time, he left work at eleven and drove towards Providence. The traffic crawled on the highway through Connecticut. New Haven was like a parking lot, and he was desperate to take a leak. "I'll never get through the city if I get off the highway," he said aloud. During a standstill, he got out of his car and relieved himself through the guardrail. The honking of cars behind him did not bother him. He gave the other drivers the finger and turned toward them to zip up his pants and yell obscenities. The horns and shouts of drivers behind him added to the din. His stopped car was slowing down the crawling traffic.

"Get moving!" The driver behind him screamed.

Barry returned to his car, gunned the engine, and closed the wide space ahead of him. He would have yelled back, but the guy looked bigger and more threatening than someone he wanted to provoke.

By the time he hit Providence, Barry was hot and sticky. Despite the car's air conditioning, the sweat pooled at his armpits and ran down his sides. He called Sam on the cell. "Hey, I can't find a parking spot, so meet me in front of your dorm. Make it quick. I'm triple parked."

It was not long before Sam arrived with a duffel, some sports equipment, and a guitar slung over his shoulder. He looked strong and confident. What a change from the dorky kid they dropped off at Brown last fall. It impressed Barry. "You look good. Working out?" He admired his son as he put on his seat belt. "You must be a chick magnet."

"I'm on the swim team. Don't you remember I won the last race against Yale?"

This was going to be a long drive if he was supposed to keep track of all the insignificant details. That was Franny's job. They drove in silence for thirty minutes. The traffic was heavy but moving. By the time they hit New Bedford, Barry was bored. He had left work early to help his son, had been driving most of the day, and the kid was giving him the silent treatment. As he watched Sam texting his friends on his phone, Barry felt left out. He wanted to know what was so interesting.

He tried another conversation starter. "Got a girlfriend? Any cute broads in your life?"

Sam gave him a sideways look. "Nah." He continued texting and reading emails, clearly not interested in talking to his dad.

Barry turned the radio to a country station and continued driving. Traffic was getting heavy as they grew closer to the Cape. Who were all these people? Didn't they have jobs? If so, they had the nerve to leave work so early to get a weekend head start.

Another hour and they were over the bridge and on the Cape. Barry turned to Sam and growled, "Okay. Where the hell are we going? You do have an address and directions, right?"

Sam checked his iPad. "Get off at the exit for Chatham and I'll get you there."

Finally, off the highway, they traveled for fifteen minutes until they were on the road that ran along the shoreline.

"Take a left on this road," Sam announced.

All Barry could see was a dirt driveway. "I don't see a street. What kind of road is this?" He turned left at a hand-lettered sign. After a bumpy ride, they arrived at a small cottage, surrounded by un-mowed grass with a hammock strung between trees. An old pickup was in the yard. Sam pushed the car door open and ran up the uneven wooden staircase. He pounded on the door and Barry followed.

"Hey, man. I'm coming." Barry heard an impatient voice and saw a tall, muscular young man with blonde wavy hair answer the door with a beer in his hand.

Barry thought this was more like it. A guy with good taste. He stayed on the landing of the bottom steps and waited.

Sam introduced himself, ignoring Barry. "I'm Sam, Chris' friend from Brown. He said you had a room for me here. We're both working in Chatham. A cottage is way better than being cramped in a dorm with other kids."

"Oh, sure. Come on in. My name is Roger, but everyone calls me Duck. Chris will be back in an hour. He went to get some pizza."

Sam left his dad standing in the yard, so Barry returned to the car and hit the horn. What was he supposed to do? He wanted to go in and have a beer with the guys. After he had taken the day off and driven Sam to the Cape, he expected a lot more than this.

Sam came out and stood at the car window. "Well, thanks so much, Dad. I hope this didn't put you out." Without waiting for an answer, he opened the door, grabbed his gear, turned, and bounded up the stairs into the cottage.

Barry was furious. Ungrateful little jerk. Was this all the thanks he got? He gunned the engine and bounced down the long driveway until he hit the main road.

Heading back down Route 6, he got off at the Yarmouth exit. He remembered taking a drive down this bumper-to-bumper stretch of road last summer and seeing 1950s motels and little tourist cottages. His internet search told him they were a lot cheaper than uppity Chatham. He could not even afford a hamburger in that town. Barry checked his handwritten list of budget places. Pilgrim's Landing, Restful Sea, and Colonial Nights. They were all along Route 28. Most looked a bit rundown. No high-priced tourist traps. His kind of place. The first one he came to was Restful Sea. He pulled into the driveway, with older sedans and small trucks parked in front of tiny peeling-paint cottages. The small, sparsely tufted grassy area in the middle had rusty playground equipment, and sported a kidney-shaped pool with no shade trees. A heavy-breasted woman sat in a vinyl chair, watching her children splash in the water. He hoped they would all die from sun exposure.

He chuckled at the name Restful Sea. This was on Route 28. No sea and no view. Did they think he was a moron? He wondered about the people who expected to be on a beach. Too bad. Buyer beware. Barry went into the dark office and checked in. Eighty-five dollars lighter, he entered a small cottage with a green, mold-stained carpet, a chipped Formica dresser, a wooden chair, and a double bed. The forty-five-watt bulb cast an eerie glow, and the room had a view of the decrepit pool with its broken-down chairs. What a dump. Tomorrow he would find a broad, stay at her place, and have a great weekend at the beach. All he needed was a little luck and a brief nap.

Ten minutes later, he lay down on the dingy bedspread and fell asleep to the humming of the window air conditioner spewing tepid air. The broken air conditioner was another strike against this place.

Chapter 37

The bright skies signified another extraordinary day in paradise, and Liza headed to the beach. She wanted as much time as possible on the sand before the crowds showed up. After setting up her chair and kicking her shoes off, reality hit. She was not on vacation and had to be at the store in an hour. What was she doing here when she invited Jeff for dinner tonight? She should cook, but looking at the beckoning sand and water, she made another plan. The local fish market had terrific chowder. With crusty bread and a salad, it would be good enough. Liza could even get a dessert at the same store. She relaxed as she convinced herself she was going to be fine.

When she returned to the cottage, she had only twenty minutes to dress and get to work on time. Licorice roused and stretched while Liza hurried. Too bad she did not have time to straighten up the place and clean the bathroom. The feline stared at her with a lazy expression in her slit, green eyes. Liza ruffled her fur and said, "In my next life, I'm coming back as a cat. Nothing to do but find a sunny place to sleep." It would be perfect.

One minute before she needed to leave for the store, she went into the bathroom, sprayed cleaner on the fixtures, and wiped them down.

After everything was gleaming, she announced to the cats, "Now don't mess up the house when I'm gone." Neither cat replied.

Liza wore her nicely tailored navy capris and the navy and white striped summer sweater she bought with her employee discount. When she glimpsed at herself in the bathroom mirror, she studied her reflection and admired her latest look. With her blonde hair, small pearl earrings, and Cape Cod attire, she could pass for a tourist.

It was the last Friday in June, and her shift would not be over until four-thirty. Liza could see that the town was bustling. She heard that summer kicked off with the first Chatham Band concert. Each Friday, mobs of people traipsed into town, putting blankets down on the green in the morning to save their places. They returned at night to have a picnic, eat ice cream, and listen to nostalgic music. It was more than a fifty-year-old tradition and a free family event. Adults and children danced and sang, ending the night with a roaring rendition of the *Star-Spangled Banner*. Chatham and the band concerts were old-fashioned Americana, and everyone loved them.

Well, almost everyone. Last summer when Liza was on vacation, the Old Cape Inn had a flyer about the band, and she and Barry went to hear them play. Barry was embarrassingly rude, making disparaging comments about the music. When the band played the *Bunny Hop*, he blatantly ogled the women bouncing up and down.

When Liza arrived for work, she found parking in town nonexistent. Luckily, she had a reserved space in the lot behind the store. She was thankful she did not have to search the narrow streets for a spot that would let her stay for six hours. Moms with large strollers were walking down the sidewalks drinking coffee. After setting out their blankets for the night's concert, they filled the morning with window shopping.

Chatham Summer's display included clothing for adults and children. Happy, well-matching mannequins. Even early in the morning, Liza would be alone until midday, when Lindsay, a new college kid, would arrive to help.

The first mom entered the store. She pushed a double-wide stroller and carried a super-sized drink. Her two children, dressed in matching seersucker clothes, looked like an ad from the Chatham Chamber of Commerce. The boy looked to be three, and the girl was a little younger. The mother was wearing coordinating seersucker capris and a white golf shirt. Liza approached them with a smile. "We have a place you can leave your stroller and beverage while you look around." She pointed to the stroller space outside the door. The mother reluctantly backed out and returned with each child clinging to one of her hands.

"Okay, Matt and Megan. You've got to be good here. Mommy will get you ice cream if you let me shop." She sprinted to the sweater table, leaving Liza with the two kids. Liza admired her. This woman was smart, but Liza had enough experience to prevent her from dumping the kids on her. "Come on and let's find Mommy." She took their sticky hands and walked them across the store to where their mother was unfolding stacks of pastel summer sweaters. Megan was pouting. Matt tugged on her hand. "She's over there." Liza pointed and smiled slyly. She would not let their mother get away with this. The family must have a full-time nanny at home, and Liza did not intend to fill that role.

The mom ignored the children and kept moving through the racks of clothes, finally pulling out an expensive blue silk blouse. "I'll try this one."

"Nice choice. The fitting rooms are in the back of the store." Liza pointed to the curtained area.

The mother moved quickly. With long strides, she headed to the back, but with her aid, Liza helped Megan and Matt catch up to her. She had too much work to do and not enough time to babysit.

Two new customers entered the store. One was an older woman with gray hair, wearing blue slacks, and a faded Liberty print blouse. Her outfit had been expensive many years ago. Her clothes were well-worn and neatly pressed. The other woman resembled her and was clearly in charge. Wearing a designer suit and sensible low-heeled shoes, she blurted out, "We need to get my mother some new clothes. Mom's been losing weight and refuses to buy anything."

The older woman interjected, "Joanne, you know I have too many things as it is. At my age, why waste money?"

"Mother, you're not going to go around looking like a homeless person. What will people say? Now, let's pick out some new outfits. I'm just here for the weekend. With my ridiculous work schedule, it's the only time I can help you."

The older woman looked at Liza. "My daughter is a prestigious attorney in Boston."

Liza nodded, wondering if the daughter was a killer divorce lawyer. She would love a consultation but could not afford even fifteen minutes of her time.

Ms. Attorney turned to her with a harried look. She was a woman, clearly used to getting her way. "We're in a hurry. Can't you find my mother some appropriate clothing?"

Liza smiled cheerfully. She saw a generous commission in her future. Money appeared to be no object for this lady.

Meanwhile, the young mother with Matt and Megan in tow was running at full speed towards her. She shoved a rumpled blouse into her arms. "I'll take this. Can you check me out now?"

"Holy crap. This is going to be a long day," Liza muttered under her breath. The children's mother gave her an irate look, and Liza hoped the other customers had not overheard her.

Five more people entered the store and needed help. Liza tried to keep everyone happy by sizing them up and directing them to the parts of the store where they would find what they requested. Preppy moms to the left and mature women toward the front. The more sedate outfits were closer to the register, so the older customers did not have to walk as far. She made a game, guessing who was going to buy a full-priced item or one from the clearance rack. So far, she scored better than fifty percent. Liza entertained fond memories of her boredom in the spring when there was an empty store, and she spent her time folding and refolding the same sweaters.

When Lindsay arrived, Liza gave her a rundown of the morning. "Fifteen customers in two hours. It was unbelievable. Make sure you get the moms to park their strollers outside. Remember to keep an eye out for children, and keep everyone from bringing food or drinks onto the floor."

Lindsay was cute. She wore a skirt with boots and a gauze shirt. Not a Chatham look, but could attract the younger set into this traditional boutique. She gazed at her with a wide-eyed, perky expression. "Okay. Got it." She did not waste words or try to appease. At eighteen Lindsay was aware of the social pecking order, and Liza knew she came in last.

More customers arrived and Liza and Lindsay kept busy ringing up credit cards and bringing new sizes to the fitting rooms. Watching for little sticky hands, which could ruin $500 of merchandise in two minutes, added to the chaos. By four-thirty, Liza was out the door and headed to the fish market. After waiting in line for twenty minutes, she wondered if she made a tactical error. "Do you mind if I go before you?" Liza sweetly inquired of the person next to her. "It's close to five and I need to get home to finish making dinner. I have guests coming at six."

The well-dressed woman looked at her incredulously and with disdain. "No, I was here first and I need to get out, too. It's summer in Chatham and you should plan your time better."

So much for nice. Liza hoped she did not wind up hating summer in Chatham. She got out of the market by five-fifteen, with enough time to put the chowder on the stove to heat. Liza raced through the cottage, picked up strewn clothing, dusted cleared surfaces, and set the table. She barely had enough time to change into clean clothes. By six, there was no sign of Jeff. Sitting in the living room wearing a fresh white blouse and jeans, Liza checked her phone. No calls, texts, or emails. The smell of the chowder in the kettle and bread heating in the oven gave off an enticing aroma. The cats circled her legs in anticipation of fish for dinner. She began talking to them, "Yes, my loves. You can have some chowder after dinner. I'm starved, and you'll have to wait until the big people eat."

Was she trying to have a rational conversation with two cats? Next, people would find her sitting on a bench in the park, drinking wine straight out of a paper bag, and regaling pigeons with her woes. A quarter after six and still no Jeff. She raged, "Screw you, Mister. I'm going to eat by six-thirty, whether you're here or not." And then, "I'm going to feed your dinner to Zeus and Licorice. So, I hope you aren't too hungry."

Liza opened a bottle of wine and poured herself a large glass of Riesling. It tasted like bliss, and she dug into the hummus and pita on the coffee table. She tried to dip and then smooth out the surface, so it still looked untouched. She was a master at sneak-eating. By six-thirty, the appetizer was almost gone. She shouted into the empty room, "Who do you think you are by standing me up? I worked hard all day and rushed home to cook dinner and clean the house. I don't have time for this. You better have a good excuse. That's all I can say." The cats moved uneasily away from the couch. She was ashamed that she might have scared them. What if Jeff was in an accident? What if something bad happened? He was one of her few friends on the Cape. She became even angrier because she thought they liked each other. She bit her lip, thinking how naïve she was to trust a man again.

With another call to her missing date, there was still no answer, and it went directly to voice mail. "Hi, this is Liza. You were supposed to come over for dinner tonight. Are you okay? Please call me back." By seven-thirty, the cats and she finished the chowder. Still no news from Jeff. She considered herself officially, stood up, and announced to her feline companions, "I'm getting out of here. Waiting around for Jeff to show is for losers. I've got other stuff to do." She drove into town to hear the Chatham Band. At least she would not be alone.

The cars lined up bumper to bumper, and the drive that normally took seven minutes stretched to twenty. She was grateful for her reserved parking place. Although it was her night off, Liza stopped in the store to say hello. Sara and Lindsay were working the late shift, vying for commissions. Customers jammed into the store, making it impossible for anyone to get help. The girls pounced on her when she crossed the threshold. Liza took pleasure in that at least someone needed her.

"Hi, Liza, can you cover for a few minutes? We're dying for a coffee. Be right back." Before she could protest, they gathered their wallets and dashed out the door.

Why did she come here? She knew the answer. She was lonely. Liza waited on a few customers and checked her watch for the girls' return. She was tired of waiting for everyone tonight. Finally, after twenty minutes, Lindsay and Sara were back. "Oh, you're a lifesaver. We owe you." They beamed winning smiles and Liza knew they had gotten away with a lot of things, being young and pretty.

Chill out. She felt like a resentful old lady. She was not that old yet. Retrieving her purse in the back, Liza glanced over her shoulder and saw three young men enter. They made a beeline for the girls. Liza's heart raced, and she rushed into the staff area and peered through the door that separated it from the store. What the hell? She looked again. It was Sam. Her palms were sweaty, and she did not know what to do. Her impulse was to run out and hug him, but she hesitated. What if he told Barry that she was here? She would be dead. Although Liza knew he was working on Cape Cod this summer, she never expected to see him walk right into Chatham Summer.

Liza crept back into the main part of the store for a closer look. She just needed to be near Sam. Hiding in the dressing room, she had a good vantage point of the whole place. The guys would not spot her unless they peeked around the corner of the room or tried something on. Not a likely scenario. They had their eyes on the girls, who were laughing and tossing their hair. It shocked Liza that Sam looked so grown up compared to when she last saw him. He was handsome and tan, wearing chinos and a dark polo shirt, with his dark hair bleached with streaks. She wanted to yell at him for bleaching his hair, but refrained. She ached, missing him so much. A moment of sanity prevailed, and Liza remained hidden behind the dressing-room curtain. Lindsay peered at him with an adoring smile. When Sam headed towards the door, Liza left the privacy of the cubicle and inched closer to listen to what he was saying. "See you guys later. We get off at ten. The party is on Orleans Road near Pleasant Bay. Be there by eleven and bring a few friends."

Maybe she could count as one of their friends? Sure, Liza, don't be ridiculous.

The girls giggled and waved as the boys left. Liza sauntered over toward them. "Nice guys." They eyed her suspiciously, as if she was going to snitch on them. "It's okay. I don't tell Mrs. Woods anything."

Lindsay visibly relaxed and beamed. "Yeah, that Sam is cute."

"How'd you meet them?"

"We met them at the coffee shop. They work at the Blueberry Street Inn cleaning up the grounds and parking cars."

"It must be fun to make new friends in the summer." That sounded stupid. They were not trying to make friends; they were looking for boys.

A look passed between the two girls, and Lindsay said, "Sure."

Liza wanted to pump Lindsay for more information, but Lindsay did not appear interested in continuing the conversation. "Well, have a great evening. See you tomorrow." Liza exited the store and checked the street for signs of her son. Although she was eager to see Sam again, she knew she had to avoid him. What a dilemma. If Jeff were here, he would know what to do. Her fists clenched. What the hell happened to Jeff? No word from him all evening.

She headed for the town green, sat on a bench, and listened to the music. The night was still cool in the early summer, and the crowd was enthusiastic. This was the America of her youth. Parents and children gorged on candy and ice cream. Everyone swayed to a waltz, and she longed for Jeff. If he were here, they could dance on the grass. Chatham in the summer could be so romantic.

Chapter 38

The sun streamed through her window, waking her. It was only seven, but it was a glorious Saturday, and Liza did not have to sell clothes until two o'clock. The flip side was she had to work until ten and close up. She would not approach the crowded town until later. With a morning to herself, she could take an early beach walk and drink a cup of coffee made by someone else. After hastily dressing in cargo pants and a Cape Cod tee shirt, Liza gave the cats a quick rub on their backs and opened a can of wet food. At the sound of the can opener, they circled her legs in anticipation, meowed, and gratefully ate with gusto. Life was simple when one was a feline.

After being stood up by Jeff last night and barely eating supper, she was famished. The thought of eggs, pancakes, and coffee was enticing. Liza opened the cupboard door and frowned. She was out of pancake mix and the refrigerator had an almost empty carton of eggs. She could go shopping before breakfast, but that was not appealing. The last of the low-fat vanilla yogurt and granola sat on the counter, but she wanted something more substantial. A cooked breakfast with fried potatoes and rye toast with butter. Just thinking about it made her want it more. She put the yogurt back into the fridge and announced, "A trip to the Lobster Roll would be perfect." She hadn't seen Bonnie in ages. Licorice and Zeus devoured their wet food and ignored her. "So, my kitties, I'm going out and

will be back in a few hours. You need me to pick up anything?"
Again, no answer. The cat lady's life had limitations.

Climbing into the car and driving out of the dirt road, Liza
noted that most of the houses had at least one vehicle in their
driveway. The summer owners and renters were here, with
beach towels scattered over the rails of the tiny decks. The
plastic riding toys on the grass in front of many of the cottages
added to the carefree feel of the place. It was lively after a
winter with no one around. Parents called their children inside
for breakfast. The cottages were so close that she could smell
the bacon and eggs from her front porch. Delicious aromas
from neighbor's grills and kitchens would waft into her cottage
all summer long. Keeping with her plan to lose weight was
going to be impossible, and Liza laughed at the power of
suggestion. Could that be why she craved a big breakfast?
Although she could have gotten a home-cooked meal in the
small greasy spoon nearby, Liza secretly hoped she would run
into Jeff at Bonnie's restaurant. Otherwise, she was going to
hunt him down. That was reason enough to drive a half-hour
away for breakfast.

Traffic was light in the early morning, and she arrived at the
Lobster Roll sooner than expected. The parking lot was still
half-empty. Soon, cars would pack the place.

"Hi, Hon. How are you?" Bonnie rushed over and gave her
a big hug. "I haven't seen you in a while. How've you been?"

Liza returned the embrace and melted into her arms. She
adored this woman. "I'm sorry I haven't been down lately, but
the store's been wild. There are so many more people in town
these days. I've been settling in and getting used to living on
my own after my hus...." She never told her she was married
before. It just slipped out.

Bonnie knowingly touched her arm. "It's okay. I won't say
anything to anyone. You can trust me."

"I do," Liza said, realizing she believed her. Bonny was a good friend.

"The college kids are here and will work until the end of August. I'll call you when they leave. Maybe you can help then." Her sincere smile was contagious. "I know you haven't forgotten me." She removed Liza's guilt about not coming down to see her sooner.

Seated at the counter, Bonnie delivered coffee with milk and sweetener without a word. Liza smiled, flattered that her friend still remembered her preferences.

Bonnie returned to the front of the restaurant to greet customers. A willowy young woman in black stretch pants and a tight tank top arrived to take her order. She swished her blonde ponytail held back with an elastic. "What can I get you?" She smiled but kept her head down, focusing on the order pad.

"I'll have the number one special. Two scrambled, two pancakes, toast, and hash browns." Liza was grateful they did not give the calorie count. It was probably enough to sustain five adults.

Without making eye contact, the server continued, "Anything else?"

"No, I'm good. Thanks."

The athletically built woman loped toward the kitchen. Liza watched with envy. Should she give her advice on how to take an order? No. She was not in charge anymore. Liza decided to just enjoy her food and keep her mouth shut.

Bonnie sauntered to the counter. "Hey, have you seen Jeff lately?"

"No. The bastard was supposed to come over last night and never showed."

Bonnie frowned. "Men. Big jerks. Jeff's usually a nice guy. Do you think something happened to him?"

"I hope it's a good enough excuse, so I won't have to kill the creep when I see him. Did you run into him yesterday?"

She smiled and shook her head. Clearly, Bonnie wanted to stay out of the relationship business.

The meal arrived, and Liza ate with enthusiasm. Pancakes oozed with syrup and butter. Just the way she remembered. It was a long time since she had breakfast cooked by someone else. What a luxury. Liza groaned with delight, ate everything on her plate, left a hefty tip, and gave Bonnie a quick squeeze as she left. The place was filling up fast. Her old boss looked swamped, greeting customers and taking names as they waited for open tables. After Bonnie returned her hug, she asked, "Any plans for today?"

"I have to work tonight, but I have time for a short drive and a walk on the beach. It's early enough so there won't be guards at the gate checking for season passes."

"Stop by again and don't be a stranger."

Liza drove down Route 28 until she reached Jeff's motel. When she was right in front of Pilgrim's Landing, she drove into the motel's parking lot, hoping Jeff did not spot her. She found his red truck parked in front of his cottage. He was home, and she was furious. Should she go into the office and talk to him? And say what? Her need to find out why he stood her up overcame her hesitancy. After she parked in her old spot, she sat in her Forester until her hands stopped shaking in anger. After five minutes, she garnered enough courage to confront him and walked into the motel office.

Jeff sat behind his desk dressed in his usual jeans and tee shirt. He smiled as if he was expecting her. "Hey, Liza, how are you?"

Liza felt her face redden. She had no patience for social niceties. "Where the hell were you last night?"

"Last night?" he replied, looking at her quizzically.

"Remember, you didn't show up for dinner at my house?" She shouted at him, not being able to control her temper. So much for keeping calm.

He sputtered, "Was that last night? I'm so sorry. I just forgot. The tourists kept checking in and I got caught up in the frenzy. Let me make it up to you...."

"You're an ass. I cooked a special meal and wound up waiting forever. I called you. Why didn't you answer your phone?"

"Phone?" He kept repeating everything she uttered. This was making her even madder. He pulled his cell out of his pocket and looked sheepish. "It's been off since yesterday."

"Off?" Now she was repeating herself. This was going nowhere. She needed to get control and took a deep breath. Like a patient parent trying to reason with a toddler, Liza continued with exaggerated calmness, "So, you forgot to come for dinner and your phone was off. Why didn't you answer when I called you at the motel? Was that phone off, too?" Her voice squeaked and was rising again.

Jeff did not make eye contact. "I got a message that my inbox was full, too. I was just going to check it when you came in. Listen, I'm really, really sorry. What can I do to make things better? Believe me, I care about you."

Liza felt frustrated. She hated being so angry, and she could not think of anything to say. She pivoted toward the door to leave.

"Please Liza, stop. How about tonight? Let's do something special this evening." He sounded desperate.

"I've got to go." She did not look back and hurried towards her car. She vacillated between wondering what was wrong with her and feeling justified for her actions. He apologized, and she knew she was not managing things well; however, she was at a tipping point. She could not cope with any more disappointment from men. She needed to walk on the beach and try to de-escalate.

The nearest beach was a quarter mile down a side street off the main drag. It was still early, and the place was quiet. She spotted a few dog walkers near the water, taking a stroll with their pets before the lifeguards and gatekeepers shooed them out. A couple of teens off in the distance were jogging on the sand, possibly training for a race. Liza hugged the shoreline, where the packed sand would be easier on her knees. Walking along the water's edge, Liza's thoughts ran rampant. What was happening to her? Trying to reason with herself, Liza was glad no one could overhear her. "Come on, Liza. You are doing great, with a steady job, and even have a few friends. You need to chill."

Liza stopped her pep talk when a middle-aged man wearing navy shorts with whales embroidered on them came near. He was walking a small fluffy dog and gave her a sideways glance as he passed. Was she talking too loudly? He should judge. The dog looked like a dust mop. What kind of man went out in public with such ridiculous shorts and a stupid-looking dog?

Maybe she should take Licorice for a stroll on the beach. The thought of her cantankerous old black cat on a leash made her giggle, remembering when Sam tried to convince Licorice to go for a walk. Her son was no older than seven. She helped him put a small harness around the cat's body and they drove to a mall. After the cat sat down and refused to move, a security guard showed up, and not so kindly, demanded that they remove the cat and leave immediately.

After fifteen minutes of hard walking, Liza sat on the sand and gazed at the ocean. Life always seemed so peaceful near the water. She would return to Jeff's place and sort out their relationship. He was a good friend. Maybe she was expecting too much from him. The phone rang as she contemplated what to do.

"Hello."

"Hi, Liza, it's Bonnie."

She wondered what she wanted. She just saw her. "Hi, Bonnie. What's up? Miss me already?"

"More than you can imagine. Remember Sherry, the girl who waited on you?"

"You mean the girl who looked like Barbie and made no eye contact?"

Bonnie chuckled. "Yes, she's the one. Well, she announced she was feeling sick and took off in the middle of the shift. All hell's breaking out here. My next server isn't due for two hours. I tried calling her to see if she'd come in early, but her cell's off. I know this is a long shot, but are you still in the area?"

Liza wanted to lie and say she had returned to Chatham, but she owed Bonnie so much, and this was a chance to repay her. "You're lucky. I'm down the road, walking along the beach. I can come in for a few hours, but I need to get back in time for my afternoon shift at the store."

"No problem. You'll be out by lunch. I really appreciate it."

"Hey, what are friends for? I'll be right over." She dusted the sand off her pants and slid into the driver's seat. Her serious talk with Jeff would have to wait until later.

Chapter 39

Barry

Barry woke to the racket of splashing, giggling children in the pool outside his cabin. He groaned, turned onto his right side, grimaced at the stained and peeling wallpaper above the dresser, and muttered, "Where am I? What a toilet. This place is roasting, and it stinks." Barry untangled his legs from the damp sheets, sat on the mattress, and continued complaining, "What happened to the air conditioning? It must have shut off when I was sleeping. It better get fixed now or I want my money back."

Looking at the bedside clock, he swore, "Damn, it's almost noon." He tried to stand, but fell back on the pillow. It was too early for him to function. Didn't this eyesore have muffins and coffee in the morning? At least that was what the guy who took his money said last night.

A mom yelled from outside his window, "If you do that again, I'll kill you!" He heard shrieking children in the background.

Barry mumbled, "Don't worry kids, I'm gonna kill all of you." His remark made him snicker, and he felt better.

A sharp smack and a loud yelp replaced the laughter and raucousness. Barry dragged himself out of bed and went to the cabin door, shouting, "Shut up all of you or else!" It became uncannily silent. "Now that's more like it." He grinned.

Barry pulled on his jeans, grabbed his shirt from the floor, and whined, "I'm hungry. Where can I get a bite to eat around this dump?" Stumbling into the bright sunlight, he squinted as he tried to get his bearings. Crap. It was too bright. Another sunny day. The sky looked like a postcard for a perfect vacation on Cape Cod. What a joke, especially when people drove here from Cincinnati and wound up sleeping in this dump. Their only views were cars crawling down Route 28.

The locked office made him furious. He pounded on the manager's cabin door. "Open up. My air conditioner's broken and my cabin's a hellhole. I want it fixed NOW. Anyway, you're supposed to have coffee and muffins in the morning. I'm hungry." No answer.

Barry left the office and went out to the pool area. A heavy woman was reading a romance novel while her two kids played in the water. Barry looked at her bulging thighs peeking out of her red two-piece suit. Yuck. She needed a reality check before she went outside and showed the world that body. He could add some real spice to her life. Big ladies always knew good places to eat. Maybe she would direct him to a restaurant with fantastic breakfasts.

He smiled brightly at her. "Hi, I'm Barry. I'm in the next cabin over there."

She answered warily, "I'm Suzanne. How are you? My husband, Ben, is still sleeping, so I thought I'd take the kids outside. I hope they didn't wake you." She did not look at all apologetic, and she returned to her book.

It shocked Barry that she had a husband. There was no accounting for taste. "So, you know any good places to eat around here? The guy last night promised coffee and muffins, but the office is closed, and I'm starved."

Suzanne looked up at him with an annoyed expression. "Try the Lobster Roll restaurant down 28. It's pretty good and they have lots of choices. I'm not sure you can still get breakfast. Maybe lunch." She looked pointedly at her watch.

"Thanks." Barry rushed off to get to his car. He was not getting anywhere with this broad. Besides, it was only noon. Of course, they had breakfast. He would deal with the motel manager later. Why did he pay in advance for two nights? Only thoughts of parties on the beach prevented him from grabbing his gear and leaving today.

Chapter 40

Liza got into her car, finger-brushed her hair, and applied make-up in a rush. Bonnie was by the door greeting customers and looking flustered. Instead of an orderly line like before, there were crowds of people clamoring for tables. Calling out names for seating from a handwritten list, Bonnie was pouring coffee and trying to look hospitable. She grabbed Liza's hand. "Thanks so much. I need somebody who knows how to wait on tables."

"No problem, but don't forget that I have to be out of here by noon. I'll need time to get back to Chatham and change before I work my shift at the store."

Bonnie smiled. "Lori will be in by twelve. She's a local college student who takes classes at night. She promised to rush over as soon as her car was back from the garage. It's been a total screw-up kind of day."

"I'm not exactly dressed for the job."

Bonnie grabbed an apron off the coat rack. "You can wear this. People are so hungry; you could bring food to them with your clothes on inside out and they wouldn't notice."

Liza took orders and brought breakfast out to the patrons. One couple tried to take their frustrations out on her. "We've been here fifteen minutes and haven't even ordered. If we knew it was going to take this long, we would've gone somewhere else."

They were indistinguishable from the more recent customers at the store. Liza smiled sweetly. "So, what'll you have? Sorry for the delay." After the summer crowd appeared at work, she discovered quickly never to give an excuse. This was something she also remembered from living with Barry. She now understood why kitchen staff got angry when an irate customer returned a meal. Liza was more than tempted to spill coffee on them, but refrained. This was going to be a long two-hour shift.

By eleven, the crowd was dispersing, and they were catching up in the kitchen. She was into the rhythm of taking orders, serving, and cleaning. It felt good to help a friend. The tips were not bad either, and she could always use the extra cash.

At twelve-fifteen, her replacement finally arrived. She was short and dark-haired, wearing a black skirt and a white blouse. Her features were full, and she had heavy eyebrows and straight white teeth.

The young server, exuding confidence, impressed Liza. The woman stuck out her hand and looked Liza in the eye. "Hi, I'm Lori. You must be Liza. Thanks for filling in until I got here. I had a flat tire last night and needed to have it fixed before work."

"You just missed the craziness. I waited on angry customers who demanded to eat instantly, and people who decided they did not like the way we cooked their eggs. Others wanted to return their food to the kitchen for something else. We were so backed up in the kitchen, we even ran out of bagels."

"Wow. That's worse than last weekend. I thought it was wild on Sunday morning. The Cape just gets busier every year."

"Speaking of busy. I need to get back to Chatham. I'm working the afternoon-evening shift at Chatham Summer tonight."

Lori appraised her. "You work there? Isn't it stuffy with fashions for little old ladies?"

Liza laughed, hoping Lori thought she was cool. "No, it's got clothes for all ages, although it leans toward an older clientele."

"Yeah, the pink and green ladies," she replied and added, "But not you."

"No, I'm not the pink and green type." Hanging the apron back on the coat rack, Liza prepared to leave. She gave Bonnie a quick hug as she headed out the door.

Bonnie touched her arm. "Now come back and see me real soon. I want to make this up to you."

"Stop that nonsense. I'm always happy to help. Wow, I'm late. I've got to go. See you again."

Liza hurried out the door and jumped into the Forester. She was desperate to get home as fast as possible. Traffic was so bad it could take over an hour to get to Chatham. Endless traffic inched down Route 28. As Liza glanced at a black Mercedes waiting to turn into the parking lot, she shuddered, remembering Barry's black Mercedes. Thank God he was in New Jersey.

Chapter 41

Barry

Anger and hunger did not improve Barry's mood. His patience worn, he wanted to get even with everyone. The traffic made it almost impossible to pull into the crowded lane to make a left turn into the parking lot of the Lobster Roll. Since he was allergic to lobster, he wondered why he was here. The fat lady better be right about the food being decent. He needed breakfast before he died from starvation. He cut off another car and slammed on the brakes. Hand gesturing, he yelled, "Get out of the way!" Where did that guy learn to drive?

While waiting for a clearing in the traffic so he could turn into the restaurant's parking lot, Barry admired a blonde lady getting into a gray Forrester. She wore cargo pants and a pink Chatham tee. The woman was not too fat, and not too skinny. He liked her nicely put together look, with her almost too-tight shirt. Barry could not get a good look at her face, but he felt like he had seen her before. What was with the cargo pants? He liked his ladies in tight jeans. Funny, she reminded him of Franny before she let herself get fat. He sat upright. His heart pounded, and he grinned. Could it be Franny, here on Cape Cod? He swiveled to get a better look at her face, but her back was toward him, and the car was heading out. Who was she? He snapped a picture of her license plate as she exited and stared at her disappearing car. If it was Franny, he had hit the jackpot. What a lucky day. He could not wait to catch up to her. He would make sure she was dead for good. Barry clapped his hands in anticipation.

Barry went into the restaurant and greeted the hostess, an ample-bodied blonde woman. Her expression was taut, and she barely looked at him. Not too friendly. Barry tried to make pleasant conversation. "Hey, you got any breakfast food left? I'm starving."

She looked up with fleeting disapproval and then a quick, recovering smile. "No, but you can get an egg sandwich and hand-cut fries. We go to the lunch menu in the afternoon."

"You gotta be kidding. Back in Jersey, we can get breakfast all day at joints like this."

She smiled thinly. "Well, guess you're not at the Jersey Shore today, but we have great food."

He sat at the counter. A petite, black-haired girl wearing a nametag came over to take his order. He read it aloud and said, "Hi, Lori. I'll have black coffee. No milk or sugar. Got it? Hmm, and I'll have the fried egg sandwich. Is it any good?"

She smiled at him. "Everything's great. You should try the chowder, it has real…"

He cut her off. "Maybe I'll eat lunch here tomorrow. Now, I just want coffee and eggs. Is that too hard to understand?"

"Sure, I'll be right back with your coffee."

He ogled as she leaned over the coffeemaker. She was young and sweet. Just the way he liked them. "By the way, I just saw a hot blonde in a Chatham tee shirt leaving the restaurant. Do you know her? I think I used to work with her and can't remember her name."

Lori put his coffee down and it sloshed on the counter. She bent down to get a cleaning cloth and her skirt rode up. "Sorry about that."

"No problem." He enjoyed the view of her skirt hiked up almost to her panties. What else could he spill? Back to identifying Franny. "So," he tried again. "Do you know that lady who just left?"

"Not really. She used to work here, and Bonnie asked her to fill in because my car was in the garage."

The server's chatter exasperated Barry. Couldn't she shut up with all this talk about her stupid car? This broad was dumber than Franny's cat. He tried to be patient and make small talk. "Oh, did your car get fixed? It's hard to find talented mechanics these days."

She smiled. "Just a flat. I must've run over a beer bottle, but it's all set."

He returned her smile and tried again. "So, what was her name? The lady who used to work here."

Lori turned to pour coffee for a woman on his left. She glanced back. "I just met her today. I think her name is Liza. Ask Bonnie. She knows her." She tossed her hair toward the blonde at the front of the restaurant.

Getting information out of these people was difficult, and he did not have all day. Was everyone on Cape Cod so stupid? Barry ate quickly, wiped his face with the back of his hand, and stood to get his wallet out to pay. He had just enough cash for the meal and would have to get to an ATM soon. He found an extra dollar shoved deep in his pocket. It would have to be enough for the tip. Too bad it was so little, but the chick was lucky to get anything. Approaching the door, Barry smiled and tried to engage the hostess again. "Great food you have here."

"Yes, we're known for our chowder."

The food was good. He might just come back tomorrow and have a bowl of their famous chowder. Barry continued, "When I came in. I thought I saw a woman I knew from work but couldn't remember her name. Lori said she used to work here."

Bonnie narrowed her eyes and looked at him closely. "What did you say your name was?" she asked guardedly.

Barry thought fast. "Sam. Sam Johnson." Not too bad for a spur-of-the-moment reply.

"I'm sorry, Mister Johnson. I don't give out employee information."

He put on his sales agent's face. "Oh, that's okay. I'm sure she'd want to see me again. We worked on a big deal together and I wanted to take her out while I'm here."

Bonnie examined him and gave a small smile. "Well then, I'm sure you'll be able to find out more about her through your mutual work friends. Have a nice day."

Barry went out to his car. He was in a rage. Confidential employee information? This was a crappy food joint, not a bank. "Don't sweat it," he said aloud. He had a first name and a license plate number. He would find her. Sitting in the front seat, he remembered the Harwich realtor, who said she saw Frannie on the Cape. Didn't the lady say the woman she recognized called herself Liza? He had a brilliant idea, reached for his cell, and called a New Jersey number. It picked up after three rings. Barry smiled. "Hey, Sal. How are you doing? It's Barry."

Sal sounded like he had just woken up. "Barry? What'd you want this early on a Saturday?"

"I gotta speak with your cop brother, Brian. I need a little help. Remember when I paid you back last month and told you I needed a little more time to get the rest of the dough?"

Sal replied, "You said you'd get it real soon."

"I need a small favor and then I'll pay back everything I owe you, plus interest. All Brian has to do is run a plate for me. It'll take him five minutes."

"What are you talking about? Where are you?"

"You know Franny's been missing for a few months. I've been going out of my mind trying to find her. Well, I'm on

Cape Cod and am pretty sure I spotted her hanging around. I'm sure Brian can get her address. Franny's got great life insurance that's worth a bundle of money. Once she's out of the way, we'll all be rich."

This got his attention. Sal sounded more awake. "Wait, a sec. I need to get a pen and paper. Give me the plate number and make of the car. I'll ask Brian to do this. He'd never speak to you."

Barry felt his heart race. He was closing in and this could be his big payoff. "Call me right back. It's a gray Subaru and has Mass plates...."

Chapter 42

The drive back to Chatham was excruciating. It was what the year-rounders called *changeover day*. Renters moved in, filling the road with families in cars with beach chairs and bikes on roof racks. To amuse herself, Liza counted the cars towing boats. Five so far. They slowed traffic even more when they tried to make left-hand turns and did not have room to maneuver on the narrow streets. Although incongruent, Liza was nostalgic for the times she went on summer vacations when Sam was a child. Wiping a tear, she recalled the time they rented a cottage on a beach in New Jersey. Sam loved the sand and built amazing sandcastles. Unfortunately, she also remembered how angry Barry got when the summer traffic was bad. He hated vacations. Barry had spent most of the week complaining that he was missing big business deals and was giving up a week to make everyone else happy. He refused to go out for meals because he thought it was a waste of money. Liza wound up cooking and cleaning the entire week. It never was much of a break for her, but watching Sam digging in the sand and running through the waves made it all worthwhile.

Until last summer in Chatham. What a luxurious place. It was part of Barry's bonus for setting up a land deal. Was this friend in the mob? She never asked. Barry would not have paid for a week at such an expensive resort if it weren't subsidized.

It was one of the few fond memories she could recall after so many years of marriage.

A loud honk accompanied by a red-faced man screaming interrupted her thoughts. "Come on, lady. Move it."

She stopped for a yellow light and the guy behind her wanted her to run it. Just making him wait made her feel good. She could do anything she wanted. She was a local, and he was a tourist. "You're a jerk, and everyone hates you," she muttered aloud. She would never be a helpless female again. She was in control and strong. By the time Liza reached the Chatham town line, she had only twenty minutes to make it to work. She was desperate for a shower, a change of clothes, and something to eat. She had not eaten at the restaurant because it was so hectic. Liza laughed because she could never remember missing a meal before she moved to Chatham. This was an unfamiliar experience. No sweat. She could do everything in ten minutes. She shook her head. Who was she kidding? She was going to be late again. Oh well, she did her best. It was a changeover day. Her boss should expect her to be a little late because of the traffic.

When she stepped into the cottage, she headed toward the bedroom and threw her clothes on the floor. Licorice jumped on the pile and began kneading the shirt. Cat hair on her clothes was becoming her signature style. "Okay, enjoy yourself. It's hot and I need to shower." She wrapped a beach towel around herself and ran around the house to the Zen-like outdoor shower. Too bad if the neighbors saw her. Showering outside was a summer ritual at the Cape. Most people did this after a day at the ocean, and she loved the feel of bathing in the open air. It was big enough for two, and best of all, there was no bathroom to clean up.

She showered and dashed into the house, dripping water everywhere. No way would she make it to the store on time. Liza tripped over the cats and her towel went flying as she stopped her fall by catching herself on the side table with her hand. "Damn," she screamed. Luckily, she was okay. "Stop worrying. No one's going to fire you at the beginning of the summer. They're dying for help here. Just get dressed and keep your cool." She used self-talk to calm down and not fall again.

"What's your problem? Ever seen me naked before? Move, you furry idiots." The cats eyed Liza and ignored her outburst. They shifted their weight, rolled over on the fallen clothing, stretched, and left the bedroom.

The place was a mess, but she did not have time to clean. She remembered when she used to be a neat freak and Barry was the slob. "Barry." She shuddered as she spoke his name. "Where the hell are you?" Just thinking about him made her back tense. "Stop. You are in a safe place."

Liza forced a deep breath and tried to relax. She glanced at the cats wandering around the living room. They liked her clothes strewn about and never criticized her. She was in charge here. "Good thing you don't complain, or I'd send you to obedience school."

Liza giggled at the thought as she dressed. She deliberated what was clean and looked presentable enough for the store. She settled on a black skirt, a royal blue shirt, and sandals. A glance in the mirror told her she looked good for a rush job.

She treaded around the playful cats and checked that they had enough water and food for the day. "Bye, guys. See you tonight." No answer. Not even a glance in her direction. She tossed her hair and wondered if she needed different companions. Maybe a dog who would be sad to see her leave. Who was she fooling? She loved her kitties, and Licorice was her faithful companion for years. On the way out, Liza spotted the smelly bag of trash she forgot to take out this morning. She propped the door open, lugged the bag outside, tossed the garbage into the green barrel, and returned to lock up.

She climbed back into the car and headed to town. When the weather was nice, the tourists jammed the beaches, and the town was less crowded. On a rainy day, she had to plan for a twenty-minute ride for the two miles it took to reach the store, and the town was impassable. "Red sky at night, traffic a fright. Red sky in the morning, cars are crawling." She repeated the old rhyme with slightly different words as she headed into town. Lucky for her. Today was a beach day.

Liza parked behind the store and quietly entered through the back door. Mrs. Woods and Lindsay, occupied with customers, barely glanced at her as she sauntered over to a woman in her thirties holding a baby. The baby had red, frizzy hair and was wiggling to get free.

The mom gave Liza an exasperated look. "She's just learning to crawl, pulling to stand, and won't stay in the stroller." The petite, red-haired woman kissed her baby on her cheek. "Her name is April, and she's a handful. So heavy. She weighs twenty pounds." The child gurgled but mom looked exhausted.

Liza chuckled as she remembered those days with Sam. This poor lady looked like she needed a nap.

The woman must have read her mind. "I haven't slept through the night in two weeks. They say it's teeth. But I don't see any new ones coming in." Then she burst into tears. "I need a blouse. With nursing and all, I can't fit into anything."

"Sure, do you want me to hold the baby while you look through this rack of blouses?"

The distressed customer handed the baby to Liza, who cuddled up with the softness. The smell of powder brought memories of the early days with a baby in her arms. April looked at her with soft gray eyes and smiled. Liza admired her beauty. With those eyes and hair, she was going to be a stunner. "Oh, she's so sweet."

"Try two a.m. She sure can scream."

"Do you have help with her?" Liza knew not to assume there was a significant other in anyone's life.

"No, it's just us. My parents have a house in Chatham and invited us for a week. They're not into babies and want her to be quiet all the time. It's rough trying to please them."

Liza was jealous. This woman's parents were lucky to have such an adorable grandchild. She could not wait until Sam got married and had a baby. "Well, let's get you something nice. You have gorgeous hair and will look terrific in this new black jersey. You just need a few new things to pick you up."

"My mom gave me her credit card and carte blanche to buy anything I want. She says I look like I've gained a ton. She thinks I've let myself go."

Unlimited credit card? That was music to her commissioned ears. Besides, Liza already hated the poor woman's heartless parents. She was ready to help this young mother spend their money.

"By the way, my name is Kelly. Thanks for being so nice to us."

"My pleasure." She hoped Sam would find a lovely girl like her. She missed her lady friends and shopping trips. They found three blouses, two dresses, and a pair of shoes that looked fabulous on Kelly. The purchase added up to over a thousand dollars.

After she left, Mrs. Woods came over to the register and scrutinized the receipt. "I know you were late again, but you almost redeemed yourself with this sale. You were lucky today, but you can't always rely on luck, you know."

Liza thought about her life and the twists it had taken. She was counting on luck to keep everything together and prayed it held.

The rest of her shift was uneventful, and she arrived back at the cottage exhausted. After she kicked off her shoes, Liza plopped on the couch. A cat landed next to her, rubbed against her arm, and meowed a greeting. "Oh hi, Zeus. Did you have a nice day? Where's Licorice?" Usually, her cat ran towards her when she came through the door. Her absence was unusual, and Liza groaned as she got off the couch to look for her pet. Momentarily annoyed, she checked her cat's favorite places. Licorice liked to nap on the rug and beds. "Come on, Baby. Where are you?"

She felt her stomach clench. Where was her kitty? Was she sick? She never hid from her. "Hey, Licorice. Come on out." Liza took the treat bag and shook it. Licorice would never ignore the opportunity for an unearned delicacy. The sound brought Zeus running. Begging for a kitty treat, Zeus rubbed Liza's legs. She threw three salmon-flavored crunchies on the carpet and continued to search, but it was futile. No sign of Licorice. Where could she be? Checking the closets and under the beds, she thought she might vomit. Liza remembered taking out the trash and propping the door open for just a few moments. Could the cat have wandered outside, enticed by a small animal running through the yard? She had opened the door like this before and neither cat had ever seemed inclined to leave the cottage.

Liza feared Licorice was gone for good and blamed herself. She left for work in such a rush she had not noticed her kitty leaving. No, no, no. Licorice would not have left the safety of her home. Would she? Making a last-ditch effort, Liza opened a can of tuna. The noise from the can opener and the smell of fish always brought her cats mewing to her feet. Zeus was front and center. Licorice's absence was undeniable. She was not inside or around the cottage. When the realization hit Liza, she cried. She pictured her pet outside and all alone. Did someone run her over? Was she dragged away by a coyote? Licorice was her last tie to New Jersey. Liza had left everything behind, except her cat. Now, no one knew who she was. She was alone.

Liza could not escape this nightmare. She paced the yard, calling her cat's name. Searching everywhere, Liza canvased the neighborhood. A neighbor was hanging beach towels over his deck's railing. "Hi, I'm Liza. Sorry to bother you. I'm looking for a black cat with a white patch on her chest. I think she got out this afternoon. Have you seen her?" Her words jumbled together.

His silence filled the air. Then he looked sad and answered in accented English, "Sorry, no cat."

"If you see her, please let me know. I live over there." She pointed to her cottage and hoped he understood what she was saying.

"Sure. No problem."

No other people were outside, so Liza tramped through Nora's yard. Her neighbor's car was not there, and Liza regretted discouraging intimate friendships. She wished she had gotten closer to her. After another unsuccessful twenty minutes, she headed back to the cottage, called Nora's cell, and left a message. Maybe, just maybe, Licorice went next door. She was doubtful, but held out the slimmest of hopes.

Licorice could be anywhere. So many small animals ran through the woods outside to tempt her. She was probably chasing a squirrel and got lost.

Liza tried to think about what her next steps should be. She needed help to search the area and would forgive Jeff for last night's stand-up. When she called him, he picked up after three rings. "Hi. This is Liza, and I need your help." She could barely get the words out.

"What's wrong? Are you okay? Do you want me to come right over?" He shot questions at her.

"Licorice's missing. I don't even know where to look."

"Oh no. Have you looked outside?" He continued with advice, "Did you check underneath the crawl space of the cottage?"

By now, Liza was sobbing. "Yes. I even used a flashlight to check inside the fireplace. I'm so scared something's happened to her. She's all I have."

Jeff responded in a quiet voice. "Just calm down and I'll be there as soon as I can."

While waiting for Jeff, she continued her search. She knew it was fruitless, but she had to do something. After ten minutes, she gave up and sat on the couch, petting Zeus. He purred and rubbed his head against her hand. Liza talked softly to the big cat with false bravado, "I know you miss her too."

They were on the couch when Jeff bounded through the door. He gave her a big hug. "I know she means everything to you. I promise I'll do everything I can. We'll find her."

"I'm scared. Something bad has happened. I just know it."

She barely got the words out before Jeff interrupted, "Let's call animal control. If anyone finds a stray, they usually call it in."

Although she was terrified of the authorities, this was too important. "She has an implanted tag, but we aren't in New Jersey anymore, so it won't help us."

Jeff took over, making a few calls. "Someone brought a cat in, but it was a tabby. No one reported finding a lost kitty with Licorice's coloring." He left both of their names and contact information in case anyone found her. He turned to Liza. "The best bet is for us to post signs around here and in town. You never know how far she went. Cats can travel five miles in a day."

"Oh no. We'll never find her."

"If you have a picture of her, tomorrow we can head to the local print shop to make a poster.

By nighttime, she was distraught. It was too dark to keep looking, and Liza had visions of Licorice being attacked by coyotes. Liza could do nothing else until morning.

Jeff warmed up a can of soup and brought her a bowl. "You have to eat something."

Sitting on the couch stroking Zeus, Liza was at a loss for words. Zeus snuggled beside her, and she swore the big cat knew something was wrong. He had terrific, comforting instincts. Liza smelled the soup and made a face. "I'm not hungry. Just leave it on the coffee table."

"Do you want me to stay over so we can look early in the morning?"

"I don't know what to do." Liza was exhausted and miserable, knowing Licorice could be anywhere. All she could do was wait and hope her kitty either returned, or someone found her and reported it.

"What do you want me to do?" he repeated.

She wanted him to guess her needs and take charge, but could not tell him. "Shouldn't you go back to the motel? Don't you have guests checking in tonight?"

Jeff was not good at reading her. What she meant was, please stay and keep reassuring her. Unfortunately, Jeff was literal. "You're right. I need to get back. It's a full house tonight. I'll call you in the morning. If you need anything or hear from anyone, please call. Don't worry about the time."

She was not concerned about waking him up. He was such a jerk for leaving her when she was distraught. After she heard his car drive off, she remained on the couch, petting Zeus and crying. "It's gonna be alright. It has to be." Zeus opened one sleepy eye and rolled over.

Too exhausted to stay awake, Liza approached the door one more time and shook the box of treats. "Hi, Honey. Where are you?" The silence was eerie. It was going to be a long, restless night.

Chapter 43

Barry

Barry spent the day at the beach. No luck finding any broads. Mostly moms with little kids and sand toys. Sunburned and drained, he picked up a clam roll for dinner. Wiping his greasy face with his sleeve, he sat on the edge of the bed and willed the phone to ring. It was an entire day, and he had not heard from Sal. He had to find Franny. Barry paced impatiently as he picked up his phone and left another message. "Did you track down that plate? I need that license traced pronto. What's taking your brother so long to find it in the police database? Should be a piece of cake. Remember, your money's riding on this. Call me yesterday."

What a moron. The whole family was dumb. Finishing his sandwich, he threw the wrapping on the floor. He might as well give the cleaners something to do since he was paying the big bucks. Barry lay down to rest his eyes for a few minutes. He would find a bar later and pick up a hot chick. He even had a motel room to take her to. The sheets were relatively clean. It was paradise.

The phone woke him from a glorious dream. He just had his hands around Franny's throat. "Who's calling now?" He glanced at the clock on his way to the dresser where his phone was playing a marimba tune. He hated that song. It was late. "Yeah," he answered. Sal better have the goods.

"Is this Mr. Blackman?" This was not Sal. Who the hell was it?

"I don't want any." No way he was going to speak to a telemarketer.

"No, wait. I have your cat."

Cat? What was this guy talking about? What a great con. He should try it sometime. "Listen jerk face, I don't have...."

The man interrupted him, "My name is Dr. Jasper and I'm at the Beachside Animal Hospital on Route 28 in Chatham. Someone found a black cat with a white patch on her chest. They turned her into the hospital and her collar identified her as Licorice. She has an implanted microchip with your contact information. Is this your cat or what?"

This was better than his dream. Barry remembered he had an outgoing message on his home phone with his cell number. When Franny brought the cat home, she must have put their home phone number on record to call if someone ever found the cat. This guy had Franny's cat right here on old Cape Cod. Franny would do anything to get the meowing piece of fur back.

"Yeah, the little angel is mine. She must have slipped out the door when I was unloading groceries. Can you keep her overnight? My car's acting up and I need to have it checked out before I drive over to get her. Where did you say the person found her?" His voice was butter.

"Someone said they found her off Barn Hill Road and brought her in. It's near Harding's Beach."

Bingo. Franny was nearby, and Barry tasted blood. "Thanks. The garage said they can look at my car first thing in the morning. I can pick her up around noon." Yeah, like he was ever going to pick up that furry dirtball. She could rot in her little cage forever. Tomorrow, he would head to Harding's Beach and find the little wifey.

Barry went back to bed with a smile on his face. *Kill Franny. Kill Franny. Kill Franny.* The phrase went round and round in his head as he nodded off.

Chapter 44

Reaching for Licorice, Liza grimaced. The other side of the bed was empty. Her heart pounded as she remembered what had happened. Zeus, sprawled out on the bedroom rug, gave her a sorrowful look. Licorice was still missing, and she needed to find her today. Where was she?

The clock's time showed eight a.m. and Liza bolted out of bed, trying to decide what to do first. She scanned the pile of clothes on her bedroom chair and selected a pair of almost clean black pants and a blue cotton shirt. They were serviceable, and not too wrinkled. Barry was right. She was turning into a slob. Shuddering at the thought, Liza needed to give herself a break. These counted as extenuating circumstances.

After showering and dressing, she gave Zeus a quick pat and ran outside, calling for Licorice. No answer. Disappointed, she returned and searched the kitchen to see what she could make for a quick breakfast. She was running late and had less than ten minutes to eat. Liza apologized to Zeus, "Hey big guy, looks like we both get cereal this morning. I'm going to be late for work again."

Liza poured a bowl of granola and put dry cat food in Zeus' bowl. "I'm sorry, Baby. I know you must miss your girlfriend." Zeus never looked up, eating with gusto. "So much for cat loyalty," she muttered.

Last night Liza made a poster with a picture of Licorice, including her name, and contact information at the bottom. She had to get to the local office supply store to make copies before work. Luckily, the copy shop opened at nine. She could distribute the signs on the way to town. Just thinking about working upset her, but she had to go in today. It was her turn to restock the shelves. "No, no, no," she yelled. It was inhumane to have to go to the store when her life was in crisis. She hated her boss. Why did she surround herself with mean people? They were everywhere. Considering the problem, Liza decided analyzing her situation would need to wait until another day. She was on a tight schedule.

Liza barely had enough time to put up posters in the coffee shop at the end of the road, on a few phone poles, and in a nearby convenience store with a bulletin board. She was halfway into the village when she realized she had left her cell on the counter. What if someone found Licorice and called? No one was around to answer the phone. Liza lived alone and did not have a spare key hidden anywhere. No way could anyone get into the house, grab her phone, and bring it to her. She was stuck all day without a way to contact anyone.

It would be impossible to drive home at lunch to get it. This time of year, she would never make it through town and back on a half-hour break. Liza sighed. It was going to be a long day. Maybe her boss would let her out early? Magical thinking, Liza. No way out of prison until three-thirty. By the time she crossed the threshold of the store, sweat was pouring down her back. She was stressed, and the day had hardly begun.

Mrs. Woods gave an exaggerated look of displeasure and looked at the clock when she arrived. One minute to spare. The manager pursed her lips but remained silent. It secretly pleased Liza that her boss wanted to reprimand her, but could not.

"Liza, I need you to restock all the beachwear. It's moving fast this time of year."

"Sure." In the back room, she pulled out boxes with bathing suits, cover-ups, and beach shoes. All the bathing suits were supposed to be available in every size and color. The mundane task helped the time go by. By eleven a.m. the store was filling with a steady stream of customers. Lovely, carefree people kept coming in all morning. After she completed her assignments in the back, she headed out to the front to wait on them.

"I need a bathing suit," the first five customers requested.

Didn't anyone ever check their suitcases before coming on a beach vacation, or was this just an excuse to buy a new one? "Sure, we have a great selection." Liza brought at least three into every dressing room and sometimes sold two to the same person.

One pert young woman exited the dressing room in a green bikini. "How do I look?"

"You look lovely in that color." It was true. The twenty-something girl looked terrific.

"Do you think it's too loud?"

"On some people, yes. But not on you. You have the right shape and coloring to carry it off."

The customer looked in the mirror one more time. "I'll take it. It'll look great at the beach party tonight in Orleans."

Liza wondered if Sam would be there. Maybe this beautiful young woman would be her daughter-in-law someday. A ridiculous thought, Liza. Just sell her the suit. "You'll look fabulous."

Finally, it was lunchtime. She looked around furtively, did not see Mrs. Woods anywhere nearby, and broke the rules. She used the store phone to make a quick call to Jeff. Maybe he would break into her cottage through a window and retrieve her phone. It seemed like a reasonable idea. No answer. Liza went into the break room, ate a quick yogurt, and counted the minutes until she could leave. The afternoon dragged on. It was nice weather, and everyone was probably at the beach. She was eager to go home. Now.

Mrs. Woods sensed her restlessness. "Liza, can you stay a few minutes extra to fold the shirts? I know you want the store to look tidy."

Liza rolled her eyes before responding, "Of course." No way was she going to give her the satisfaction of seeing how angry she was.

The boss gave a curt smile and went into the back room. The woman probably was just asking her to stay to show her power.

After refolding fifteen shirts, Liza approached Mrs. Woods. "All done. See you Tuesday." It was almost four, and she needed to get home. Tomorrow was her day off. Thank God or she might kill her.

"Okay. You did well today, Liza. Keep up the excellent work." The woman's phony smile never reached her eyes.

Traffic crawled near Harding's Beach Road, and Liza sped down her dirt lane. She felt sick to her stomach, but ignored it. She was impatient to get to her phone in case someone found Licorice. After parking haphazardly, she unlocked the door and raced into the kitchen, grabbing the phone off the counter. Tears flowed. Only one call from a blocked number and she had no way to return it.

Chapter 45

Barry

After a restless night, Barry grabbed a cup of burned-tasting coffee from the motel office and headed down Route 28 toward Chatham. He turned onto Harding's Beach Road, spotted the poster with Licorice's picture taped onto a phone pole, and got out of the car to make sure it was his cat. He smiled, recognizing his former pet in the mug shot. Franny and the cat would get what they deserve. Best of all, now he had Franny's cell number. She was just a phone call away. He drove up and down the side streets but did not see any sign of her car. He would love to surprise her with a memorable visit. One she would remember until her death. He chortled.

He blocked his number and called from his car. It rang and rang but went to voice mail. "No way am I tipping her off." He left no message.

Barry called the Beachside Animal Hospital. "Hello, this is Barry Blackman. You called last night, and you have my sweet cat."

"Sure. We need you to pick her up. We checked her over, and she seems fine. Please make sure you have her carrier when you get her."

Oh, crap. A carrier? He bet she needed food and a litter box, too. What else would the princess need? This could cost big bucks, but it would all be worth it because Franny would pay. That was the bright spot in this scheme. "I'm in Chatham now and will be over in an hour."

Barry had to keep the cat alive until Franny came to get her, although he would prefer to deliver the ugly hairball right to her door. He chuckled at the thought as he located a hardware store with pet supplies. "Where's the cheapest cat carrier you have?" he asked the man behind the counter.

"Back here. We only have one type." The guy eyed Barry with disdain.

Barry picked up the bare necessities, including a traveling litter box. He would not need the crap for more than a few hours, but he did not want Licorice to pee on his stuff. Once in the car, he carefully folded the receipt. He could return everything and get his money back. He would not even use it for a day.

When Barry arrived at the animal hospital, a cute technician greeted him. She looked hot in her white uniform. "I'm Heather. Come this way, Mr. Blackman. She's right here." She pointed to the cage with Licorice curled up in the back.

When Licorice spotted Barry, she hissed at him. Barry smiled sheepishly. "Oh, Furball. You were a naughty girl to run away. Everything's going to be fine. Daddy's here."

Heather eyed him warily. "Are you sure everything is okay? She seems skittish."

Barry laughed. "No problem. She's my wife's baby and gets jealous sometimes. Isn't that right, Licorice?" He put his fingers through the woven metal and tried to pet the cat, but she arched her back and moved away from him. "Hey. Why don't you put her into the carrier for me? She seems to like you."

Heather eyed him with suspicion, reluctantly opened the little steel door to the cat carrier, and put Licorice inside. When she bent over, Barry tried to look up her skirt. The cat wailed.

The young woman straightened. "You need to pay for the visit and checkup. It'll be two hundred dollars."

"Two hundred..." Barry stopped himself. What thieves. They find your cat and charge a fortune to get her back. It was ransom, but worth every penny. Hell, it was cheaper than a hitman.

After leaving the vet, Barry returned to his motel room and sat on the bed. The cat was in the carrier, wailing. "Shut the hell up!" Licorice cried louder. He could not think with all the noise. He had to get rid of the cat and Franny. Barry gave a menacing grin in the kitty's direction. "Listen, Rat Ball, if you don't calm down, you're dead."

He needed it quiet so he could concentrate on how to convince Franny to come to him. The victory was near. Who could he call? He could not think of anyone else besides Sal, who was still ignoring him. Not only did Sal sell drugs, but he also had a cop brother. What a screwed-up family. Barry dialed a number and Sal answered on the third ring.

"Hey, Sal. I've been calling you all day about the license plate. What's going on?" Barry tried not to sound too eager.

"Oh, Barry. I meant to call you back. What time is it? Who's that yowling?"

Barry ignored his questions. "I figured you were too much of a loser to help me."

Sal whined, "No, I tried. My brother couldn't find the license number."

"Right," Barry replied sarcastically. "You forgot to call him, didn't you?"

"Well...I've been pretty busy," Sal began, but Barry cut him off.

"Listen, forget about the car. I need to hook up with a person who I can trust. No questions asked. You get me?"

"Like, what do you need?" Sal sounded helpful again. He would do anything to placate Barry and get him to pay off his loan.

"Just some stuff. Better you don't know too much," Barry replied. "Do you have a Massachusetts contact or what?"

"I need to know something about the job, so I can pass the information along."

"I need some elimination work done."

Sal hesitated before answering, "Are you stupid? You're not in New Jersey. You could get in big trouble and wind up in jail."

Barry would not take no for an answer. He was so close. "Listen, are you going to help me or what?"

After a few seconds, Sal responded, "Well, some of the good stuff comes from Boston, but our connections are real mean dudes. Barry, trust me, you don't want to get mixed up with them."

Barry did not, but he was impatient. "Get me a Cape Cod contact."

"Me?" Sal stammered.

"Yeah, and you have ten minutes to set it up. I'll even add a hundred bucks on my loan if you get it done right."

Sal repeated, "Barry, don't get mixed up with these guys."

Barry screamed into the phone, "Don't tell me what I want! Just do it." The cat howled even louder. Barry hung up and went outside into the courtyard. He needed some peace. They were all idiots. No one could do anything without screwing up.

Nine minutes later, the phone rang. Barry returned to his room for privacy. The space was unexpectedly quiet. Maybe the cat was dead? He could only hope.

"Hello," Barry answered.

"This Barry?" A man with an accent he could not determine sounded angry.

"Yeah," Barry replied. "Who's this?"

"No names. I got a call from Sal. He says you need a guy on the Cape that can get you anything. Somebody needs to go on a long trip?" He cackled at his own joke.

This was better than Christmas. "Great. How do I get in touch with him?"

"It's gonna cost you."

Barry checked his wallet. He could still get some money out of the bank machine with one of Franny's old debit cards. "How much?"

"Depends on what you need."

Barry hesitated. He knew he had to give this man information if he wanted to complete the deal. "Well...," he began, "I need to keep it neat and clean. No way to trace it to me."

The man waited and calculated aloud. "Hmm. About a thousand bucks should do it."

"Okay." Barry had no choice. This better work. It would practically wipe him out.

"Go to the Main Street Coffee Shop in Yarmouth. My man will meet you in forty minutes. Bring cash."

"How will I know who he is?"

"Don't worry. I already sent your picture to him. The internet is a beautiful thing. No?" The laughter on the other end gave Barry the chills. If he did not need to do this today, he would hang up and try to find another solution. However, he had limited time to get Franny to meet him and he could not stand having Licorice around any longer.

"No problem," Barry answered with false bravado.

"Don't be late. Time is money." The phone went dead.

Barry sat on the edge of the bed with his head in his hands. What had he done? For the first time, he was terrified. These guys were bad. He knew he had to be careful. He said to the restless cat, "I can take care of myself. It'll work out when she's dead. I'll inherit the house and her life insurance and will find a great place to start over. Somewhere with hot chicks in bikinis."

It was five p.m. He called Franny again. This time, she answered.

Chapter 46

Liza willed the phone to ring. When it finally happened, she was thrilled, anticipating it might be a call about Licorice. "Hello?" When there was no response, she repeated, "Hello." The silence on the other end was ominous. Then she heard a throat clearing. "Who's this?" Because it was from a blocked number, she was cautiously optimistic. If it was a telemarketer, they would not be happy with her next words.

"Well, well, well, Franny. It's lovely to hear your voice." His mockery was sickening.

"Barry?" Her heart pounded, and she felt a cold sweat run down her back, recognizing the familiar malevolence.

"Yes, Franny or Liza or whatever you're calling yourself today, it's me. So, how're you doing? I've been eager to find you." Barry sounded both calm and menacing.

"What do you want?"

"Well now. That's not polite. I've been worried about you. How've you been?" he laughed.

Barry never changed. He was vile. "Yeah, sure Barry. You have thirty seconds to tell me why you're calling before I hang up."

"Have it your way. You always did," he replied coldly.

Liza counted aloud, and when she almost reached ten, she moved her finger to end the call. Barry's next words startled her.

"Well, Wifey. You always wanted everything fast, so I'll give it to you straight. I've got Licorice. Your *lost cat* posters were so helpful. Thanks for your phone number."

She could not believe it. "What?" she stammered, as bile rose in her throat. How could this have happened? She prayed the cat was unharmed.

"Yup, your little kitty is right here. Meow for her, Girl."

Liza identified the wail in the background. It was Licorice. "What do you want?" she snapped, both furious and scared. He was on Cape Cod and had her cat. Things could not get much worse.

"Now you're talking, Love. We're going to meet, and I'll give the little furry rat back to you. Oh, and you know how much I love her. I wonder how she'd look with a flaming tail."

His icy laughter unnerved her, and Liza trembled. She willed herself to remain calm. Barry was trying to rattle her, and he was succeeding. She needed to show him she was not the same scared mouse who ran away from New Jersey a few months ago. She hardened her tone. "What will it cost?" It was always going to be about money. She knew him too well for it to be anything else.

Sure enough, he replied, "Just a divorce and you walk away and never see me again. I get the house, the trusts, and all the joint bank accounts. You'll be free of me. Isn't that what you always wanted?"

Liza tried to think of her next move. She kept quiet, stalling for time to figure out how to manage things. She was not stupid and knew he would never let her walk away. No matter what he promised, he was a liar. He would kill her and her kitty, and what she did next could mean life or death. For both of them.

Barry continued, "I expect you at the Restful Sea Motel in two hours. It's in Yarmouth on Route 28. Should be easy to find. Your cat is getting extremely hungry, and I'd love to play with her some more...."

"Wait," Liza responded sharply. No way was she meeting him alone in a motel room.

"What's the problem? Don't you trust me?"

She rolled her eyes. "Barry, let's act civilized. I know what you want. Money. If you want an easy divorce and a large settlement, you need to meet me on my terms. I'll see you at seven p.m. at the Lobster Roll in Yarmouth. It's also on Route 28, not too far from your motel." She knew she might risk Licorice's life, but it was the best she could think of on such short notice. At least it was a public place, and she had friends there.

He waited a few seconds before replying, "Okay, you win. The Lobster Roll at seven p.m. Don't be late or you'll never see your little princess again."

While he was threatening her, Liza could hear the cat hissing in the background. Poor Licorice. She understood how her kitty felt. "My cat better be alive and well or you'll be sorry." With that, she disconnected.

Zeus rubbed his back against her legs and looked at her with slitted eyes. She swore his expression was almost human. She told the cat, "I'm sorry about leaving Licorice with him, but it's the only way to get her back. Everything will be okay. I promise." The big cat closed his eyes and lay near her feet.

Liza dialed Jeff. No answer. She left a message. "Please come to the Lobster Roll at seven tonight. Don't be late. Barry's got Licorice, and he's planning to kill both of us. I need help. Bring your friends." She knew she sounded unhinged, but she was frantic, and Jeff misinterpreted subtleties. The voicemail was straightforward, and she prayed he would listen to his messages and meet her at the restaurant. Otherwise...

Chapter 47

Barry

Barry was furious. He took a deep breath, snarled, and thought about meeting Franny at the restaurant and killing her without getting caught. Barry knew how stubborn Franny could be, and he did not want to blow it when he was so close. Chuckling, as it came to him, he would hold the cat back in his room for an exchange. Franny would not want the cat to sit in a hot car too long. It just could work. She was so gullible about her stupid pet.

First things first. He needed a clean weapon so he could eliminate his lovely wife. Sal's contact better show up with the goods. Barry got in the car and drove to the meeting place at the Main Street Coffee Shop. If he hurried, he would make it on time. Time was money, his. He parked two blocks down the street from the café and walked. He hoped the guy would not get his license number that way.

On the way, he passed a branch of a bank that held joint accounts for Franny and Sam. He gained entrance by inserting Franny's debit card, the one she left in their dresser at home. Her code was a joke. He entered Sam's birthdate and continued the transaction. Barry prayed this old account had enough money for the deal. He held his breath and exhaled when it worked. The account held just enough dough, and he had the cash in less than three minutes. He put the cash in a plastic grocery bag and sauntered towards the restaurant.

When Barry reached the address for the meeting, he opened the door and scanned the restaurant. The place was empty. *What the hell?* His plan was dead if this guy did not show. He ordered coffee at the counter and sat in a booth.

A burly man entered, dressed in black, and despite the heat, wore a hoodie that mostly covered his face. He sat at the adjacent booth with his back against Barry's. "You Barry?" The guy's voice was raspy, almost inaudible.

"Yeah," Barry could barely get the words out. He tried to turn to get a look at the man.

"Don't even think about it."

Barry wanted to run from the room. This guy was scary. "Sorry."

"Boss says you need something to help a friend sleep?"

Barry smiled. One way of putting it. "Yeah, for a long time."

"First, I need something from you."

Barry passed the plastic bag with the money behind his back. It felt like an hour waiting for the man to count the cash. "Everything alright?" Barry's stomach hurt and his palms were slippery. Although Barry tried to act tough, he was not used to anything like this.

The man replied, "This should work. A heavy dose of insulin. Not traced on most autopsies. Stay for five minutes and relax. Don't open your package. Understand?"

Barry nodded. He felt the paper bag land in his lap. The man must have slipped it over the top of the booth. Barry turned his head. The guy was gone.

Barry wiped his hands on his pants, checked his watch, remained in his seat for five minutes, paid for his coffee, and returned to his car.

When he got back to the motel room, he dumped the contents of the bag onto the grimy bedspread. A sealed *EpiPen* box fell out. Barry lifted and shook it. It felt like the real thing. He removed the legitimate *EpiPen* that he always carried in his inside jacket pocket and replaced it with the phony one. Franny would expect him to have the medicine on him, as he almost died from eating lobster when he last vacationed on Cape Cod.

The room was roasting, and the business deal exhausted him. He glanced out the window and saw a hot blonde in the parking lot. Too bad she would have to wait until later. Barry grinned, stripped off his clothes, climbed into bed, and passed out. When he woke at six p.m., the place was silent, except for the whimpering cat. He growled at her. "Shut up, you monster. I should have ended your miserable life years ago."

He rushed to get dressed. The heap of clothes on the floor was all he had left to wear. Barry dressed in jeans, his last almost-clean shirt, and the navy blazer with the hidden weapon. He admired himself in the chipped mirror over the dresser. "I look fantastic." He whistled at his reflection.

Barry went over to the metal cage and sneered at the cat, half-asleep from the heat and exhaustion. "Just a little longer, and you'll be out of here for good. Enjoy a little time alone, Mouse Breath." He was not about to feed her because she would be dead soon. He assumed he would have enough insulin leftover from Franny's demise to shut the cat up for good. It was time to meet his not-so-perfect wife.

The fist pounding on the door startled him. Who the hell was pestering him now? It must be the stupid manager coming to fix the air conditioner. He did not have time for this. He yelled, "I'm busy. Come back later."

The hammering increased, and Barry was furious. "What's the matter with you? What don't you understand? Leave me alone." That should take care of it.

The door splintering open made him back into the corner. "What the actual hell?"

"Hello, again." The man from the diner in the hooded jacket stood before him. Although Barry never got a good look at his face, he recognized the voice.

He tried to bluff. "What do you want? How did you find me?" Barry's voice was wobbly, and he felt a trickle of urine down his leg. This would not end well unless he got the upper hand.

"Following you to this dump was not spy movie material. You've pissed off some of my friends." The man glared at him.

"I didn't mean to offend you. What did I do?" Barry put his arms out in a friendly gesture.

"First, I don't like people who mistreat animals."

"Is this about Licorice? You can have her." Barry motioned to the cage on the floor.

The man chortled. "You don't get it, do you?"

"I'll do anything. Please don't hurt me."

"Now, that's more like it." The intruder shoved a pile of papers at Barry and barked, "Sign these."

"I haven't read them yet." This was unreal. What did this guy want?

Tapping his boot on the floor, the man looked at his watch. "You have exactly five minutes. I hope you learned to speed-read in school."

Barry stared at the thick packet of forms, with a summary sheet on top. They were for a divorce and included a statement of facts signing over his share of the house, all the bank accounts, and joint assets to Franny. The papers were pre-witnessed and notarized. "I can't sign these."

"No problem." The man removed a knife from a sheaf on his waistband and cleaned his fingernails.

"You're asking me to do this under duress. It'll never stand up in court."

"Are you an idiot? You want the judge to know about the death threats, stalking, and kidnapping of your wife's cat?" He pulled out his phone. "I have it all recorded here."

Barry gasped and tried to stall. "How do you know I'm married?"

The man rolled his eyes. "After you set up the meeting, I called my buddy. Your wife has lots of friends around here. One of them knows a hotshot divorce lawyer in Brewster. She drew up these papers and dropped them off. They're all legal and everything...in case you were thinking of welching out."

The bed creaked as Barry sat down hard. This was not going the way he expected. Who was this guy, and did he really know Franny? He begrudgingly had to admit his wife was not the same woman who cowered in the living room six months ago.

The tip of the knife came perilously close to his neck. "Well? What do you want to do?"

Barry pulled out a pen and signed. All his hard work for nothing. "Anything else?"

"I never thought you'd ask. Drive to the restaurant, return the cat, give your wife the papers, and say goodbye. This is your choice. You can disappear on your own...or I can help you vanish. For good."

Barry understood what the man meant. He'd tell his boss it was an emergency and get an advance from work. Barry would use it to help him move somewhere where neither Franny nor her friends would ever find him. He nodded and grabbed the carrier. Licorice was awake and howling. "You sure you don't want the cat? She's a perfect companion."

The tip of the knife shut him up and Barry put the packet inside his blazer, headed to his car, and hoisted the cage onto the back seat. It was not until he pulled in front of the Lobster Roll that he stopped shaking. He was not too late and the bogus *EpiPen* box was still in his pocket. If he acted fast, he could still kill Franny. Who would believe a bunch of thugs from Cape Cod? He was a respected business executive.

The delicious blonde hostess smiled at Barry, and he thought about pinching her. When he reached for her bottom, the woman glared at him. Chagrined, Barry headed to one of the red vinyl-covered stools at the counter and faced the door. His perch was ideal, and it gave him a splendid view to watch for Franny. She was late, as usual. A server with a tight tee approached. "What'll you have? Can I interest you in our special chowder?"

When did he last eat? He could not remember. "Is your chowder made from real clams? Not those frozen strips?" He loved good chowder.

"Yes, sir," she answered. "Fresh clams every day. Our soup's so special because we even put in...."

Barry cut her off. He had no time for conversation. "Just bring me a cup. Make it fast. I'm meeting a friend to finish some business."

Chastised, the server turned around and rolled her eyes. Another tourist. She walked into the kitchen and finished her sentence, "We even put in fresh lobster." Barry never heard her.

Chapter 48

No word from Jeff. Liza frantically called, left messages, sent emails, and texted. Almost giving up, she called Bonnie. When her friend answered on the first ring, Liza began talking without the usual social pleasantries. "You won't believe this. My revolting husband, Barry, is on Cape Cod, and he's kidnapped Licorice."

"What?" she replied. "How did he find you?"

"I'm not sure. I've been so careful. He's extremely dangerous. He wanted to meet me in his motel room, but I insisted on the restaurant. I'm so sorry to get you involved."

"What can I do to help?"

"I can't see him alone. Can you get friends for backup?"

"Don't worry. My staff will be here, and we'll look out for you. If he even crosses his eyes, I'll call the cops. Most of them are regular customers."

Liza put on a black shirt and capris. Her stomach lurched and her hands shook. Zeus was sleeping on the couch, and she gave him a quick hug. He rolled onto his back for a belly rub, purring loudly. "Hey, Zeus. You're such a good boy. Licorice will be home soon." It felt better to say it aloud. Liza wanted to believe her own words.

She fought off a sense of panic. What if something happened to her or both her and Licorice? Nope. She could not think like that. Barry threatened, but would he really hurt them? She shivered at the thought and climbed into the car. The reality that she might drive to her death left a cold sweat running down her back.

Traffic went ahead at a slow crawl, and Liza thought she would never get there. She wanted to be early, to have time to cover all the details. At a stoplight, Liza tried Jeff's phone again. Still no answer. Where the hell was he? She left another message. "Hi, Jeff. This is Liza again. It's an emergency. Meet me at the Lobster Roll at seven. Barry's gonna be there. I need help." Wiping tears from her face, she tried to be brave. Not since she first arrived on the Cape had she felt so hopeless or alone.

Liza arrived at the restaurant a little later than she hoped, still optimistic she would beat Barry to the rendezvous. No such luck. When Liza peered through the front window, she saw him seated at the counter. Despite the weather, she shivered. This was it. She watched him gaze at a cup of soup in front of him, calmly adding oyster crackers. He dipped his spoon into the cup. She gasped, and he must have heard her because he looked out the window and smiled. A stone-cold smile.

She muttered, "Stop thinking like Franny. Franny is gone for good. You can do this." She yanked the door open and strode in. "Hello, Barry." She forced her voice to remain calm.

He rested his spoon on the counter and smirked, "Well, well, Franny. So happy you could make it. I bet poor Licorice will be glad to spend eternity with you." Liza remained silent, and he continued, "Why don't you sit down and have a nice dinner with me?"

"I'd rather eat poison," she retorted with false bravado. All she wanted was to find her kitty and get away from this demon. "Where's my cat?"

"Oh Franny, I'm so pleased to see you. Why so hostile?" His laughter sent chills down her spine.

"Be right back. Don't choke." She sprinted to the kitchen to find Bonnie. No way was she going to confront him without witnesses.

Bonnie was stacking plates of food on a serving tray. She lifted the tray off the counter and headed toward Liza, who was standing at the swinging door. "Is everything okay?"

"Hey, I need you," Liza whispered. She did not want to take a chance that Barry might hear her.

"No problem. Mike and Laura will be out right behind me. I told them you're confronting the world's meanest bully and they're ready to help."

Liza nodded. Mike was a big guy and had been a cook there for years. Laura was tough. She never let the customers get away with anything. They moved closer to the door.

"No one's going to let you go back in there alone." Laura crossed her arms.

When they single-filed through the doorway into the dining area, Liza heard a woman's voice yelling, "Call 9-1-1."

"Got it," answered another.

People crowded around the counter, and Barry was on the floor. What happened? The next few minutes moved in slow motion. Barry was struggling for air. Liza saw what he had eaten and knew what had happened. "Oh my God," she screamed. "I bet he ate the chowder made with lobster. He's allergic. He usually keeps an *EpiPen* in the car."

A woman in a red dress reached into her purse and rushed toward them. I carry an *EpiPen*. I'm allergic to peanuts. She held it out to Liza.

Barry gasped, "Help me." Liza had a choice. She could save his life or let him die. No matter what, she would have to live with the consequences. Liza grabbed the woman's pen and shoved it into his thigh. When Liza put her ear next to his mouth, she could hear his breathing was less labored.

Barry begged, "Help me."

At that moment, three EMTs pushed through the door and the crowd dispersed to let them near the patient. Two strapping men put Barry onto a stretcher. The taller of the two said, "How do you know this guy?"

"He's my husband." The words sounded brittle to her. Already she wondered why she saved him.

When the two men carried Barry off to the ambulance, the third walked over to Liza. "We'll be taking him to Cape Cod General. You can meet us at the ER."

Liza gathered her things to follow the ambulance. Jeff arrived in the middle of the commotion and ran over to her. "Oh my God, what happened? Are you hurt?" Liza collapsed into his arms while he murmured, "I'm so sorry I'm late. I was on a boat and couldn't get back any sooner."

The next few moments were a blur. One minute she was terrified and the next she held onto Jeff, sobbing. "Barry had an allergic reaction to lobster, but he's alive. I don't know where Licorice is." Liza was close to hysterical.

Jeff looked at her and promised, "I swear I'll make it up to you. You'll see, it's all going to be okay. You're safe now."

"I need my kitty. How are we ever going to find her?" Liza was frantic. She did not want to go to the hospital, but could not leave Barry alone. "I don't know what to do."

Jeff grimaced. "First things first. Let's check Barry's car. You said he was planning to return the cat tonight. Then we can worry about your, er...husband."

Liza ran into the parking lot and located Barry's car unlocked. Spotting the cage on the back seat, she found her cat curled up and limp. "Oh, my God. She's dead," she screamed.

"Whoa, Honey. Remember about nine lives and all?" Jeff opened the back door, removed Licorice from the cage, and handed the cat to Liza.

Liza felt the cat's heartbeat next to her chest. "She's alive."

"Let's get her some water and I'll call a vet friend of Doc's to meet us at the hospital parking lot."

"Do you know everyone on Cape Cod?"

"If they fish, I probably do." Jeff had his arm around her.

"What should I do? I need to make sure Barry's okay, but I don't want to leave Licorice."

"We can drive over together, and I'll stay with the cat and watch the vet check her out. Bonnie can get the cat some food and water to go."

"Already done." Bonnie's voice behind them brought a smile from Jeff. She had a bowl of water and a covered plate with cooked chicken.

Liza felt hot tears on her cheeks. "I love you guys. How can I ever thank you?"

"Just make sure you're okay, too." Bonnie gave her a brusque hug.

The emergency room was chaotic, but Liza located Barry in one of the small rooms behind the check-in desk. When she reached him, a large man in a hooded sweatshirt was slipping out the back of the curtained room. Liza did not see his face, but thought he looked familiar. They propped Barry up on pillows and he sipped from a glass of ice water. Liza approached. "Hello, Barry. How are you and who was your friend?"

Barry looked cowed. "Just someone. Not important."

Liza struggled to speak. "Why did…?"

Barry smiled. "Cat got your tongue?"

Just thinking about poor Licorice infuriated her. "How could you?"

"After today, you will never have to think of me again. I had a guy I know bring me some papers. You can have a divorce and the house."

"Why now?"

"Just say I'm feeling generous after you saved my life." He handed her the manila envelope with the papers he had signed earlier. "I can't wait to leave this dune. It was the worst vacation of my life."

Liza suspected he was lying, but took the packet and glanced inside. The divorce settlement was on top, and she gasped in pleasure. She wondered if Jeff or one of his many fishing buddies had something to do with this. "What now?"

"You go your way and I'll go mine. I expect we won't be seeing each other again."

Liza did not care what he said. She was almost free. She turned her head when the hooded man returned.

"Everything all set?" he asked. The look he gave Barry was chilling.

"Sure, Buddy. I gave Liza her papers and plan to skip this hellhole as soon as they release me."

The man nodded and stared at Liza. "Need anything else?"

Liza clutched the envelope to her chest and slipped out of the small room. She would have a long conversation with Jeff later. No way would Barry have signed divorce and settlement papers without a court order.

By the time she reached the car, the vet was still with Licorice. The cat was drinking from a bowl in the back seat of Jeff's car, and they were sharing fishing stories.

"How's my baby?" Liza interrupted them.

"She's tough as nails. Going to be just fine. A bit dehydrated, that's all. Lucky for her, she's a desert animal and will bounce back from this."

It took many hours and a lot of comforting back at the cottage before Licorice forgave Liza. Although endless treats, belly rubs, and wet food helped. By bedtime, Zeus and Licorice cuddled together on the couch, and looked like they were never apart. Licorice did not hold a grudge and seemed to forget that Liza had abandoned her. Later, the cats crawled into bed with her and Jeff. Things were back to normal.

Chapter 49

Barry

After being discharged from the hospital, Barry called a taxi to take him back to the restaurant to pick up his car. Although he hated paying for a ride, there was no one else he could call. Sam did not have a car and explaining everything to his son would be too difficult. Shuddering at the memory of the hooded man, Barry was glad that was over. He never wanted to see anyone else on Cape Cod as long as he lived.

Driving to the motel, the sight of another traffic jam in paradise enraged Barry. He needed to find a place with more opportunities. Las Vegas. He always loved gambling and entertainment. He would drive to New Jersey, pick up his stuff, and head out west. Maybe Sam would come to visit him when he moved, and he could show him some action. He would make sure the kid would keep his mouth shut so no one would ever find him in Vegas. Goodbye to the men he owed money and good riddance to Franny forever. Yes, that would be great. He never spotted the gray truck tailing him as he pulled into the motel parking lot.

Barry entered his motel room and rejoiced that it was silent. There was no stupid cat to bother him. If only the air conditioning worked, he could get a decent night's sleep. However, he did not want to alert the manager to the damaged door. It closed, although not as securely. Given the filth and broken air conditioner, he would slip out early, before anyone noticed. Tomorrow was going to be fine. Lots of luscious babes in Las Vegas. He could start all over again. He smiled at his brilliant plan.

The next morning, Barry awoke, still in his clothes. Might as well forget the stale donuts. He could almost taste the endless buffets with delicious food in Las Vegas. He could double his money at the craps table. Yes, it was going to be a new adventure. He looked at the sky. Today was another not-so-perfect day on Cape Cod. Blue skies and fluffy clouds. He grabbed the rest of his stuff from the stifling room, packed his car, and peeled out of the parking lot. *Adios* to this sandbox.

Chapter 50

The man in the hooded sweatshirt tipped his hat as Barry snuck out of his room at seven a.m. He was sure Barry never saw him, and he laughed at the ruse. Jeff was right. The guy was as dumb as a bag of rocks and just as predictable.

Jeff arrived in his truck and joined Doc and Rocky in the parking lot. Juggling three paper cups of coffee and a bag of donuts, he smiled at his friends. "You guys were great. How did you find out Barry was planning to kill Liza?"

Doc grinned. "The owner of the café, Amos, is one of my fishing buddies. Barry's friend Sal contacted Amos to get Barry a weapon. When Amos and I were out on the boat, Amos bragged about a deal he made with a guy from New Jersey. He said he was supposed to provide a weapon to kill a loser's wife named Franny. Liza slipped and told me her name was Franny when I fixed up her hand. Since the description of the woman's situation sounded exactly like Liza's, I contacted Rocky, and we made a plan. We had to split the money Barry paid me with Amos, so he'd let us take over the deal. To make sure you couldn't get implicated, we arranged an all-day fishing trip for you."

"You guys put yourselves out for Liza and me." Jeff hit Rocky on the arm and continued, "I also can't believe you scared Barry off."

"He was a frightened bully. My favorite kind. Let's fix the door and get out of here."

"Yeah. I don't want the motel manager to track Barry down for repair money," Doc added.

The three men worked in silence, substituting a new door for the splintered one. "This place looks better than the rest of the units." Jeff admired their handiwork.

"Maybe this will give your motel some competition." Doc laughed.

Rocky handed Jeff a paper bag. "This is the rest of the cash. It's for Liza. I bet the worm stole it from her."

"She's going to be thrilled. Thanks, guys. We owe you big time."

All three returned to Pilgrim's Landing, and Jeff was at peace. Compared to the place Barry stayed, his place looked impressive. He worked hard to maintain the grounds, complete with gigantic blue and white hydrangea blossoms surrounding the garden. Next winter, he would redecorate the rest of the rooms and redo the front office. Until he collected the money from this summer's tourists, the old-fashioned Americana décor would have to do.

The men seated on the plaid chairs in Jeff's office helped themselves to the plate of cookies Jeff put out for his guests. Rocky said, "We were lucky. If we hadn't intervened, Barry would have murdered Liza."

Doc agreed. "That's why I set up the sting. I thought it was an amusing touch when you had Charlie get the divorce and settlement papers pre-notarized at the motel. All you needed was Barry's signature."

Rocky sipped the last of his coffee. "Charlie's a brilliant lawyer and a loyal friend. When I told her what was happening, she was glad to bend the rules but wanted the actual documents to be nice and legal. I never laughed so hard when she showed up in short shorts and a tight tank. Barry was so busy staring at her, he never noticed she was handing over a large packet of papers to me."

The friends sat in silence. No one had gotten hurt, and Barry was out of Liza's hair forever. Jeff said, "I don't know what I'd have done if anything happened to Liza. She's an amazing lady."

"Doc smiled. "That's what friends do. Playing a tough guy was a lot of fun. I scared the crap out of Barry."

Jeff turned to Doc. "What was in the *EpiPen* box, anyway? I never asked."

"You mean the one Rocky sold him? Nothing but an old marker from my house." Doc snickered. "I figured the guy would be too stupid to even check the box. It was a good thing that the woman at the restaurant had a genuine *EpiPen* with her. Otherwise, Barry might have died."

Jeff stared at his friend. "Remind me to never play high-stakes poker with either of you. You guys can bluff."

"Let's go see that girlfriend of yours and make sure everything's okay." Doc headed towards the door.

Chapter 51

The next day, Licorice was back to normal. She was eating, drinking, and displaying her usual antics.

Jeff moved a lock of hair off Liza's face and asked, "Are you okay?"

"Not really, but I'm getting there. I'm still processing what happened. When I had the chance to kill the bastard, I didn't. I'm wondering why."

Jeff touched her arm. "Because you're a good person, and despite Barry being a sociopath, you'd never harm him. That's why I love you."

Upon this declaration, Jeff took Liza's hand and led her into the bedroom. Liza knew things were different.

He looked at the jumble of covers and cats. "A bit crowded, don't you think?" Licorice and Zeus were in bed with them, and the sheets and blankets were in disarray.

After an intimate breakfast of bagels and lox, Liza picked up her phone. "I need to call Sam."

"What are you going to say?"

"I don't know, but I'll figure it out. I have to tell him about his father."

She dialed. "Hi, Sam."

"Mom? Is that you?" He sounded excited.

"Yeah, Sweetheart. I've missed you so much."

"Where've you been? Why did you leave us? Where are you?"

So many questions, most unanswerable. "Listen, Honey, there's too much to discuss on the phone. I'm on Cape Cod and I heard you were, too. Where are you staying? How about I come and pick you up?" She was glad he did not challenge how she knew he was here.

"Does Dad know where you are? He's on the Cape, too."

Liza guffawed. She figured Barry had left as quickly as he could, but this was not the time or place to have that conversation. Jeff went back to the motel to give them time alone. She drove to the Blueberry Street Inn and brought Sam back to the cottage. After Sam explored the rooms and played with Licorice and Zeus, they sat in the living room.

"Who's the new cat?" he asked.

"I'm cat-sitting for a friend. His name is Zeus, and he's a love." Funny way to start this conversation.

"Wow, this is a fabulous place. How did you find it?"

"It's part of the cat-sitting arrangement. It feels like home." This got a quick response. Small talk was over.

"Why'd you leave us, Mom? Dad and I were worried sick about you. He was trying to find you. I thought you were dead." His voice was shaky.

This was rougher than she expected. "Sam, I've been living here since I left New Jersey. I needed a breather from everything."

"Even me? Why didn't you call?"

"I never wanted a break from you. I love you." She did not want to trash Barry, but Sam was old enough to know the truth. Maybe a sanitized version, but she needed Sam to understand what had happened. "I'm sorry we didn't talk about this before, but I needed to get away. It had nothing to do with you. I didn't want you to worry, but I had no choice."

"What do you mean, get away? Why?"

Liza gulped her coffee. "Sammy, remember when Dad and I used to argue a lot?"

He nodded. "When I was little, I thought you guys were mad at me. I hid in my room."

"Dad used to hurt me. He was getting more violent, and after you left, things got worse. I had no other options but to leave."

"How come you didn't tell me?"

"I didn't want you to hate your father."

"Do you think I'm like him?" Sam looked sick to his stomach.

"Of course not, Honey. You're a great guy. Have you ever even yelled at one of your girlfriends?"

"No. I'm so sorry, Mom. I kind of knew what was going on. I wish I had stopped him."

"You couldn't have done anything to stop him. It was between your father and me. Dad and I met last night, and we agreed to a divorce. We won't be in contact with each other, and neither of us will go back to New Jersey to live." She omitted the fact that the papers were pre-signed, and Jeff and his friends made sure Barry understood he had to disappear. "This is the best for all of us."

"What about the house?"

"I'm going to hang onto the house until you graduate from college and decide where you want to live. I'll rent it out for now. You'll be part of any decision I make."

Sam had tears in his eyes, and she hugged him. He had gotten so slim, and she could feel his ribs through his shirt.

Although it seemed like hours, it was only minutes before Liza could continue the conversation.

Sam asked, "So, where's Dad now?"

"I'm not sure. When we met for dinner, Dad had an allergic reaction to lobster and went into shock. I revived him with an *EpiPen*, and the EMTs rushed him to the hospital. We discussed the situation and decided it was time for us to split up. Later, he went back to his motel room. I'm sure he'll call you soon."

"I love you, Mom." Sam clung to her, and she knew everything was going to be all right. It would just take time.

Chapter 52

The conversation with Sam and the events of the weekend were exhausting. Liza called Rebecca at Cape Cod Summer and offered to exchange her shift for another later in the week. The young woman agreed, and Liza found herself with an afternoon off. It was summer, and she needed a beach day. This seemed like a perfect way to spend time.

Liza put on her new bathing suit and cover-up and glanced at the mirror. She had lost a significant amount of weight and was looking great. So much had happened over the past few months, and she never expected to feel good about herself again.

After loading a beach chair, a towel, two books, a bottle of water, and snacks into the trunk of her car, Liza headed to Harding's Beach. It was a weekday, and the parking lot was not too full. She parked at the second beach and walked to the left of the lifeguard chair. The tourists were more spread out. With unobstructed views of Harding's Light and the waves crashing on the sand, Liza felt tears in her eyes. She had finally made it. She was in one of the most beautiful places on earth.

A warm hand on her back startled her, and Liza turned to find Jeff. He unfolded a large plaid blanket and spread it on the sand. "Hi, Darling. I thought I'd find you here."

"Why?"

"It's a perfect day and your car was not in the driveway. I took a quick run down to the store and spoke to a lovely young lady. She told me you were not coming in. Where else could you be?"

"Maybe I had a hot date." Liza's eyes twinkled.

"You do. Come join me." He eyed her approvingly as she slid off her beach chair onto the blanket. "Now, this is more like it."

"What about the motel? Don't you have to work today?"

"I will always have time for this. I promise."

Liza took his hand and understood he meant it. She was safe. She was home.

Acknowledgments

It took extraordinary efforts, help, and friendship for me to finish Liza's Secrets, and end up with an actual book. My writing group, beta readers, husband, and friends gave generously of their time and ideas and supported me every step of the way.

In the early 2000's, I took Paul Kemprecos' writing class on Cape Cod and dreamed of writing a novel. Years later, I brought my notebook of story beginnings to a writing seminar and met a group of women who would change my life forever. We met over coffee and lunch from 2007 until 2020 and read our pieces, celebrated successes, and mourned over losses. Thank you to Barb I and Pat for their early reads with careful critiques, edits, and suggestions. Also, to Carol, Nikole, and Jerri for cheering Liza Kasner to a happy ending and listening to my original manuscript. Special kudos to the rest of the group for staying together three-times a week with on-line gatherings. I never could have made it through the pandemic without you. Acclaim to Catherine, my partner in crime and legal guru, and Barb II, who was inspirational and willing to share writing and publishing tips. I want to complement Anita, who never forgot a character or plot line, and Yvonne, a fellow Black Rose Writing author. Special thanks to my late friend Joan, Liza's first editor and champion.

My early beta readers Carol, Linda, Monique, Ed, Elaine, Mariann, and Chris helped me improve my writing. They made sure the characters were authentic, and the plot was believable. Over the years, between my first draft and publication, I edited, re-edited, and rewrote most of the novel based on their feedback. Thanks to my latest group of beta readers, Kerry, Barb II, Catherine, Linda, Peggy, and Deborah who read my final draft and gave me the confidence and help to complete my book. I would also like to give a shout out to my fellow Black Rose Writing authors, Karen, Lucille, Marie, Trey, Lee Anne, Laurel, and Caroline for their suggestions and reviews.

Commendations to Black Rose Writing, and Reagan's hardworking team. I have learned so much from all your suggestions. I am proud to be one of your family. From my first encounter with you, you guided me and made me a better writer.

To my Cape Cod and Boston area friends, thanks for your support and encouragement all these years. Sometimes pushing me to find a publisher was the last thing I wanted to hear, but it paid off. Cape Cod is a unique place and I want to commend the independent bookstores that thrive here and support writers.

Gratitude to my storytelling late brother Ray and my sister-in-law Linda. She was an avid first reader with critiques, friendship, and support. Special acknowledgments to my author brother Joseph for teaching me the ropes and his sage advice on publishing, marketing, and social media. You all validated my work and helped me through this voyage.

My daughter Miriam constantly tells me I flunked retirement. She is correct. I have many more Liza Kasner stories to share with the world. Gratitude to my son-in-law Nate for contract advice, my son Nathan for sharing the business side of the art world, and his partner Nicole for marketing ideas.

No acknowledgments would be complete without mentioning all the cats that have graced my life. From ones long gone, to my sweet tabby who is watching me type, I am grateful for your companionship, entertainment, and trust.

And not last nor least, to my husband of over 50 years, Bill. He has been with me every step of the way and has always made sure I had the space, technology, help, and love to write my stories. Thanks for the journey.

About the Author

Iris has an infinite curiosity about seemingly routine interactions in her world. Even an ordinary woman sunning on the beach can inspire a story. When not removing green paint from her cat's paws, Iris is painting landscapes, singing, and crafting her Liza Kasner suspense/mystery books. Iris is a retired, international presenter on bullying prevention and an occupational therapy educator. She lives with her husband on Cape Cod. There she finds inspiration in the gardens, endless beaches, and sand dunes on one of the most stunning places on earth.

Readers can contact Iris at www.IrisGLeigh.com

Note from Iris Glazner Leigh

Word-of-mouth is crucial for any author to succeed. If you enjoyed *Liza's Secrets*, please leave a review online — anywhere you are able. Even if it's just a sentence or two. It would make all the difference and would be very much appreciated.

Thanks!
Iris Glazner Leigh

We hope you enjoyed reading this title from:

BLACK ROSE
writing™

www.blackrosewriting.com

Subscribe to our mailing list – *The Rosevine* – and receive **FREE** books, daily deals, and stay current with news about upcoming releases and our hottest authors.
Scan the QR code below to sign up.

Already a subscriber? Please accept a sincere thank you for being a fan of Black Rose Writing authors.

View other Black Rose Writing titles at www.blackrosewriting.com/books and use promo code **PRINT** to receive a **20% discount** when purchasing.

Printed in the USA
CPSIA information can be obtained
at www.ICGtesting.com
LVHW092258220624
783697LV00001B/2